PARCHMENT
AND OLD LACE

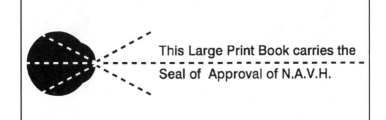

This Large Print Book carries the
Seal of Approval of N.A.V.H.

A SCRAPBOOKING MYSTERY

PARCHMENT AND OLD LACE

LAURA CHILDS
WITH TERRIE FARLEY MORAN

KENNEBEC LARGE PRINT
A part of Gale, Cengage Learning

GALE
CENGAGE Learning®

Farmington Hills, Mich • San Francisco • New York • Waterville, Maine
Meriden, Conn • Mason, Ohio • Chicago

GALE
CENGAGE Learning·

LIBRARY OF CONGRESS CATALOGING-IN-PUBLICATION DATA

Childs, Laura.
    Parchment and old lace / Laura Childs with Terrie Farley Moran. — Large print edition.
        pages cm. — (A scrapbooking mystery) (Kennebec Large Print superior collection)
        ISBN 978-1-4104-8332-4 (paperback) — ISBN 1-4104-8332-0 (softcover)
        1. Bertrand, Carmela (Fictitious character)—Fiction. 2. Women detectives—Louisiana—New Orleans—Fiction. 3. Murder—Investigation—Fiction. 4. Scrapbooking—Fiction. I. Moran, Terrie Farley. II. Title.
    PS3603.H56P37 2015b
    813'.6—dc23   2015031379

Published in 2015 by arrangement with The Berkley Publishing Group, an imprint of Penguin Publishing Group, a division of Penguin Random House LLC

ACKNOWLEDGMENTS

Heartfelt thanks to Terrie Farley Moran, who contributed her energy, humor, and writing to this book. And to the usual suspects — Sam, Tom, Amanda, Bob, Jennie, Dan, and all the fine folks at Berkley Prime Crime who handle design, publicity, copywriting, bookstore sales, and gift sales. An extra special thank-you to all the scrapbook shop owners, bookstore folks, librarians, reviewers, magazine writers, websites, radio stations, bloggers, scrappers, and crafters who have enjoyed the adventures of the Memory Mine gang and who help me keep it all going.

And to you, dear readers, I promise many more mysteries featuring Carmela, Ava, Gabby, Tandy, Baby, Boo, Poobah, Babcock, and the rest of my crazy New Orleans cast. As well as a few surprises!

CHAPTER 1

Commander's Palace wasn't just the most storied restaurant in New Orleans. For Carmela Bertrand it was pure magic.

Carmela knew this for a fact because she was sitting in their Garden Room at this very minute. And not only was she nibbling soft-shell crab and sipping an awesome Montrachet, but she was staring into the inquisitive blue eyes of her fella du jour, Detective Edgar Babcock.

Maybe it was the wine, no doubt crafted by wily Bacchus himself, that had cast such a luscious spell. Or maybe it was the soft, warm light from the gilded candelabras, the old-world charm and formality of the place, or that crazy second course of oysters baked in absinthe and buttered crumbs. Whatever the reason, Carmela was definitely feeling it. Luxuriance, exhilaration, and romance. Sweet, bubbly romance.

"This is so lovely," Carmela said, trying to

pitch her voice an octave lower so it was sexy and seductive, kind of like Kathleen Turner in *Body Heat.* Or maybe Lauren Bacall in one of those old black-and-white movies from the '40s.

"You're lovely," Babcock replied.

And Carmela really was. Her blue-gray eyes, fine features, and tawny-colored hair (this week's color, anyway) gave her an air of exuberance and creative curiosity. She was toned and fairly athletic from lots of dog walking with Boo and Poobah, but still enjoyed a few sweet curves. And, yes, she could be stubborn, but was generally quick to administer a hug or kind word.

Carmela took another sip of wine. "I have to say, this dinner has been pure perfection. If every restaurant reviewer in the universe hadn't already bequeathed four stars to this place, I would have sprinkled them on myself."

Babcock smiled and reached across the table to gently take her hand.

"Why are you talking that way?" he asked.

Carmela's eyes went slightly round. "What way?"

"Like you've got the beginnings of a head cold. Or are doing an imitation of a character from *The Simpsons.*"

"Oh." Then, "I didn't mean to."

"You've just fallen completely under my spell, is that it?"

"Well . . . yeah," said Carmela, reverting to Valley girl speak. Now she wasn't sure if he was flirting with her or putting her on.

Babcock gave a low chuckle. "You're such a little cutie, you know that? One of these days we're seriously going to have to . . ."

"Carmela!" A loud, impassioned shriek suddenly split the air.

Startled, Carmela and Babcock both whipped their heads sideways, only to find an exuberant-looking blond woman grinning at them, all teeth and gums and big Southern hair.

"Uh . . . hi," Carmela said as she scrambled to dredge her memory, to put a name to this face. "Isabelle?" She said it tentatively because she really wasn't sure that was the name of this young woman who'd just hit an earsplitting high C as she stormed their table like a pirate commandeering one of the king's galleons.

Isabelle's smile got even wider and brighter, and she said, "You remembered."

"How could I forget?" Carmela said, when she really had forgotten. Well, almost.

"Has Ellie been keeping you in the loop about all my big wedding plans?" Isabelle asked. Ellie was Eldora Black, Isabelle's sister and the tarot card reader who worked at Juju Voodoo, the little shop across the courtyard from Carmela's French Quarter apartment. The voodoo shop, a kind of funky, fun tourist trap, was owned by Carmela's very best friend, Ava Gruiex.

"Ellie *has* shared a few things with me," Carmela said, lying as gracefully as she could. She glanced over at Babcock. "With us." Now she gave Babcock an encouraging nod. "You remember Isabelle, don't you? She's one of the assistant district attorneys."

"We've met," Babcock said politely.

"Just two more weeks," Isabelle said. She held up two fingers and then fluttered her hand nervously as her engagement ring caught the light and glittered like a disco ball.

"That's some gorgeous ring," Carmela said.

Now Isabelle preened a bit. "Isn't it? Three carats, a VS2."

"Sweet," Babcock said, gamely trying to interject himself into a conversation that had suddenly turned girly.

Flustered by the attention, Isabelle took a step back from their table. "I hope you two are still planning to attend my wedding."

"Absolutely," Carmela said. She had an awful feeling that she hadn't actually mailed back her RSVP. She'd been busy and scattered lately, what with teaching a series of card-making classes at her scrapbook shop, Memory Mine. Oh well, maybe she could short-circuit things and give her reply to Ellie. Yeah, that oughta work just fine.

Isabelle glanced across the room where two of her friends waved at her, one tall and blond, the other short and dark haired. "Well, I'm afraid I have to hustle off. I've been tasting cakes with Naomi and Cynthia and a few other folks from the wedding party." She rolled her eyes. "And now I have a thousand other things to nail down."

"I'll bet you do," Carmela said. She gave a little wave as Isabelle scampered away. "Bye-bye. Good luck." Then, when Isabelle and her friends were out of both sight and earshot, she leaned across the table and said, "Do you recall me inviting you to her wedding?"

Babcock shook his head. "Nope."

"Do you want to go? Do you want to be my plus-one?"

Another head shake. "Nope."

"Come on," Carmela said. "Don't be an old poop. Weddings are exciting, romantic events filled with dancing, champagne, good food, and excellent cake." Carmela was particularly fond of cake, though champagne wasn't too far down her list, either.

"I'm pretty sure I have to work," Babcock said.

"You don't even know when her wedding is," Carmela snorted. "So how do you know if you'll be called upon to bust an international smuggling ring of ladies' designer flip-flops or chase down a homicidal maniac?"

But Babcock didn't answer. He was suddenly frowning at the check that had been surreptitiously deposited at their table, running quick computations in his head.

Hmm. He was good at dodging bullets, that's for sure, Carmela decided. Probably from all the practice he got as a police detective.

She narrowed her eyes and studied him carefully. He was quite a catch, this guy. Tall, lanky, ginger-colored hair, nice high cheekbones. A man who walked into a room and immediately projected a certain weighty presence. Plus he had a penchant for snazzy clothes. Really snazzy clothes, like Ralph Lauren Black Label and Moncler. Tonight he was wearing a Burberry Brit jacket that widened his shoulders and nipped his waist. Always a good thing.

Babcock glanced up and gave her a warm

smile. "Ready to go?"

Carmela returned his smile. Her upper lip dipped in a soft Cupid's bow, a luscious, rounded lip that most women would kill for. Or pay good money for in a plastic surgeon's office.

"I could get used to this, you know," Carmela said. She meant the dinner, the togetherness, and then some. The *and then some* meaning the two of them would eventually head back to her place for a nice Sunday-night canoodle.

"So could I," Babcock said. He held out a hand and helped her up from the chair. Then, he slid both arms around her, pulled her close, and gave her a quick kiss.

"Uh-oh," Carmela cautioned. "PDA."

Babcock arched back an inch. "What's PDA? Some kind of women's political group? A new design project?"

She brushed her lips across his cheek, feeling his warmth and energy. "You know, public display of affection."

"Oh, that." He chuckled and grabbed her hand. "Come on."

Outside the restaurant, the November evening had turned cool and breezy. Though it was full-on dark, the exterior of Commander's Palace twinkled with multiple

13

strands of lights. Turrets, columns, gingerbread swirls, and balustrades were all shown off to full advantage, gilded and glittering like a Mardi Gras float. Turquoise and white awnings flip-flapped in the wind while the restaurant's trademark neon sign hummed softly.

The whole of the Garden District was spread out around them, stately and sublime, as if it were its own proud principality governed by some unseen archduke. Lush gardens and wrought-iron fences surrounded block after block of palatial Greek Revival homes, with a few Queen Annes and Victorians thrown in for good measure. And, if you strolled down First Street, you might even encounter a fanciful Gothic home, owned by a famous author of vampire books.

Carmela and Babcock walked down Coliseum Street, heading for Babcock's blue BMW, which was parked at the end of the block. Across the scuffed blacktop, where dry leaves scritched and scratched, hurried along by little puffs of wind, stood the notorious Lafayette Cemetery. Dark and ominous-looking, this was one of New Orleans's oldest and most infamous Cities of the Dead. Here, crumbling tombs, ancient crypts, and hulking mausoleums stood shoulder to somber shoulder, more than seven thousand residents interred in a one-block area, attracting and terrifying swarms of tourists as well as locals.

A chill gust of wind suddenly blasted them, and Carmela turned her face into Babcock's shoulder.

"I was thinking that we should —" she began.

An ungodly scream suddenly pierced what felt like a fragile night.

"Heeeeeelp!"

Carmela clutched Babcock's arm. "What was that?"

"Nooo!"

Another agonizing scream rolled out, but was immediately cut off.

Babcock swiveled his head like a periscope. "Cemetery," he said sharply. He took off running, as if a starter's gun had sounded, leaving Carmela standing all by herself on the sidewalk. In the dark.

She weighed her options for all of one second. "Wait!" she cried. And took off after him.

But Babcock's longer legs had put him easily twenty strides ahead of her. And when he reached the cemetery's fence, he simply grabbed hold of the top tines, wedged a toe into a curlicue, and vaulted over it slick as you please.

"Where are you . . . ? Oh jeez!" Carmela cried. She knew she couldn't climb over that foreboding-looking fence in her tight skirt, so she pounded down the block to the formal entrance at the corner, lost her balance and almost spun out, then ducked through the narrow entry.

"Babcock," she called out. "Where are you?" She slid to a stop and listened intently. When she didn't hear anything, she called again, "What's going on?" Then, "Are you okay?"

"Over here." Babcock's faint shout drifted toward her.

Carmela glanced around, decided that his voice had to be coming from practically the epicenter of the cemetery, and then took off at a gallop. She dodged around a row of low, flat, humpy-looking tombs, then sped down a narrow gravel walkway between two mausoleums that were iced by a finger of moonlight. The night felt even darker, more dangerous, in here. Fear trickled coldly down her spine, and the exertion of a full-out sprint made the blood pound in her ears.

Still she kept going, moving and darting ahead.

What could have happened? Carmela

16

wondered. Had someone been attacked? That had to be it. None of New Orleans's cemeteries were particularly safe after dark, and visitors were constantly being cautioned to avoid them. Had Babcock been able to foil this robbery attempt or attack or whatever it had been? Had he given chase to the attacker?

Carmela spun around a stone angel whose upturned face had eroded away over the years from the constant onslaught of heat, wind, humidity, and hurricanes. She dashed past a row of oven tombs, stumbling as her toe caught on the corner of a marble tablet that the earth had heaved up. Righting herself, she listened again but didn't hear anything. So she ran left in a sort of zigzag pattern, still trying to get a bead on where Babcock had called to her from.

Gray clouds boiled up, and the sliver of moon, which had served as a small guiding beacon, slipped behind them. Now Carmela was practically running blind, feeling her way along, touching and grasping cold stone. If only she could . . .

She ran her fingers along the edge of a marble tomb, cool and smooth as picked bones. She glanced up — hoping that the crescent of moon might put in an appearance again. But the night seemed to turn darker, holding a hint of ever more danger.

Carmela scuffed along quietly. She figured she was fairly close to where Babcock might have called to her from. Now if she could only see . . .

A sound, soft and muffled, as if someone might be hunching themselves back into the shadows and hiding from her, caused Carmela to stop dead in her tracks. On high alert, hair on the back of her neck prickling like crazy, she listened as though her life depended on it. And maybe it did.

What was that? What did I hear?

Flattening herself against the side of a large, hulking crypt, she tried to modulate her breathing as best she could. Tried to make every sense keenly alert to what was going on around her.

But, after a few moments, she heard — and felt — nothing.

Carmela slowly released a breath. She was spooked, yes, but she wasn't going to let her emotions run wild. She was going to keep bumbling along and find Babcock. After all, he was in here somewhere.

Carmela moved ahead two steps, then three, her right shoulder still brushing against the side of the crypt, using it as a sort of touch point. She was just about to cry out to Babcock again, to try to get a fix on his position, when she heard a strange, low, creaking sound and caught a rush of something.

The initial spark in Carmela's brain told her it was a shadow coming at her — a grid of light and dark projected by a far-off passing car. At the last moment, she realized it was a rusty iron gate. The heavy, flaking wrought-iron door of the crypt had been flung open on squeaking hinges and was creaking inexorably toward her.

Shocked and totally unprepared, Carmela had barely two seconds to get a hand up in front of her face, a pro forma protest at best, before the gate struck hard against her, pinning her tightly against the crypt's outside wall.

She let loose a startled yelp as her forehead went numb and bright stars danced and flashed before her eyes. She suddenly felt like a captured butterfly pinned inside a display case. Angry, stunned, and struggling to pull herself back to the here and now, she gripped the gate with her hands and managed to croak out, "Help!"

Then she heard footsteps lightly running away from her as she was finally able to shove the heavy door or metal gate or whatever it was off her body.

"Stop!" she cried out. Now her fear had

been replaced with fury.

But whoever had smacked her with the gate was long gone.

Carmela gently touched a hand to her nose, mindful of sudden tears that clouded her eyes.

Broken?

She prodded carefully. No, she didn't think so. Just sore. But whoever had tried to waylay her had been fairly successful. They'd stopped her cold. She figured she'd probably feel battered and bruised come tomorrow morning.

Deciding the smartest thing, the *safest* thing, to do right now was get herself out of the cemetery as fast as she could, Carmela scuttled left, found a sort of pathway, and hurried along it. She was angry and scared and hurt. If she could make it out to Babcock's car, she'd hopefully meet up with him there.

Boy, did she have a story to tell!

But as Carmela lurched along, her eyes scanning to either side of the path, she almost tripped again. She caught herself at the last moment, glanced forward, and let loose a startled cry.

What is that? What am I seeing now?

Someone had flung a coat across a gravestone?

Carmela blinked and struggled to focus. Wait a minute. Maybe that wasn't a coat? *Is that a person lying there? Oh dear Lord.*

Carmela moved forward as if in a trance. She was suddenly hyperaware of every crunch of gravel underfoot, every looming grave, every sigh and hiss of the wind. *Who is it? Is it the person we heard screaming?*

Had to be.

As if compelled to bear witness, Carmela drew closer and closer to the grave where someone — she was pretty sure it was a woman — was sprawled in a totally unnatural pose, as if they'd been hurled there by some uncaring, unfeeling giant.

Carmela was five feet away when her brain blipped out a warning message: *Be careful, be careful.*

Babcock. Where was Babcock? Now she really had to find him.

She opened her mouth to cry out, but no sound emerged. Because, by this time, she was standing directly in front of the slumped body (slumped *dead* body?), feeling not only shock, but paralyzing fear.

Get a grip, she told herself. *Try to breathe. Make a sound. Any sound.*

Carmela gritted her teeth and tried to rally her courage. She wasn't sure if this woman

21

was dead or very badly injured. But she knew she had to try and help this poor soul . . .

Tentatively, Carmela reached out a hand. And just as the tips of her fingers were about to touch the woman . . .

"Carmela," came a harsh voice. "No!"

CHAPTER 2

Carmela jumped back as if she'd been jabbed with a hot wire.

Then footsteps sounded and Edgar Babcock slalomed to a stop next to her. He grabbed her arm, jerking her backward.

"No, Carmela, don't touch her. She's gone."

Carmela staggered back against Babcock, turned, and bumped her forehead again. "Ouch!" Then she stared up at him with questioning eyes. "What . . . what happened?"

"She's been assaulted," Babcock responded. "Strangled." He was using his cool law enforcement tone of voice, the same calming tone he used when he was tasked with speaking to relatives of crime victims. When he had to show up on someone's doorstep and say, *I'm sorry, but there's been an accident.*

"Strangled just like that?" Carmela said.

She was a little incredulous. "You mean the woman is *dead*?"

"I got here just in time to find her like this and then see someone disappear into the graveyard," Babcock said. "I took off after him, but . . ." He gave a kind of feral snarl. "I lost him."

"I saw him, too," Carmela said. "Well, I sort of *encountered* him."

Babcock stared at her. "What are you talking about?"

"Somebody . . . well, I guess it might have been the killer, was hiding just inside one of those big crypts. Anyway, when I came along he swung the door open and tried to nail me."

Babcock gripped both her shoulders. "Are you hurt?"

She pointed to the bridge of her nose. "Just kind of banged up."

"You shouldn't have followed me in here, Carmela. This could have been a bad scene." Then, as she glanced at the body draped across the tombstone, he added, "Worse than it already is."

Carmela made a slight move toward the body. "Do we know who . . . ?"

"Carmela, don't," Babcock said. Now his voice was uncharacteristically harsh.

"What?" Carmela asked. She studied

24

Babcock's face, saw something lurki: there, and said, "What aren't you telling me?"

"I've already called this in," Babcock said. "So the best thing we can do now is . . ."

"No," Carmela said. Then, "Something's really wrong, isn't it?"

When he didn't reply, Carmela edged closer to the body. She bent down and asked, "Do we know her?"

Babcock pulled a hanky from his pocket, carefully draped it across the woman's hair so he wouldn't obliterate any evidence, and turned her head gently. As he moved the body, Carmela caught a glimpse of the woman's pale face.

"It's Isabelle!" Carmela said in a hoarse voice. "Please, no, it can't be her."

But it was. And she knew it.

"What happened?" Shock and anger bubbled up inside Carmela.

"Look here," Babcock said. His index finger hovered close to the dead woman's face, then dipped down to indicate her neck. "She's been strangled."

"Dear Lord," Carmela gulped. "With what?" She really didn't expect an answer, because she was leaning in close herself, eyes finally adjusting to the darkness as she gazed in horror at the body.

25

"You see?" Babcock said. Now even he was slightly choked up.

Carmela tried to look past the awful purple and black welts, at the twisted piece of fabric that was buried deep in Isabelle's neck. "It's a piece of lace," she said, sounding almost incredulous. "Isabelle's been strangled with a piece of lace."

Five minutes later the cemetery was a hub of activity. Police cruisers rolled up, their blue and red pulsing lights cutting through the inky darkness and attracting a gaggle of onlookers. Uniformed officers streamed in, along with two EMTs who'd brought along a clattering metal gurney.

Too late for that now, Carmela thought. Now they would need the crime-scene techs with their myriad tests and equipment.

Police radios burped as more officers arrived, along with Babcock's right-hand man, Detective Bobby Gallant. They talked in low, concerned voices, their shoulders hunched, their heavy cop shoes scuffing gravel. Nobody paid much attention to Carmela.

Carmela wandered away from the circle of law enforcement that clustered like blowflies around Isabelle's dead body, and stared at a row of dark, curious faces that peered through the wrought-iron fence. The lights and hum of activity had attracted these onlookers, and she wondered if any one of them might have had a hand in poor Isabelle's murder. Was the killer standing over there right now? Watching the drama unfold with dull, appraising eyes?

"Carmela?" Babcock was waving at her. "Stay close," he cautioned.

"You think her killer's still out there?" she asked. Her eyes were once again drawn to the dark faces at the fence.

"We don't know," Babcock said. "We've got officers searching the area right now. Talking to people."

"Okay," she said woodenly. She could hardly believe it. Thirty minutes ago, Isabelle had been inside a cozy, warm restaurant with a group of friends. Now she was lying dead atop a cold, impersonal tombstone. It simply didn't compute. None of this did.

The crime-scene team arrived, deposited a half dozen black leather cases on the ground, and set up three stanchions with super bright lights. They were here to process the body.

"Careful now," Babcock warned as they pulled on latex gloves. The techs nodded perfunctorily. They knew their jobs and they were always careful.

Carmela hunched closer to Babcock. Under the glaring bright lights, Isabelle's body looked pale and ethereal. "Why is there a crust of blood on her mouth?" she asked.

"Probably bit her lip during the struggle."

Carmela frowned and looked around. The cemetery was dark, lonely, and foreboding. "Why would Isabelle even come in here?" she asked. "I mean, she'd been tasting *cake,* for goodness' sake, with a bunch of friends. Why would she bother coming in here at all? Do you think she was taking a shortcut or something to get to her car?"

"Maybe," Babcock said. "Or it's possible she knew her attacker."

Carmela's head pivoted in Babcock's direction. "What did you just say?"

"There's a chance that she knew him," Babcock repeated. "That she was comfortable with her attacker and never sensed she was in any sort of danger. It would certainly explain why she came strolling through here."

Carmela swallowed hard. She didn't respond because she didn't know quite what to say. But . . . maybe Isabelle *knew* him? That made the circumstances surrounding the woman's death even more frightening.

A sudden scuffle nearby caused everyone who'd been hunkered around the body to immediately turn and stare.

"Stop it! Let me go!" shouted a man. He was angry and struggling like crazy as two uniformed officers half walked, half dragged him into the circle of light.

"We found him lurking just outside the gate," one of the officers said to Babcock.

"I wasn't lurking, you idiot, I was getting into my car," the man cried. He was tall, with an aquiline nose, Dudley Do-Right square jaw, and a shock of blond hair that swept across his forehead preppy style. His face was practically beet red to match his crewneck sweater. The man glowered at Babcock. "Are you in charge here?" he snapped.

Babcock stared at him. "Who are you?"

"My name is Julian Drake and I'm —" He broke off his words suddenly as he gazed past Babcock. "Dear Lord, what happened?"

"You don't know?" Babcock asked.

"No, I don't know," Drake snapped. "What's going on? I need some answers *right now.*"

"Are you familiar with a Miss Isabelle . . . ?" Babcock turned toward Carmela.

"Black," Carmela said. "Isabelle Black."

29

Drake sagged visibly. "Something happened to Isabelle?" He sounded stunned.

"I guess he knows her," Carmela said.

"She was murdered here tonight," Babcock said. He was watching Drake intently.

"Murdered? Here?" Drake said. He spoke the words as if they were completely foreign to him. "Seriously?"

Babcock stepped aside. "See for yourself."

"Oh no," Drake said, as he caught sight of Isabelle's lifeless body illuminated by the harsh lights. "Oh no." The two officers released him from their grip, and he lurched forward and caught another quick glimpse of the body. Then he moaned and staggered sideways toward a low stone tombstone. He plopped down hard on top of it and dropped his head into his hands. "This can't be happening," he rasped.

"It's already happened," Babcock said.

Drake slowly lowered his hands so just his eyes were visible. "She's really gone?"

"I'm afraid so," Babcock said.

"Gracious." Drake fumbled in the pocket of his khaki slacks, pulled out a white hanky, and mopped his face. There was a loud honk and then he peeked out again and asked, "What happened?"

"She was strangled," Carmela said. She

was watching Drake carefully. He seemed like a man in shock. Then again, you never know.

"You were well acquainted with the deceased?" Babcock asked.

"I am . . . I was supposed to be the best man at her wedding," Drake said.

"So you were at the cake tasting tonight," Carmela said.

Drake stared at her. "Yes, of course." He paused. "Who are you?"

His question was ignored. "Did you see Miss Black leave Commander's Palace with anyone in particular?" Babcock asked.

"We all kind of straggled out," Drake said. He licked his lips and nervously jiggled a leg. "Am I under arrest?"

Babcock was noncommittal. "We'd like you to come downtown with us and answer a few questions. Give us the names of everyone who attended your party tonight."

"Sure. But I don't know how much help I can be," Drake said. He wiped at his eyes and gave a loud snuffle.

"You can try," Babcock said.

Ten minutes later it was all over. Drake was escorted to a patrol car, and the crime-scene techs packed up their equipment. The two EMTs took great care as they loaded Isabelle's body onto a gurney. Now they were going to hump it back out through the graveyard, with everyone shuffling along in their wake.

Carmela shivered. Isabelle was getting her procession after all. It just wasn't the grand wedding day procession that she'd probably dreamed about.

CHAPTER 3

Gabby poured a steaming cup of chamomile tea into a shiny black mug and handed it to Carmela.

"Here," Gabby said. "Maybe this will help."

Carmela didn't think it would help, but she took it anyway. Standing in Memory Mine this early Monday morning, she felt discouraged and weary. Gabby, her trusted assistant, was being her sweetest self, but even that wasn't giving her much comfort. Really, nothing could wipe out the shock and pain of seeing Isabelle's body splayed out on that awful tombstone last night.

"I can only imagine how terrible Ellie is feeling," Gabby said. "For her own sister to be murdered . . ." She shook her head, almost choking on her words.

"I'm sure she's numb with grief," Carmela said. Then thought, no, Ellie was probably sick with grief. She herself was the one who was still feeling numb.

"And what about Ava?" Gabby asked. "How did she take it when you talked to her last night? Or *did* you talk to her?"

Carmela nodded. "Oh yeah, I figured I pretty much had to. After Babcock dropped me back at my apartment, I ran across the courtyard to Ava's place. Kind of dropped the whole thing on her like one great big nasty matzo ball."

"And she was upset?" Gabby asked.

"Ava was stunned. She felt terrible about Isabelle and was worried sick for Ellie. I mean, Ava and Ellie are fairly close. Ellie's been working at Juju Voodoo as a tarot card reader and astrologer for well over a year now."

"So you and Ava didn't go over to Ellie's house?" Gabby asked.

"We talked about going over there, but felt like we'd be horning in. Anyway, Babcock and Bobby Gallant went there to make some sort of formal notification . . ."

"Which must have been an awful thing for them to do."

"Yes," Carmela said. "And then we figured that Ellie would want to commiserate with her family. Or with Isabelle's fiancé."

"So sad," Gabby said. "Especially since they were supposed to be married in . . .

what was it? A couple of weeks?"

"Two weeks," Carmela said. She took another sip of tea. "What a tragedy." For some reason, the fact that she'd forgotten to RSVP to Isabelle's wedding made her feel all the more guilty and sad.

Gabby was silent for a few moments, and then said, "Do you think it's kind of creepy that we're scheduled to have a wedding workshop tomorrow afternoon? I mean, we're even going to be working with *lace*." She gave a little shiver.

"It is a little weird," Carmela said. "Even though Isabelle wasn't registered." Their workshop was all about creating concept boards to help brides-to-be narrow down their choices on colors, theme, flowers, and décor. "The thing is," Carmela continued, "it would have been too late for Isabelle anyway." She considered her words and sighed deeply. "I guess we were *all* a little too late for Isabelle."

Gabby reached across the front counter, where multiple packets of beads and brads were displayed on metal racks, and patted Carmela's hand. "You're always so strong, Carmela. And you were very brave to go chasing into that cemetery after Babcock."

"I don't feel particularly brave. Especially since I didn't do much of anything to help."

35

"Not yet anyway," Gabby murmured quietly. Then she brightened. "Carmela, what if we unpacked all the new boxes of paper and rubber stamps this morning? That might help take your mind off things."

Carmela eyed Gabby. "You think?"

"No, but why don't we give it a go anyway." Gabby pushed a few strands of honeyed-brown hair out of her eyes and set her full lips in a smile. She was a woman who was blessed with optimism, warmth, and compassion. With her cheerful nature, luminous complexion, and penchant for pencil skirts and cashmere sweaters, Gabby was everyone's favorite. And even though she was married to Stuart Mercer-Morris, the somewhat stodgy owner of multiple New Orleans car dealerships, Gabby always managed to project abundant good humor.

Carmela and Gabby set to work then, ripping open cardboard boxes, exclaiming over some of the brand-new scrapbook paper, and then carefully placing the paper in their floor-to-ceiling wire bins.

"Look at this," Carmela said. She held up a sheet of pastel pink paper. "Handmade silk paper. Can't you just envision this as the background for a wedding- or anniversary-themed scrapbook page?"

Gabby handed her a floral design rubber

36

stamp that she'd just pulled from one of the boxes. "And this is the perfect rubber stamp to enhance that theme."

Carmela was beginning to relax and ease into a slightly better frame of mind. Then again, working at Memory Mine always did make her feel happy and fulfilled. She'd opened the scrapbook shop several years ago in what she'd always figured was the quintessential French Quarter space. That is, a quaint shop with brick walls, sagging wooden floors, and a bow window in front with ample space to display finished scrapbook pages, memory boxes, handmade cards, and altered books. She'd added a counter, paper racks, and shelves to display albums, scissors, and rubber stamps. Two flat files housed their larger-format specialty papers. The former antique dealer tenants, who'd fled the spot, had left behind an enormous table. So that was moved to the back of the shop and became their designated craft table. As luck would have it, there was even a cubbyhole space where Carmela could set up a small office.

And business had been good. Carmela had sweated out her first year, of course, but she was a practical, focused business-woman. She offered dozens of classes and demos, invited potential customers in for free make-and-takes, and promoted her shop like crazy. In the end, all her good efforts had paid off. Memory Mine was now the premier scrapbook shop in all of New Orleans. Really, in all of the surrounding parishes.

At 10:00 A.M. the bell over the front door did its trademark *da-ding* and Gabby chirped, "There you go, first customer of the day. That always brings good luck."

But when the door pushed open all the way and the customer stepped into their shop, they saw it wasn't a customer at all. It was Babcock.

"Oh no," Carmela said. Even though she was really thinking, *Now what?*

"Dear me," Gabby said, looking slightly rattled.

"That's one heck of a welcome," Babcock said. He was dressed in khakis, a light blue poplin shirt, and a brown leather jacket. He looked like he was ready to hop into an Aston Martin and take a jaunt up to Baton Rouge for Creole food at Juban's. But Carmela noted that his face looked tired and drawn, and she figured he'd probably endured a very long night with little to no sleep.

"What's up?" Carmela asked. For some

reason this looked like it might be an official-type visit, not just a pop-in-and-say-hi visit.

"How are you fixed for coffee?" Babcock asked.

"I can whip up a pot of chicory in about two minutes," Gabby offered.

"Do it," Babcock said.

Then, while the coffee was perking and the two women were giving each other glances, wondering exactly why he was here, Babcock reached into his pocket and pulled out a stiff white envelope.

"What have you got there?" Carmela asked. One side of her mouth twitched. "I hope you're not serving an eviction notice." Carmela always enjoyed a little droll humor at the expense of her landlord, Boyd Bellamy, especially since he was a world-renowned curmudgeon.

Without answering, Babcock gestured for the two women to follow him as he walked to the back of the shop and stopped at the large craft table. He upended his envelope and a piece of fabric fluttered out.

"Ribbon?" Gabby asked. Eyebrows raised, she was wondering just what was going on.

But Carmela suddenly had a good idea of what Babcock had brought them.

"Lace?" she said. "Please don't tell me it's

from last night." She couldn't bring herself to say last night's *murder.*

Babcock nodded slowly. "I'm afraid so."

Gabby put a hand to her chest, as if to still a fluttering heart. "Whoa." She seemed stunned. "You mean this is a piece of the actual lace that strangled that poor woman?"

"A shred of it anyway," Babcock said. "As much as the crime-scene techs would allow me to spirit away from the lab."

Gabby moved a step closer to the table and gazed at the snippet of lace as if it was a horrible, tainted thing. As if it had the power to curl up like a serpent and slither around her throat, slowly choking off her breathing.

"Why did you bring it here?" Carmela demanded. "What do you want from us?"

"I've got our forensic people checking into various types of lace," Babcock said. "But I wanted to know if you two had ever seen anything like this before? I know customers are always coming in here with bits and scraps of paper and fabric."

"There's no law against it," Gabby said.

"I realize that," Babcock said, keeping an even tone. "But what I really want to know is, have you ladies ever set eyes on *this* type of lace before?"

Carmela leaned forward and focused on

40

the fragment of lace. She'd been too shocked last night to take a really good look at it. Now she saw that the piece of lace was about an inch and a half wide and had a design, a raised floral pattern running down the center. And it was definitely antique-looking, in a color that could best be described as ivory.

"Maybe I have seen something like this," Carmela said. "Although I can't remember exactly where. Gabby? What do you think?"

Gabby peered at the lace. "It's pretty, in a horrible kind of way. And it looks like it might be made of silk."

"Maybe French silk," Carmela said. "And I'm guessing it's fairly old. Probably even antique."

"Which would make it expensive," Gabby said.

Babcock stared at them. "Really? You think this piece of lace is some sort of collectible?"

"It could be," Carmela said.

But Gabby was more definite with her answer. "Very much so," she said. "If you're into antique fabrics and laces."

"Do you know anyone who collects this type of thing?" Babcock asked.

"Not specifically," Carmela said. She thought for a minute. "Why don't we go

41

into my office? I'll pull up a couple of antique lace websites and we can take a look. See if there's anything similar."

"Good," Babcock breathed. "Now we're getting somewhere."

Gabby and Babcock hovered over Carmela while she sat at her computer, running her fingers across the keyboard.

"This site," she said. "Lace and Grace. They always feature a lot of antique laces, shawls, table runners, and bridal veils."

"I had no idea there was even a market for this old stuff," Babcock said. "I mean . . . why?"

"Because it's lovely," Gabby said, coloring slightly. "And because it's handmade, whereas everything today is cranked out by machine. Usually in sweatshops in India or China."

"Okay," Babcock said, as Carmela continued to click along.

"Take a look at this," Carmela said as she scrolled down. "Here's a piece of lace similar to the sample you brought in."

Gabby studied it, too. "The floral pattern is similar, but not exact. See," she said to Babcock, "your lace doesn't have an intricate lattice border like this one does."

"It's called a strangling vine pattern,"

Carmela said.

Gabby's face blanched white. "Oh my."

Babcock tapped the screen as he read the caption below the photo. "And they're asking three hundred fifty dollars for that piece of lace? Hmm. Expensive."

"For one point five yards of lace, dated to between 1800 and 1850," Carmela said. She scrolled down some more. "Look at this antique lace shawl. The asking price here is seventeen hundred dollars."

"Amazing," Babcock said. "Why so expensive?"

"Because it's old and rare," Carmela said. "Most lace from that era, if it hasn't been properly stored and cared for, has long since disintegrated with age."

"Is lace really strong enough to strangle someone?" Gabby asked. "Especially if it's antique? Wouldn't the threads be awfully fragile?"

"I'm afraid that piece last night was strong enough," Babcock said. "The lace is stretched and tattered now, but it obviously held up."

Carmela swiveled around in her purple leather chair. "We know that Isabelle was at Commander's Palace last night for a cake tasting, right? Do we know how many people were there with her?"

Babcock pursed his lips. "Seven other people. Three bridesmaids, the groom, and various assorted friends. Well, you met one of them last night. Julian Drake. The best man."

"Is he off the hook?" Carmela asked.

Babcock nodded. "Probably, pending a few lab tests. We've got nothing solid to hold him on."

Carmela wondered if Drake had been the dirtbag who'd swung the crypt gate at her and bonked her on the nose. Or was he the innocent he claimed to be?

"And the groom was at the cake tasting, too?" Carmela asked.

"Edward Baudette," Babcock said. "Yes, he was there, but he apparently left early."

"Really?" Carmela said. "That's . . . interesting."

"Maybe," Babcock said. "Or maybe it doesn't mean spit. Anyway, we know there was a whole group there just to taste cake." He shook his head dismissively. "Cake."

"But wedding cake is important," put in Gabby. She was a huge champion of romance and marriage. "And a cake today costs upward of eight or nine hundred dollars. So you really need to know what you're getting. What you're paying for."

"Wait a minute," Babcock said. He'd just

been gobsmacked by her comment. "That much money for cake?" He seemed bewildered. "Can't you just . . . I don't know . . . walk into a bakery and *buy* one?"

"Well, no," Carmela said. "It doesn't quite work that way." In the distant future she might have to educate her beloved on the finer points of planning a wedding. For now she just tapped a finger against her keyboard to bring him back to the issue at hand. "What I'd really like to know is, with that many people surrounding Isabelle, how did she get lured away from her group?"

"Maybe because she wasn't lured," Gabby said. "Maybe she thought she was with a friend, someone she trusted." She hesitated. "Only then her friend . . ."

"Murdered her," Babcock said.

Carmela gazed pointedly at Babcock. "Last night you kept referring to Isabelle's killer as a he. Are you positive about that?"

"I'm guessing that it was a male," Babcock said. "Just because Isabelle was overcome through sheer brute strength."

"Still," Carmela said, "it could have been a female. A strong female."

"Could have been," Babcock said. "We're not ruling anything out."

"Because a man using a piece of lace . . ." Carmela looked dubious. "It strikes me as being somewhat odd. I mean . . . wouldn't a man be more comfortable using a hunk of rope or a plastic cord?"

"You know," Gabby said, "I don't think comfort was ever a consideration."

CHAPTER 4

Just as Carmela was shuffling through a stack of French ephemera, the front door swung open and a frazzled-looking woman swooped in, propelling her young, tween-aged daughter ahead of her.

"You don't want to do this now," the mom was saying to the reluctant-looking girl, "but I guarantee you'll thank me when your photos are all organized and your scrapbook comes together."

The girl shrugged her shoulders so high that her bright pink, cropped T-shirt rose to reveal a silver chain around her waist. Interlocking stars dangled from it, winking and twinkling in the light. Then she dropped her shoulders and the chain slipped back down over her nonexistent hips.

Carmela was amused. *Good girl,* she thought, *just a chain, no pierced navel.*

She put on her helpful shopkeeper's face. "May I help you ladies?"

"I hope so," the woman said. She flipped open her oversized canvas bag and pulled out a brown envelope stuffed with photos. "We took a family trip to Yellowstone National Park and the Grand Canyon this past summer, and I'd really like to turn our mishmash of photos into a well-organized scrapbook." She smiled at her daughter. "We're hoping it can be a kind of *family* project."

"That sounds like fun," Carmela said. She led them to the table in back, the one they'd dubbed Craft Central, grabbing a few sheets of colorful paper along the way. "I've got some paper that's edged with trees and mountains." She smiled at the girl. "And did you know that Paper Wizard even makes a National Parks Collection?" She set the pages down on the table.

"Let me see those," said the girl. She picked them up and studied them. Her eyebrows rose in twin arcs. "Not bad."

Then Gabby dashed back with a roll of ribbon that featured a repeating pattern of ducks swimming along, the mama in front, with five babies behind.

"These are like the birds we saw, right?" the girl said to her mother. "Flying over the canyon?"

"Well," mom said, "I think the really big

48

ones were turkey buzzards. But we did see ducks at the lake."

"Cool," said the girl. She was definitely warming up to the idea.

The mother beamed at Carmela, then grabbed a basket, and the two of them began to shop. They gathered up sheets of paper, rubber stamps, ink pads, and, finally, they selected a lovely album. Carmela rang up each item, packaged everything in a brown kraft paper bag with raffia handles, and then stuck a colorful crack-and-peel sticker that said *Memory Mine* onto the side of the bag.

The two shoppers had barely left when Gabby returned to the subject that was first and foremost in their minds — the death of Isabelle.

"If I recall," Gabby said, "Isabelle worked in the district attorney's office."

Carmela nodded vigorously. "Yes, she was one of their attorneys. And I have a feeling I know where you're going with this."

"Mm hm," Gabby said. "Isabelle's murder could easily have been related to her job."

"That's what I've been thinking, too."

Gabby continued. "Isabelle probably helped put some pretty unsavory characters behind bars. Then they sat there stewing in their own juices, with nothing to do but plan for the day when they'd be released."

"Except when they were busy pumping iron or surfing the 'Net," Carmela said.

Gabby grimaced. "Still, there have to be a few guys who plotted to exact their revenge. Who wanted to get back at the folks who helped put them away."

"I'm sure there are," Carmela said. "And when the wrong one gets released . . ."

"Because of good behavior!"

"Something awful like *this* happens."

"Exactly," Gabby said.

"I'll have to ask Babcock if he thought that might have been a real threat. You know, something he should look into." Carmela shuddered as she recalled seeing Isabelle's body last night. She reached for her can of Diet Coke, took a sip, and said, "We've got to change the subject or we'll be bummed all day."

"Maybe I should run out and get lunch," Gabby offered. "That always cheers you up."

"It does if we get po-boy sandwiches."

"From Pirate's Alley Deli." Gabby grinned. "What are you up for today?"

"My usual. The fried oysters. How about you?"

"I've had a hankering for a shredded beef po-boy ever since I woke up this morning. When Stuart came out of the bathroom and saw me grinning, I do believe he thought I was fantasizing about him."

"But you didn't bother to set him straight?"

"And damage that fragile male ego? Of course not." Gabby grabbed her purse and glanced at Carmela. "So . . . another Diet Coke?"

"What else?"

By the time Carmela had unpacked a box of washi paper, found a package of silver brads she'd been looking for, and answered a few phone calls, Gabby was back.

"Here you go," she said, handing a white paper bag to Carmela. There was a big grease spot blossoming on one side of the bag, a sure sign the oysters had been deep-fried to perfection and slathered with mayonnaise. "And I stopped by the Merci Beaucoup Bakery for some of their pecan pie mini muffins."

But when Carmela sat down at her desk, ready to sink her teeth into the golden, crusty roll that was stuffed with all that rich oyster goodness, the phone suddenly shrilled.

What? Oh no. Jeez, I hope it's for Gabby.

Of course, it wasn't. Not only that, it was her BFF Ava Gruiex calling. And the poor dear was howling like a wounded banshee.

"Carmelayagottacome, Idunnowhatado!"

"Ava, calm down." Carmela gazed long-ingly at her sandwich. "Just slow down, try to enunciate, and tell me what's wrong."

"Cher," Ava cried, "I need you to come over to Juju Voodoo right away. I can't do a thing. I can't seem to help her!"

"Help who?"

"Ellie," Ava said. "She's here. Now."

"What? *Your* Ellie, Isabelle's sister? She shouldn't be at work today."

"Crying hysterically?"

"Oh dear . . ."

"I didn't know who else to call. You're always so . . . competent . . . when it comes to this emotional stuff."

Carmela began wrapping up her po-boy. "Okay, okay, I'll be there in a jiffy." She took a quick hit of Diet Coke, hoping the caf-feine would see her through.

Carmela practically sprinted the few blocks through the French Quarter to Ava's shop. Down Governor Nicholls Street, over Royal Street, and hanging a right on Toulouse. The day was chilly with a scud of gray clouds hanging overhead and maybe a hint of rain in the air. So she felt a genuine tug of relief when the glossy red front door of

Juju Voodoo suddenly came into sight. As she drew closer, she could see the red and blue neon sign — an open palm with head, heart, and life lines glowing in the multi-paned window. The neon lights reflected eerily on the black-and-white painted Day of the Dead figures and purple bottles of assorted potions that lined the inside window ledge. The wooden shake roof dipped down in front, giving Ava's shop the impression of a cute Hansel and Gretel cottage. Still, it was the home of spells, fortune telling, and gris-gris.

Carmela pushed the door open and stepped inside. As always, the interior was cool and dark, lit by dozens of votive candles that glowed mysteriously. The odor of mystery and magic hung redolent in the air — opulent patchouli oil, lavender, and white sage. Overhead, wooden skeletons clacked softly in the breeze.

"Hello?" Carmela called out. At first glance the place looked deserted. Then her eyes grew accustomed to the darkness and she noticed Ava standing behind the counter, fussing with a display of white muslin voodoo dolls. She was dressed in her trademark skintight black leather pants and spiked-heel shoes.

When Ava heard the door creak open, she

turned and placed both hands daintily on her chest, nearly covering the ample cleavage exposed by her slinky leopard print top. Her mass of dark, heavy hair was pulled back behind one ear and held in place by a tortoiseshell comb studded with pearls. Like they say, a little bit country, a little bit rock and roll.

"Thank goodness, you're here," Ava breathed. Her fine-boned face was highly expressive, and she moved with catlike grace. A former beauty queen and self-professed glamour puss, she still considered herself the cutest thing since sliced bread.

Carmela looked around. "Where's Ellie? Is she still here?"

Her question was answered by a piteous wail that drifted out from the octagon-shaped reading room at the back of the shop.

"Okay," Carmela said. "I think I just got my answer."

"C'mon," Ava said, waggling her fingers. "She's really in a bad way. Nothing I say seems to help at all. Maybe *you* can calm her down."

They walked through the shop, past rows of saint candles, racks of evil eye necklaces, and elegantly decorated sugar skulls, and into the small reading room. The walls were swathed in heavy dark green velvet draperies and contained two stained glass windows that were lit from behind. Scrounged from an old orphanage, the windows depicted two angels each cradling a small white lamb. It was a soothing and gentle environment, yet Ellie was sobbing like it was the end of the world.

"Oh, honey," Ava said. She moved over to where Ellie was hunched across her tarot table and stroked her hair gently. "You see, I brought Carmela. You remember Carmela?"

Ellie lifted her head and nodded. "Yes," she snuffled. "Thank you for coming."

Carmela shuffled forward and took a seat next to Ellie. "Why are you even here?" she asked. Ellie Black, known as Madame Blavatsky to her tarot and psychic customers, was wearing a purple skirt, deep red blouse, and paisley shawl. She was dressed like she was ready to tell someone's fortune. Though, clearly, with a recently murdered sister, she was not in that frame of mind at all.

Ellie wiped away a few tears. "I didn't know where else to go. Isabelle was my only family. I thought if I came here . . . well, no, that's not it." She let loose a harsh laugh. "I obviously *didn't* think this through."

Carmela bit her lip. She hadn't realized that there were only the two of them. "What about Isabelle's fiancé?" she asked softly.

"I tried to get hold of Edward," Ellie said. "But he's not answering his phone. Maybe he's . . . I don't know . . . at his mother's house?"

"Probably in a blue funk," Ava said. "I mean, who could blame the poor guy?"

"Can you call his mother?" Carmela asked. She thought that Ellie should rightly be with people who were also missing Isabelle.

"No," Ellie said. "That just wouldn't be . . . proper."

"Why not, honey?" Ava asked.

"His mother's not exactly the warmest person in the world," Ellie said.

Ava glanced at Carmela. She was clearly at a loss, but so was Carmela.

Then Ellie bowed her head forward and knocked it against the table so hard she practically left a permanent dent. "It's all my fault," she muttered. "Isabelle is dead and it's all my fault."

Startled by the woman's words, Carmela put an arm around Ellie's shoulders and tried to pull her upright. "No," Carmela soothed. "Sweetie, no. How could this possibly be your fault?"

Ellie lifted her head and wiped her nose on her sleeve. "Because I . . . I should have been there. I should have been there with Isabelle."

"At the cake tasting?" Carmela asked.

Ellie nodded. "She kept asking me to come, but I'd already committed to work a private party at the Hotel Bonaparte. It was a big deal, I'd been booked for months, and . . . I needed the money." She dipped her head, embarrassed. "You know, because of the economy."

"We understand," Ava said as Ellie broke into defeated-sounding sobs.

Carmela tried to comfort her. "Ellie, none of this is your fault. There's no way you could have . . ."

But Ellie cut her off. "But it *is* my fault. If I'd been with Isabelle, she would still be alive."

"You don't know that," Carmela said.

Ellie was suddenly frantic. "Yes, I do. I know that I wouldn't have let her go tromping through that creepy cemetery all by herself!"

Carmela couldn't argue with that.

As Ellie gazed at Carmela, her eyes seemed to glow with intensity. "But *you* were there," she said. "Ava told me how you ran into the cemetery to help."

"Yes," Carmela said. "And I couldn't save her, either. So you see?"

Ellie grasped Carmela's hand. "But maybe you could still help!"

Carmela frowned and shook her head. "I'm not sure I'm following you. What exactly are you . . . ?"

"Ava told me all about how smart you are," Ellie said. "How good you are when it comes to solving crimes and things."

"Oh, not really," Carmela said. She knew Babcock would kill her if she got involved.

"I told her about that thing with the Ghost Train," Ava piped up. "How you figured everything out. Who the killer was and all."

"I'd say it was pretty clear to both of us," Carmela stammered. "I mean . . . there at the end." She was trying desperately to downplay her role. "It's really best to leave the investigating to Detective Babcock. That's his business. And he's very good at it."

"Please, Carmela," Ellie said. "I really need an ally here, some sort of advocate."

Now Ava crept forward. "Pretty please? You really are *good* at this."

Carmela felt torn. "Oh dear." She really did want to help Ellie. But what could she do?

CHAPTER 5

"Maybe you could just sort of ask around," Ellie said. "Unofficially, of course."

"Unofficially," Carmela said. That sounded to her like a shadow investigation. On the other hand, there was a part of her that thought a shadow investigation sounded rather intriguing.

"Come on, *cher,*" Ava cajoled. "You're the Nancy Drew of the French Quarter. You've got a big, bad rep to uphold."

That made Carmela chuckle. "You guys put up quite a convincing argument, but I don't . . ." When she saw their faces fall, she said, "Okay, maybe I . . . well, how about this? I'll try to look into things, but I dare not step on any official toes."

Ellie threw up her hands with a sigh of relief. "Agreed. No toes will be stepped on or harmed in any way." Then she focused on Carmela again, anxiously searching her face. "You really meant what you said?

You'll help?"

"I'll snoop around," Carmela said. "Best I can. But you're going to have to give me a little background information."

"Ask me anything," Ellie said. "Anything you want."

"Okay," Carmela said. "When was the last time you saw Isabelle?"

"Yesterday afternoon," Ellie said. "I was just heading out for my job and Isabelle was getting ready for the cake tasting." She sniffled. "She was trying to decide between her purple suit or her black slip dress."

"And that was it? After that she didn't call you or text you or anything?"

"Not that I know of," Ellie said. "Then again, I was pretty busy."

"Was there anything going on in Isabelle's life that seemed to be upsetting her? That had knocked her off her stride? Work? Friends? Anything you can think of?"

Ellie sniffled into a tissue. "Just the wedding, really. There were tons of pesky details to take care of, and I know Edward's mother kept butting in like crazy." She hesitated. "Actually, it was more like butting heads."

"Edward's mother is . . . ?" Carmela prompted.

"Vesper Baudette," Ellie said.

"Oh." Carmela sat back in her chair.

"You know her?"

"Only by reputation," Carmela said. Vesper came from old money and was one of the more notorious doyennes of the Garden District.

"What reputation is that?" Ava asked.

"She has money," Carmela said. "More money than many small countries."

"And I understand Vesper sits on a number of boards of directors," Ellie said.

Which means she has powerful friends, Carmela thought to herself. "Okay, so Isabelle and Vesper were not seeing eye to eye about the wedding?"

Ellie sighed. "Whenever a problem came up, Edward would just say, 'Whatever you two decide, darlin', is fine with me.' He left Isabelle to battle the old witch all by herself."

"Because he couldn't?" Carmela asked. "Or wouldn't?"

"I don't know," Ellie whispered.

"Now I need to ask you a couple of really tough questions," Carmela said.

Ellie swiped at her eyes. "Like what?"

"I want you to think about everyone who was involved with Isabelle, everyone she knew or had a passing acquaintance with."

"Okay," Ellie said.

"Does anyone jump out at you? Was there

someone who might have caused a little trouble in her life? An old enemy, a business rival, someone she might have had legal dealings with? A person in the court system, perhaps?"

Ellie's face took on a pensive look. Finally, she shook her head. "I can't think of anyone."

Ava leaned in. "Think hard, honey. If you were doing a tarot reading for a client who wanted to solve a problem, what information would you be seeking from the spirits? Look deep within your soul and see if you can find an answer."

Carmela and Ava waited a few expectant heartbeats, and then Ellie slouched down. "It's no use." She put a hand to her heart. "I'm so sad, it's difficult to even think. Or feel."

Carmela decided to ask about the one person from the cake tasting that she'd met in the cemetery. "What do you know about Julian Drake?"

Ellie shrugged. "I only met him a couple of times, but he seemed like a nice enough guy. I know he and Edward had been friends for a long time. They were roommates at Tulane."

"What exactly does Drake do?"

"He's the vice president in charge of

development at that new casino they're building over in the Gentilly neighborhood. They're planning to rip down the old amusement park that was blown all hurly-burly during Hurricane Katrina and has been an eyesore ever since.

"Mmn," Ava said. "The one with the tunnel of love."

"It's probably a tunnel of horrors now," Carmela said. "That old place is in shambles." She took a deep breath and tried to focus. "Think hard. Is there anyone who doesn't feel right to you?"

Ellie cocked her head, lost in thought. Then she frowned distractedly and shook her head no.

Carmela decided to switch topics. "Okay, let me ask you about the lace that was, uh, discovered at the scene. Do you know anyone who collects lace or might have a piece of antique lace in a fabric collection?"

"In a collection? No."

"Collecting lace sounds kind of quaint and outdated," Ava said.

But Carmela was watching Ellie's face. The girl had started to twitch and bounce her foot. It looked as if she *did* want to say something, but was afraid.

"I get the impression," Carmela said, "that

63

there might be something you want to tell me."

Ellie gave a half nod. "I really hate to say this," she said in a low voice, "but going back to Edward's mother, Vesper . . . well, the woman pretty much despised Isabelle."

"Oh no," Ava said. "I can't believe that."

"Believe it," Ellie said. "Vesper thought Isabelle was too low class for her precious son." She swallowed hard. "She even kept a list of 'unmarried young ladies from good, moneyed families' who she thought would make a more suitable bride for Edward."

"How do you know she had a list?" Carmela was incredulous.

"Vesper mentioned it the day she hosted an engagement tea to introduce Isabelle to her friends," Ellie said. "I guess she was still holding out hope."

"That's awful!" Ava said.

"Isn't it?" Ellie said.

"Still," Carmela said, "disliking someone is one thing, but killing them is completely over the top. Are you saying that Vesper is deranged?"

Ellie bit her lip. "She's pretty crazy."

"And you think Vesper could have actually strangled Isabelle to make sure the wedding never happened?" Ava asked.

Ellie sighed. "I don't know. But if anybody

could do it, Vesper could."

Carmela peered at Ellie. "Does Vesper collect lace? Or antique fabrics?"

"Not that I know of," Ellie said. "Then again, I hardly know anything about the woman. I've only been to her house maybe twice."

"Even if Vesper was guilty," Ava said, "that lace would probably be untraceable. It's like . . . the perfect murder weapon."

The thought of old lace wound tightly around her sister's throat brought Ellie to tears once again.

"Shh," Ava said, trying to comfort her. "Don't worry. Carmela's brain will start percolating all this information and *something* will pop out."

"I'll give it a try anyway," Carmela said.

Ava gazed at Carmela. "You do that, honey. Meanwhile, I'm gonna go to the funeral home tonight and help Ellie make the arrangements."

"I think that's a good idea," Carmela said.

Ava pulled a tiny juju guardian doll from her pocket and handed it to Ellie. "Keep this close to your heart. It'll help protect you."

Ellie clutched the little blue and black feathered doll like it was a lifeline. "Thank you."

"Okay," Carmela said, ready to finish up. "Is there anything else?"

Ellie fidgeted with the doll, looking nervous.

"What?" Carmela asked. Was there more?

Ellie nibbled at her lower lip. "I *really* hate to say this, because it's completely awful and total conjecture on my part."

"Spit it out anyway," Ava urged.

Ellie swallowed hard and stared at Carmela. "I think . . . mind you, I don't *know* . . . that Edward Baudette might have been trying to postpone or even weasel out of his own wedding."

"Whoa," Carmela said. She felt like Ellie's words had just sucked the air out of the room.

"You're telling us the groom had cold feet?" Ava gasped. "But I thought they were the perfect couple." She clasped her hands together. "I thought they were blissfully happy."

"I really believed they were at first, too," Ellie said. "In fact, they were both terribly besotted with each other." Her words were tumbling out now. "But these last few weeks . . . well, I think Isabelle had this weird feeling in the pit of her stomach that if she called off the wedding, Edward wouldn't exactly shed a tear. That he'd breathe a lot easier."

"That's a mighty big assumption," Carmela said. "Do you have any sort of evidence to back this up? Did Edward actually say something to Isabelle? I mean . . . this is a fairly serious accusation."

"Like I said," Ellie said. She began to play with the tablecloth, wrinkling it with her fingers, then spreading it flat with her palm. "This is pure conjecture on my part. There's no concrete evidence. Just a feeling I sort of *intuited* when the two of them were together."

Ava looked shaken. "And your intuition is pretty dang good."

"Yes, it is," Ellie said. Now they both looked at Carmela.

But Carmela was deep in thought. Intuition was one thing, but collecting hard evidence for an honest-to-goodness murder was something else. Still, Isabelle had been killed in what appeared to have been hardcore, brutish rage. Was Vesper capable of that? Was Edward?

The fact that Edward had left the cake tasting early bothered Carmela. He could be a complete innocent, of course, rushing off to an important meeting.

Or, he could have been the one who'd waited for Isabelle in the dark cemetery, biding his time among the tilting tombstones. Had he popped out to playfully spook her, and then, when Isabelle had dropped her guard, viciously strangled her?

Dear Lord, Carmela thought to herself. She fervently hoped Edward wasn't the killer. The thought was just too grisly to bear.

CHAPTER 6

Gabby was in full mother hen mode when Carmela walked in the front door of Memory Mine.

"Oh, you're back!" she cried. "I hated to see you dash out of here so fast." She reached behind the counter and pulled out Carmela's po-boy. It was carefully sheathed in shiny tinfoil, looking like a lost part from the International Space Station. "Here, I saved it for you. I wrapped it up tight so it should still be relatively fresh."

Carmela accepted the hermetically sealed sandwich, and they both walked back to the craft table. "You're so sweet to take care of me like this." She plopped down in a chair, unwrapped her sandwich, and helped herself to a bite. "Mmn."

Gabby beamed. "Good?" She slipped into a chair across from Carmela.

"Delish." The oysters were lukewarm, but the lettuce had kept the mayonnaise from turning the whole thing into a soggy mess.

Gabby leaned forward and put her elbows on the table. "Well? Are you gonna give me the 411 on Ellie? I mean, is she okay? What happened over there at Ava's place?"

Carmela sighed. "Ellie came in to work today because she had no other place to go. Turns out Isabelle was her only family."

"What about her fiancé and his family?"

"That's where it starts to get complicated," Carmela said. "Ellie has a few . . . well, let's just call them suspicions."

Gabby's brows bunched together. "Really? How could she? You said that Ellie was nowhere near the cemetery when Isabelle was murdered."

Carmela wiped a glop of mayonnaise from the corner of her mouth. She really *was* enjoying her sandwich, even though they were talking about bloody blue murder. Go figure. "The thing is," she said, "Ellie's suspicions right now are directed at Edward and his mother."

Gabby's eyes opened round as two saucers from an antique tea set. "Huh?" she said, rather inelegantly.

So Carmela laid it all out for her. Edward leaving the cake tasting early, Vesper's ongoing hostility, Isabelle feeling overwhelmed, Vesper's list of replacement brides, and a certain lack of enthusiasm and prenuptial bliss on Edward's part.

"So you're telling me their marriage might have been over before it even began?" Gabby asked. "That it was doomed?" She looked stunned.

"Something like that. Only now it's *definitely* over."

"So how much of Ellie's rant do you actually believe?"

"That's the tricky part," Carmela said. "I have to sort out her anger and rage from the melancholy and mourning."

"I see," Gabby said. She crossed her arms. "Though Melancholy and Mourning sounds more like the name of a very sad law firm."

"If it were only that easy," Carmela said. She paused. "And of course they twisted my arm a bit and asked me to look into things."

"We know you're good at making like Miss Marple. So now you have to figure out whether Edward is devastated or hugely relieved?"

"Something like that." Carmela nibbled at her sandwich. "According to Ellie, Isabelle had noticed changes in Edward's demeanor and behavior toward her. Isabelle started out being engaged to a man who adored her. But then, in these last few weeks, his ardor seemed to have cooled."

"Kind of like our weather," Gabby said. "But the thing is, engagements are broken off all the time. Everybody's heard some crazy story about a runaway bride. Or, to give equal opportunity its due, a runaway groom."

"And then there's the ever-amusing runaway husband," Carmela said. She was referring, of course, to her own Shamus Allan Meechum, who'd slipped into his boogie shoes, dodged out the back door, and left her holding, well . . . absolutely nothing.

"So why didn't Edward just man up and call the whole thing off?" Gabby wondered. "Be a gentleman like days of yore and let Isabelle keep her fancy ring? And then be done with it?"

"You mean make a clean break of things?"

"Well, it would have been a little messy, but yes."

"I don't know," Carmela said. "Somehow I think calling off a wedding is more complicated than that. Plans are in place, deposit checks written, invitations have gone out. So a person who's scared or wants to get out probably carries his secret burden deep inside himself until it's too late."

Gabby snapped her fingers. "Which accounts for all those dead newlyweds on cruise ships. Honeymooning husbands and wives are forever falling overboard — or being pushed — and are never seen again."

"That must be it," Carmela said. "If you feel cornered and can't figure out a graceful or logical exit strategy . . . then kaboom . . . all hell breaks loose."

"Do you think Edward went kaboom?" Gabby asked.

"That's what I intend to find out."

Ten minutes later, Gabby helped a woman select a few dog-themed rubber stamps, while Carmela gathered up supplies for a commercial scrapbook. It was going to be for a friend of hers, Jade Germaine, who wanted to . . .

Da-ding!

The bell over the front door tinkled, and there was Jade, looking around expectantly and carrying a large pink neoprene portfolio under her arm.

"Jade," Carmela called out. She hurried to the front of the store, her heels beating a rat-a-tat-tat against the wooden floorboards.

"Carmela," Jade said, giving her friend a hasty double air kiss. Jade was a burst of color today. Her cinnamon-colored suede shirt was belted tightly over a pair of dark

73

red jeans. Dancing blue eyes, a slash of smiling red lips, and a spill of blond hair were topped with a bright yellow tam set at a rakish angle over one eye.

The word *rainbow* popped into Carmela's mind, then she shook her head to dispel the thought and said, "You're right on time, Jade. Come on back and we'll get things rolling."

Jade followed Carmela to the craft table and hefted her pink portfolio up onto the table. It promptly tipped over, its handles flapping and scattering the scrapbook supplies that Carmela had so neatly arranged.

"Oops," Jade said. They both scrambled to set things right.

"How's the tea party business so far?" Carmela asked. Jade had just started a brand-new company called Tea Party in a Box. She'd laid in a huge supply of teapots, teacups and saucers, and three-tiered serving trays. And she'd developed at least a dozen tea party menus. Now she was determined to make a living by catering tea parties all over town — in private homes, in businesses, you name it.

"Business is starting to pick up," Jade told Carmela. "I catered a tea party for the Library Society last week, and I'm doing high tea at Tulane University tomorrow afternoon. For a bunch of big-buck alumni."

"That's wonderful," Carmela said. "Sounds like you're off to a great start."

"Word of mouth has worked so far," Jade said, "But now I need one of your super-duper commercial scrapbooks. Like the one you did for Lotus Floral. I really think prospective customers will understand my tea party concept so much better if they can see actual photos of my tea table arrangements, my fancy English tea ware, and all the sweets and savories that I can cater for them."

"And you brought photos?" Carmela asked.

"Tons of photos," Jade said. "I've been working on this project for almost a year now, so every time I bake a batch of scones, I arrange them on a pretty tray and snap a picture. Ditto for my tea sandwiches and desserts." She popped open her portfolio, and dozens of four-color photos spilled out onto the table. Photos of golden scones nestled in baskets, tiny triangle sandwiches stuffed with crab salad, amazing petit fours, and exotic pastries. "Look at this." She grabbed one of the photos. "Here's a sterling silver tea service that I picked up for a song at an antique auction up in Natchitoches."

"It looks very elegant set against that bowl

75

of pink peonies," Carmela said. "You know what?" She reached behind her and pulled out an album covered in pale gray silk shantung. "Your tea service photo would be perfect on the cover."

Jade held the photo of the silver service up against the album. "Mmn, I do like that." She gently rubbed two fingers over the richly tactile fabric. "And I adore this fabric."

Carmela had gathered up several silk flowers in shades of mauve and pink. Now she placed them next to the photo and arranged them along with some forest green velvet leaves.

"I can't believe what you just did," Jade said. "That design looks spectacular, like a graphic designer struggled over it. But you just . . . well, it was so spontaneous."

Carmela smiled. "Isn't that what you were aiming for?"

"Sure, but I didn't think it would come together this fast."

"We're not there yet. We need to select the right kind of paper for your inside pages, too." Carmela spread out a small array of paper that included an oyster white stock, cream vellum, pearlescent paper, and one called Champagne Cream.

"I like them all," Jade said. "Can we

somehow incorporate all four paper choices?"

"We could," Carmela said, "but I think it would look more polished if we chose one paper stock and let that be our background throughout the album. Let your photos shine as the star of the show."

"I see what you mean," Jade said. She narrowed her eyes as she studied the different sheets of paper. Then she reached out and touched the Champagne Cream with her index finger. "I think this one. It reminds me of a cream tea."

"Excellent choice," Carmela said. "Now, you brought along your brochures, too?"

"Yes," Jade said, pulling a flutter of brochures from her portfolio. "I figured one of them should be on the first page. Oh, and here are a bunch of business cards." She pressed a stack into Carmela's hand. "Take a bunch and pass 'em out to all your friends."

"I'll do that," Carmela said. She was eyeing the cover again. "Maybe just a few more touches for your cover? The more elements we add, the richer the effect."

"Like a good gumbo," Jade said.

Carmela nodded. "I was thinking about some purple velvet ribbon or a piece of crepe de Chine."

"Hold that thought," Jade said. She reached in her handbag and pulled out a small snippet of antique lace. "What about something like this?"

The lace surprised Carmela. "Where on earth did you get this?" She stroked the bit of lace with her finger and decided it felt old, perhaps even as old as the lace that had strangled Isabelle. What were the odds that two different pieces of antique lace would turn up in two days? Probably zero to none. Yet, here was another lace.

"Carmela," Jade said, "I would think you of all people would know about that new shop over on Orleans Avenue."

"What new shop is that?" Carmela's antennae were suddenly pinging like crazy.

"It's called Folly Française and, boy, is it ever a treasure trove for Francophiles. They offer a little bit of everything — flea market finds, some fairly authentic-looking antiques, hand-milled French soap, French perfumes, silk scarves and gloves — you name it. Oh, and there's jewelry, too. I saw some darling earrings that were cast in antique jewelry molds. Can you imagine? Just like something the Empress Josephine might have worn!"

"And they have lace," Carmela said.

"And lace," Jade said. "Yes indeed, they

carry quite a bit of old lace. That's why this piece caught my eye. I thought it might add a bit of old-world charm to my scrapbook. Oh, and I swear the owner has a few vintage Chanel bags tucked under the counter. You really have to swing by. I guarantee you'll love it."

"On Orleans Street, you said."

"Right next to that little book and map shop. You know, the one that sells those elegant little leather books that always smell so musty?"

"But it's authentic must," Carmela said, smiling. "Eighteenth century."

"Must be," Jade said, grinning back.

The idea of antique lace percolated in Carmela's brain for the rest of the afternoon, even when she was helping a customer pick out paper butterflies for a mixed-media collage and making suggestions to another woman on how to turn a cigar box into a leather-look suitcase complete with leather handles.

Finally, when the big hand on the clock crawled toward four, Carmela grabbed the sample of lace that Babcock had left behind and said, "Gabby, do you mind handling things from here on?"

"Not a problem," Gabby said. Then her

nose wiggled like a curious rabbit and she asked, "What's up?"

"I want to check out that shop, Folly Française, that Jade told me about."

"Because of the lace," Gabby said, suddenly turning serious.

Carmela nodded, equally serious. "Because of the lace."

A tiny bit of sun slanted across the rooftops of the French Quarter, gilding the redbrick buildings and giving everything a slightly ethereal feel, as Carmela ambled down Royal Street. The lacy wrought-iron balconies above her were festooned with cascades of bougainvilleas and azaleas. A saxophone player who leaned against the wall outside Ritter's Antiques played a pensive blues song. Two tourists, a man and a woman, happily dropped some bills into his open instrument case. The musician nodded his thanks but never missed a note.

At the corner, Carmela paused to let a red and yellow horse-drawn jitney go clopping by, and was suddenly struck by the chilliness of the wind that whooshed in from the Mississippi. How fast the seasons seemed to rush by. They were heading into winter again. Halloween was past, and Reveillon, a recently revived Creole custom that entailed lavish four- and five-course holiday dinners, would be celebrated in many of the fancier restaurants in just a matter of weeks. Christmas, Chanukah, and New Year's Eve were just around the corner, too.

Crossing the street, Carmela paused to look in the window of Chittenden's Antiques and Estate Jewelry. Cartier pendants, strands of Tahitian pearls, and a selection of old mine-cut diamond rings were nestled in black velvet boxes in the front window. Beyond those tasty baubles, a half dozen chandeliers hung from the ceiling, twinkling with what looked like thousands of crystals. A green leather-topped desk sat just beyond the window, looking worn but inviting. Like something Tennessee Williams might have had in the library of his Garden District home.

When Carmela finally pushed open the door to Folly Française, she was greeted by the mingled scents of vanilla, jasmine, and lavender. Like wandering through a French meadow, she decided. Or into Ava's voodoo shop, though those scents were definitely a shade darker.

And, yes, there was an enormous display of tiny French perfume bottles and dozens of elegantly wrapped soaps. On her right was an antique wooden drying rack that held a dozen colorful shawls, from the sheerest organza to whisper-soft cashmere.

Charmed, Carmela gazed around the rest of the shop. The walls were painted white, but roughed up, à la the Martha Stewart country French look. Small crystal chandeliers hung from the open rafters, and there were eye-catching pieces everywhere — jewelry, lorgnettes on gold chains, antique watches, handbags, charming and cheeky hats, French glassware, hankies, and christening gowns. And a gold velvet dress with an empire waist that literally took her breath away.

Glancing up from a polished brass cash register, a woman smiled and said, "Would you care to try it on?" She had just the hint of a French accent.

"I'm not sure I would fit into it," Carmela said. She studied the dress carefully. "It's quite old, isn't it?"

"From the Victorian era," said the woman. She reached out and gently touched the dress.

"Ooh, those women were so petite."

"You are not so large yourself," the woman said. She was early fifties but had an unlined, patrician face with elegant white hair pulled back into a chignon. Posing languidly in her black cashmere sweater, swishy black silk skirt, and single strand of pearls, she looked like she might have once been a ballerina.

"Well, thank you," Carmela said. "But I'm more in the mood to take a look around. You certainly have some beautiful things here."

"We have many items to please the eye, so do take your time and enjoy," said the woman. She extended a hand gracefully. "I am Mignon Cenas, the owner."

Carmela shook hands with her. "Nice to meet you. I'm Carmela Bertrand. I'm the owner of Memory Mine Scrapbook Shop over on Governor Nicholls Street."

"Oh," Mignon cooed. "I only opened my shop a few weeks ago, so I've not yet had the pleasure of meeting so many of my neighboring shopkeepers. I'm still trying to get organized and add to my inventory." She picked up a lace hanky. "So many things are quite difficult to locate. You see this lace handkerchief? Would you believe it's nearly one hundred years old? And the embroidery is still in perfect condition."

"It's beautiful," Carmela said. This might be the opening she was looking for.

"These must be hand washed," Mignon continued. "A machine would surely tear this delicate fabric to shreds." She picked up a lace camisole that looked like it had been hand sewn in some French convent. "Same with this garment."

"You seem to know a lot about lace," Carmela said. It was a statement, not a question.

"In the eighteenth and early nineteenth centuries, clothes were all fairly standard in cut. It was the decoration that made them fashionable and unique. Ribbons and lace pretty much defined French fashion. French *merceries* specialized in ribbons, braids, lace, buttons, and trims, all the items that made a dress highly distinctive. Today we call such things notions. And that makes them sound unimportant, but at that time . . ." She shrugged. "This type of décor was the height of *chic.*"

Carmela knew she'd come to the right place. "I have a piece of French lace," she said. She dug in her handbag and pulled out the piece of ivory lace that Babcock had allowed her to keep.

"It's lovely," Mignon said, peering at it.

Even though handling the lace made her skin crawl, Carmela said, "I was wondering if you might take a closer look at it? Maybe render your expert opinion?"

Mignon picked up a pair of tortoiseshell half-glasses and put them on. She leaned forward and studied the lace carefully, then smiled at Carmela. "Your lace is definitely handmade, but I'm afraid it's not French lace."

"It's not? Then what is it?"

"Just offhand, I'd say this might be Point de Venise flounce lace."

"Which is what, please?"

"Belgian linen lace. Also handmade, of course, but an even finer quality." She pointed. "You see that high sculptural relief of the floral motif?"

"Yes?"

"That's what sets it apart from more delicate French lace." Mignon took the lace from Carmela, held it up, and turned it slightly to catch the light. "You see — it looks like carved ivory."

"And the linen fabric means it's strong?" Carmela asked.

"Strong?"

"I mean like tensile strength. If you looped it around something and, um, pulled hard."

"Oh, definitely," Mignon said. "This is the type of lace that, how do you say it? Could choke a horse."

Carmela grimaced. That's exactly what she was afraid of.

CHAPTER 7

Minced garlic sizzled in a pan of virgin olive oil while fresh basil perfumed the air. A large stockpot filled with near-boiling water sat on the rear burner of the stove in Carmela's small galley kitchen.

She was cookin' tonight. Pasta Primavera. Stirring the beginnings of her creation with a big wooden spoon while she slow danced to "If I Ain't Got You" by Alicia Keys. Boo, her sweet little fawn-colored Shar-Pei, wiggled her chunky backside along with her, showing off with her own doggy dance moves. Poobah, a spotted Heinz 57 dog that Carmela's ex had rescued from the streets, was sprawled on his cushy, overpriced dog bed, solemnly gazing at the two of them. He'd get up when the food was *ready,* and not a moment sooner.

Carmela finished crumbling the basil and slipped it into the pan. While she stirred the aromatic mix, she reached for her phone and hit speed dial.

"Babcock," he said.

Carmela smiled. Her honey had answered on the second ring.

"I'm in my kitchen and the fragrant aromas of garlic and basil reminded me of you. Of our most recent dinner together."

"Carmela?"

"Of course, it's me! Who did you think it was, the counter boy at Pasta Pete's?"

Babcock chuckled. "Tell me more about that garlic and basil. What else comes with it? And are you offering me dinner?"

"Actually, I was calling to offer you a snippet of information, thank you very much."

"That's a switch. Usually you're trying to wheedle a few investigative details out of me."

"That lace you brought in this morning?" Carmela said. "You did say it was important, didn't you?"

"Very. And please don't be coy, Carmela. Just spit it out if you have something."

"Here's the thing: I had a client come into the shop today with a similar bit of antique lace."

"Who's that?" he asked.

"Not important," she said. "The big news is that I found out about a new shop in the French Quarter called Folly Française."

"Never heard of it," Babcock said.

"When my birthday rolls around you will. Anyway, I dropped by this shop and talked to the owner, Mignon, who I'm pretty sure is full-blooded French."

"Okay."

"And I showed her that snippet of lace you gave me."

"What'd she say?" Now Babcock sounded interested.

"She said it wasn't French lace at all, that it was probably Belgian lace. Made from linen, but strong enough to choke a horse. Her words, not mine."

"No kidding. Belgian lace? Who knew?"

"Thanks to me, *you* do," Carmela said.

"But your French lady . . . she didn't have any idea as to its origin?"

"She just said it was old. Antique."

"Huh." Babcock was mulling the information, falling silent as he often did.

"Did I do good?" Carmela asked.

"You did great," Babcock said. "Although I'm not sure if knowing the lace is Belgian in origin will advance our investigation all that much. It would be nice to find the exact source. If it was purchased from a shop somewhere or at auction."

"So I'll keep digging."

"Whoa," Babcock said. "I only want you

to keep checking on the lace part. Nothing else. No freelance investigating and no messing around with the Baudette family."

"What's so special about them?" Carmela asked. She knew, but she wanted to hear it from him.

"You have no idea."

"Enlighten me."

"Friends in high places," Babcock said. "Very high. So please try not to get yourself embroiled in one of your usual sticky messes."

"I won't do that," Carmela said. "I'm reformed." She winced at this little white lie. But really, what could a few questions here or there hurt?

"And for heaven's sake, be careful!" Babcock said.

"You know I will."

"Actually, I don't know that at all."

Carmela had no sooner hung up when, five seconds later, her phone rang. She grinned to herself, deciding that Babcock was probably calling back to whisper sweet romantic words. And snatched up the phone.

"Miss me?"

But it wasn't Babcock calling at all.

"*Cher,* I miss anyone who can serve as the voice of reason in this group."

"Ava?" Her friend sounded upset, verging on crazed.

"It's me all right," Ava said. "I'm over at Bothell Brothers Funeral Home trying to help Ellie plan a semi-decent funeral for Isabelle. But there's a whole barrel of crazies here who can't agree on *any*thing." She paused. "I know this is above and beyond the call of duty, but can you come over here and be the voice of reason?"

"You want me? What can I do?"

"Bring a gun and put me out of my misery? No, seriously, *cher*, I know I keep pulling you into this mess like it's quicksand, but we're desperate. *I'm* desperate."

"What's going on?"

"Vesper Baudette, also known as Edward's mother and the Gargoyle of the Garden District, is bound and determined to impose her iron will on every piddling detail. If Ellie even opens her mouth to make a suggestion, Vesper shoos her away like she's a stray dog."

"What about Edward? What's his part in all this?"

"He's like a puppet with his strings cut off. When he's not leaking tears, he just bows his head like a docile cow and says, 'Yes, Momma.' Seriously, Ellie and I need reinforcements. Somebody with the tenacity of a junkyard dog. Somebody like *you.*"

Carmela sighed and turned off the stove. Dinner was going to have to wait. This just wasn't her day for meals eaten on time. "Where exactly is Bothell Brothers?"

"Over in the Faubourg Marigny," Ava said. "The dreary part. And hurry. Please hurry!"

When Carmela pulled up in front of bothell Brothers Funeral Home, she saw that Ava had been right about the dreary part. In fact, her first impression was that the place had the look of an abandoned building. The hulking stone front, of what had probably been a prosperous-looking mansion in its day, was streaked with decades of grime.

Nice, Carmela thought as she got out of her car. Just what she needed. The actual place where they filmed the movie *Psycho.* On second thought, compared to this wreck, the original *Psycho* house looked like it was designed by Frank Lloyd Wright.

Carmela gave a little shiver as she mounted the steps to the portico. In fact, she half expected Lurch of Addams Family fame to throw open the front door. And she almost swore she heard him groan as she pushed the heavy door inward.

But there wasn't a living soul around to greet a living visitor.

Okay. Now what?

She glanced around expectantly. The lobby was shabby with mismatched furniture that included two armchairs with gray stuffing sticking out of torn seams, and a large wooden reception desk that was unattended. Organ music, low and tragic, moaned from a speaker. The fireplace looked as though it hadn't been lit since Andrew Jackson charged into town to settle the War of 1812.

Carmela took a breath and wrinkled her nose. What *was* that smell? Dead flowers that had been left to rot in an unchanged bowl of water? Probably. And chemicals, too. The really nasty ones you didn't want to think about too much.

"Hello?" Carmela called out. "Anybody home?"

Her voice echoed hollowly in the reception room.

She knew Ava, Ellie, and the rest of the crew must be tucked away in an office somewhere. But where?

Carmela glanced around, saw a shard of light to her left, and figured that was as good a place as any to start. She crept across the carpet and ended up in front of a partially open door. A tarnished plaque hung to the left of it, slightly crooked, as if a screw had gone missing. The words *Slumber Room 1* were etched in the center.

Easing open the door, Carmela peeked in. *Are they in here?*

All she could see was the wizened body of an old man lying in a satin-lined casket.

Oops.

As Carmela's eyes became accustomed to the gloom, she saw two women dressed all in black sitting on rickety black folding chairs. Black gauze obscured their faces. Backing away slowly, her only thought was that this looked like a scene from a Wes Craven movie.

She whirled around, determined to find someone, anyone, and found herself face to face with a dark-haired woman.

"Eek!" Carmela was so surprised she took a step backward and thudded up against the door.

"May I help you?" the woman asked.

Carmela put a hand to her chest. "You scared me."

"My apologies," the woman said. She wore a severely tailored black skirt suit and tons of dark eyeliner, and her raven black hair was cut in a pageboy à la Cleopatra. "I'm Louise Courtland, one of the funeral coordinators. How may I help you?"

"I'm looking for Ellie Black," Carmela said. "And, I guess, Edward and Vesper Baudette."

"Of course," Courtland said. "They're downstairs in our casket showroom. Won't you please follow me?"

Carmela followed the Cleo look-alike across the lobby and down a long hallway. It was hung with black-and-white photos of antique horse-drawn hearses.

"Nice place you've got here," Carmela said. "So homey, but without that overdone decorator look."

"We like it," Cleo said.

They passed a closed door marked *Office* and then descended a flight of stairs, the faux Oriental carpet whispering beneath their feet. Halfway down, Carmela could hear voices, raised voices, drifting toward her. It sounded like a knock-down, drag-out fight from a heated Louisiana political caucus. But when she got to the doorway of the casket showroom, it turned out to be Ava, Ellie, and company.

Or, rather, bad company.

A short, rotund woman with gray hair done up in a vintage French roll, was arguing forcefully with the entire group. This woman, Carmela decided, had to be the

94

domineering socialite Vesper Baudette. And surrounding her in a half circle were Ava, Ellie, a bereft-looking fellow who had to be Edward Baudette, and an unknown young woman who cradled a tiny fluff ball of a dog in her arms.

Coffins were stacked three high against the walls, making the place look like some bizarre discount mart of death. It seemed like an awful place to have an argument. And it certainly wasn't conducive to making any kind of important decision.

"Why can't anyone follow my reasoning?" Vesper brayed loudly. She was a woman who was used to getting her way. She bullied her family, her banker, her stockbroker, and all the people (the *small* people, as she called them) who worked for her. "All we need to do is select a modest coffin, sign the papers, and be done with it."

Edward Baudette sighed heavily and said, "It isn't your decision to make, Momma." Edward may have been a mortgage banker who handled million-dollar deals, but Momma was much harder to deal with.

"Of course it is," Vesper said. She smoothed the skirt of an expensive-looking dress that perfectly matched the iron color of her hair. "I offered to foot the bill, didn't I? Therefore, my generosity entitles me to a

95

good deal of say in what goes on here."

Deciding to make her presence known, Carmela deliberately banged the door against the wall. Six sets of eyes suddenly drilled into her, including those of a string bean funeral director she hadn't noticed before.

"Who are you?" Vesper demanded. Her eyes looked like two steel ball bearings.

"I'm a friend of Ellie's," Carmela said. "And Ava's." She breezed into the showroom. "Here to lend a hand." *Hopefully.*

Vesper held up a chubby hand in protest and shook her head dismissively. "No, no, no. This is a private family matter. We don't need input from some random person." She looked directly at the string bean funeral director and said, "Mr. Bothell, can you kindly show this interloper out?"

Ava jumped up. "Hold everything. Don't bother getting your granny panties in a twist, because Carmela *will* be staying. I asked her to join us because we're in dire need of her cool voice of reason."

"That's right," Ellie said, finally mustering her courage. "Carmela stays."

"It's okay with me," Edward said.

"What*ever,*" Vesper said, clearly unhappy.

"Come sit over here, *cher.*" Ava sat back

down and patted the empty chair seat next to her.

Carmela strode purposefully into the room and took her seat between Ava and the woman with the dog.

"We were just discussing . . ." Ava started. "Ahem, *trying* to discuss what type of coffin is most suitable."

"The black one," Vesper said. "It's simple and dignified."

"It's made of plywood," Edward moaned. He was tall, with a long face and square jaw. He had that slick, do-nothing preppie look about him that said, *I was born into money, own a sailboat, drive a Porsche, and snarf thirty-five-dollar lobster salads for lunch.*

"Absolutely not," the woman with the dog screeched. "The only clear choice is the white coffin with the ruffled velvet interior and mother-of-pearl inlaid skulls. It's very Alexander McQueen, the early years."

Carmela turned in her chair. "And who are you?"

The woman stroked her little dog. "I'm Naomi Rattler."

"The ex–maid of honor," Ava filled in.

"I'm widely regarded as one of the top fashion bloggers," Naomi said, giving a snarky smile. "I write the very popular blog *Haute to Trot,* so I'm extremely keen on style. And this is my baby girl Bing Bing," she added, carefully adjusting the pink and rhinestone-studded collar on her dog.

As if in answer, Bing Bing let loose a series of high-pitched yips.

"What is she exactly?" Carmela asked.

"I think some kind of long-haired ferret," Ava said.

Naomi's mouth opened and closed in protest. Obviously, she was deeply wounded by Ava's comment. "I'll have you know this is a Pomkatoo."

"Say what?" Ava said.

"Bing Bing's a very delicate mixture of Pomeranian, Karelian, and toy poodle."

"Oh sure," Ava said. "One of those Mix Master dogs."

Vesper clapped her hands loudly. "Excuse me. Could we please stick to our agenda?"

"You mean *your* agenda," Naomi said. "You want this funeral to be all dark and dreadful, when it could be quite stylish. Practically a photo op."

Carmela leaned forward and addressed Ellie. "What do *you* want, hon? What would you prefer?"

"I wanted the simple walnut casket," Ellie said. "But I was voted down."

Then Edward got up from his chair and walked over to an obviously high-end mahogany and brass casket. The wood glowed richly, and each corner was decorated with small bouquets of brass roses. The inside was lined with silk and trimmed with lace. His hand gently stroked the casket's highly polished exterior. "I think this one's the most fitting," he said.

Vesper was at his side in a heartbeat. "You want silk and fancy lace?" she snarled. "Be serious. It's a casket, not a wedding dress!"

Which set Ellie to crying piteously and Naomi to looking angry and stunned.

"Can you believe this?" Ava said to Carmela. "Are these not the most dysfunctional people you've ever met?"

"Not really," Carmela said. "You forget that I was married to Shamus." Shamus Allan Meechum was Carmela's ex-husband and heir to the Meechum banking family. Shamus (he of the wandering eye), his big sister Glory, and the rest of their snarling clan took the grand prize when it came to dysfunctionality, if that was even a legitimate word.

"Can we please make a decision?" Vesper cried. "Mr. Bothell here has work to do. After all, we've got the viewing tomorrow evening and then the funeral the very next day."

"Where's the funeral?" Carmela asked Ava.

"St. Patrick's Church," Ava said. "You know. That lovely Gothic church in the . . ."

". . . Seedy part of town," Carmela finished. "Okay. I'm getting a fairly clear picture here."

"Ellie doesn't have a lot of money," Ava whispered.

Naomi suddenly jumped up, tossed Bing Bing into Carmela's lap, and dashed over to hug Edward. They embraced warmly for a few moments, and then she smiled and whispered something in his ear. Now Edward was smiling as well.

"What's with those two?" Carmela asked. She winced as Bing Bing dug sharp little claws into her leg.

Ava shook her head. "You mean the hot mess and the cold fish?"

"Are they old friends?" Carmela decided their embrace bordered on more than a little friendly. Did this warrant looking into?

"Can we *please* get back to the casket selection?" Vesper demanded.

Carmela jumped up, the fuzzy little dog dangling from her outstretched arms. Talking over everyone, she said, "I've got an idea. Let's take another vote. All those in favor of the simple walnut casket, raise your hand."

CHAPTER 8

Three hands shot into the air. Hands that belonged to Carmela, Ava, and Ellie.

"Excellent," Carmela said. "We've got three votes for the walnut casket. Now who wants the whorehouse mahogany one?"

Edward tentatively raised his hand.

"I'm seein' a trend here," Ava muttered.

"And who likes the Snow White casket?" Carmela asked.

Naomi voted for the frou-frou white casket, and the voting continued with Vesper being the lone vote for the plain black casket.

"That's it," Carmela said. "Ellie's choice of the simple walnut casket wins. Meeting adjourned."

"That wasn't fair," Vesper protested. "We were railroaded!"

"Momma," Edward said, "just sign the papers so we can be done with this, okay?"

Even though Vesper humphed and

bumphed in protest, she still pulled out her American Express Platinum Card and shoved it into Mr. Bothell's hands. She'd capitulated, but not very graciously, like Germany surrendering to France at Compiegne.

Which gave Carmela a chance to pull Edward aside, introduce herself, and have a few words with him.

"How are you doing?" she asked finally. She was using her I'm-gonna-pull-the-truth-outta-you-if-it-kills-me nicey-nice voice.

Edward bobbed his head, looking somewhat relieved. "Hanging in there. I guess I should thank you for coming tonight. We were all sort of going in circles, chasing our tails."

"Not a problem," Carmela said. She paused, and then said, "I'm sorry I didn't get to meet you at the cake tasting."

Edward looked surprised. "You were there last night? At Commander's Palace?"

"Having dinner with my boyfriend, Detective Edgar Babcock."

Edgar aimed a finger at her. "I talked to him. Last night and again today."

"I'm sure you'll be talking to him lots more." Then Carmela decided to dive right in. "Do you have any idea why Isabelle might have ventured into that cemetery?"

Edward seemed genuinely stumped. "I don't know. I've thought about it long and hard these past twenty-four hours. There was no reason for her to be in the cemetery alone, especially at night."

"There must have been *some* reason."

Edward squinted at her and scratched his chin. "Isabelle could have been taking a shortcut through the cemetery to get to my house."

"You live close by?" Carmela asked.

"Well, my mother does. Her house is on Prytania Street, just a block or so away."

"And Isabelle thought you might have gone there? After you ducked out of the cake tasting?" Carmela eyed him carefully, trying to see if she could pick up any sort of vibe. "Because I understand you did leave early."

"Look, it's traditional that I have dinner with my mother on Sunday night. So, yes, I did leave early. I mean, I was there lobbying for chocolate cake, when everyone else wanted vanilla cream." Edward shrugged. "I was completely outvoted, kind of like tonight, so what exactly was the purpose of my staying?"

"Poor you," Carmela said. "So who else might have noticed which direction Isabelle was headed?"

"You should ask Naomi. She's been incredibly involved. She was there last night for the whole thing."

Carmela thought about the last few terrifying moments in Isabelle's life. Lonely moments. "Well, not exactly," she said. She patted Edward's hand and then turned to talk to Naomi. The girl was stuffing Bing Bing into an oversized tote that was littered with *G*'s. Or maybe they were *C*'s. Carmela wasn't sure.

"Naomi," Carmela said. "You're just the person I need to talk to."

"The white coffin would have been better," Naomi grumped. "Then we could have surrounded it with a backdrop of purple violets."

"I'm sure your taste is impeccable," Carmela said. "But I have a couple of questions for you."

Naomi blinked.

"About last night," Carmela said. "Do you have any idea what Isabelle was doing in that cemetery?"

Naomi rearranged her face into wide-eyed innocence. "Gosh, I don't know. Isabelle just took off in a flash. In fact, we all kind of scattered to the wind." One hand fluttered to stroke her dog. "I just assumed she was heading for her car."

"Or to Edward's mother's house?"

Naomi shrugged. "Maybe. Gee, I really don't know."

One more *gosh* or *gee* and Carmela decided she was going to buy the girl a '50s-era pink poodle skirt. Was this girl just a simpleton or did she really know something? Turning back to Ava and Ellie, who were pulling on their coats, she asked, "Who needs a ride?"

"Me," Ava said, holding up her hand. "Ellie's got her own car here so she's heading directly home. Poor girl is dead on her feet."

"I am," Ellie said. "But I'm feeling a little better." She gave Carmela a quick hug. "Thanks to you."

"Not a problem," Carmela said, even though the entire evening had been one big, ugly, matted fur ball of a problem.

Carmela and Ava trailed everyone upstairs, where every light but one seemed to have been shut off. Then, when they got to the portico, the two of them held back, watching as the rest of the group dispersed on the street.

"Who's got the big-time limo?" Ava asked. Then a liveried driver suddenly snapped to, opened the car door, and Vesper climbed in.

"Oh. Her."

"I don't think it's hired, either," Carmela said.

"I never met anybody before who had a car and driver," Ava said.

"Driving Miss Daisy."

Ava snorted. "Huh, more like *Driving Miss Poison Ivy.*"

They watched as Edward and Naomi sauntered over to a candy apple red Porsche 911. Edward climbed in and then rolled down the window so Naomi could talk to him.

Ava bumped Carmela's shoulder. "What do you think's going on with those two?"

"Dunno," Carmela said. "But I don't think it has anything to do with the funeral."

Naomi leaned forward and her tinkling laughter drifted toward them.

"It sounds like you're suspicious of them," Ava said.

"Are you kidding? I'm suspicious of this whole crazy wedding party."

"Except now it's a funeral party."

Carmela peered at Naomi and Edward through the gloom. "But those two," she muttered. "It does feel like something might be percolating."

"Maybe they're just friends?" Ava said.

"And maybe they're not. Come on, jump

in, let's see what happens."

Ava jumped into Carmela's car, a two-seater Mercedes that Shamus had popped for several years ago. "We're going to tail Edward?"

"Oh, I don't know. Maybe we're just all going in the same direction."

But when Edward drove back through the French Quarter on Tchoupitoulas Street, and then angled off on Poydras and cut over to Perdido Street, Carmela followed.

"Where's he going?" Ava wondered. They were right on the edge of the Central Business District, or CBD, now. It was an area that had fallen on hard times, and then been rejuvenated when real estate developers bought up parcels of land. Luxury hotels, condos, and town houses had been built and the prices jacked up sky-high.

"He must live here," Carmela said. "There. He's pulling into the garage in one of those row houses."

"Sweet."

The row houses were sleek, three-story contemporary-looking town houses. The garages were on street level with two living levels right above them.

"Do you see Naomi's car?" Carmela asked.

"No," Ava said. "I guess she didn't follow him."

"Do you know what she drives?"

"Maybe a green Prius?"

"She's a pain in the butt," Carmela said. "But at least she's reduced her carbon footprint."

"Something's gotta give."

They waited on the street, watching Edward's town house as the lights came on upstairs. But Naomi never showed up.

Because Ava hadn't eaten yet, either (and Carmela felt guilty for taking her on a wild-goose chase), Carmela invited her over for a late supper. While Ava skittered across the courtyard to change, Carmela greeted Boo and Poobah, and then heated up what had been the beginnings of her pasta primavera. As her herbs and oils sizzled yet again, she deftly chopped carrots and celery, and dug a bunch of spinach out of the refrigerator. Then she turned on her water to boil.

A few minutes later, the doorbell dinged and Ava came swishing in. She'd changed into a black-and-white zebra-striped caftan and had added a wide black belt embedded with jewels. Carmela thought she looked like something out of *1001 Arabian Nights*.

"I didn't know what you were cookin',

cher, so I brought both red and white wine."
Ava held up two bottles. "See? A Merlot
and a Chardonnay. What's your fancy?"

"Let's do white," Carmela said. She
noticed that her water was boiling, so she
tossed in two handfuls of fettuccini pasta.

"White wine it is," Ava said. She pulled
open a kitchen drawer and grabbed a
corkscrew. "Who says I don't know my way
around a kitchen, huh?"

"You're going to have to learn to cook
someday," Carmela said.

"Why? When I've got you." Ava grabbed
two wineglasses and poured out servings of
wine. Generous servings.

Of course, Boo and Poobah couldn't bear
to be left out of the fun. So they danced
around, pawing at Ava's caftan.

"Be careful with Auntie Ava's outfit, dar-
lings," Ava told them. "Satin pulls, but
organza rips forever." She took a quick sip
of wine. "Ah, just what I needed. So, tell
me . . . what was your overall impression of
the Battling Baudettes?"

Carmela twirled the pasta as the water
bubbled and roiled. "I always thought
Shamus's sister, Glory, was the most irritat-
ing woman on earth, but Vesper could
certainly give her a run for her money."

"A face-off," Ava said.

Carmela continued. "Vesper is annoying, bossy, and egotistically wrapped up in her own son."

"Baby boy."

"That's exactly how she treats him, too," Carmela said. "Like he's a little prince."

"And did you see how he acquiesces to her?"

"Yes," Carmela said. "And how dare Vesper be so rude to Ellie. If the wedding had taken place, Isabelle and Ellie would have been family. I mean, how do you think Vesper would have behaved toward them once they were related by marriage?"

"She'd probably act the same way," Ava said. "Rude and obnoxious."

"This whole situation just breaks my heart," Carmela said. "And, you know, earlier this afternoon, when Ellie was telling us her suspicions about Vesper . . . well, I kind of blew that off. But now that I've met the woman, I think she does have a violent streak."

"Vesper obviously knew about the cake tasting at Commander's Palace," Ava said.

"She'd have to."

"So maybe she was lurking outside?"

"Maybe." This still felt a little thin to Carmela.

"And they had a confrontation," Ava said.

"Or . . . better yet, maybe Vesper was suddenly *nice* to Isabelle."

"You're saying Vesper might have caught her off guard," Carmela said.

Ava snapped her fingers. "Yes, that's it! And then they just kind of wandered into the cemetery. Or Vesper got her talking and Isabelle just figured it was a shortcut."

"Could happen," Carmela said. "I guess." She turned, drained the pasta, and then quickly tossed it with the oil and vegetables. Once she'd transferred two servings into yellow Fiesta bowls, she sprinkled each one with freshly grated Parmesan cheese.

Ava took a deep breath as they carried their bowls to the table. "I don't know what smells better, your primavera or this cheese topping. I loves me an aromatic cheese."

"You usually refer to them as stinky cheeses," Carmela said.

"Hey," Ava said. "I'm tryin' to be a lady here."

They ate and sipped wine for a while, enjoying the companionship and the simple meal.

Then Ava said, "I wonder what the deal is with Naomi?"

"She turned out to be a real crazy," Carmela said.

"Crazy about Edward is what I think."

"She did seem to be putting the moves on him."

"No kidding," Ava said. "Naomi was pulling out all the stops." She tossed back her mass of dark hair and said, "Honey, if I put moves like that on a man, it would mean I was seriously angling for a diamond."

"Huh," Carmela said. "So something to think about."

The jingle of the telephone interrupted their conversation.

Ava gave a wicked leer. "Maybe that's Babcock calling. Mooning around for a little romance."

"Could be," Carmela said as she jumped up.

"Tell him to bring another bottle of wine." She burped slightly. "Preferably a really pricey Cabernet."

Carmela snatched up the phone. "Ava says you can come over, but only if you bring an expensive bottle of Cabernet."

A deep male voice let out a rumbling chuckle. "If I did that, darlin', Baby would have my head on a stick."

"Del?"

Del Fontaine was a well-known, high-priced New Orleans attorney. He wore two-thousand-dollar suits and played golf at the exclusive Commodore Club. He was also the husband of Baby Fontaine, one of Carmela's best friends and avid customers.

"I'm sorry," Carmela laughed. "I thought you were someone else."

"Carmela, honey," Del said, "I haven't had an offer anywhere near that exciting since, oh, maybe last night when Baby asked me to bring her a nice cup of chamomile tea. I'm not much in the kitchen, but that sweet little brew I concocted was well worth it." He chuckled again.

"What can I do for you, Del?" Carmela was well aware that Baby's birthday was this Friday and figured Del's call had to be related. She was right.

"I know you and Ava are planning to come to our big party Friday evening at Parpadelle Restaurant . . ."

"We wouldn't miss it," Carmela said.

"The thing is," Del said, "Baby might *suspect* about the party — the fancy dinner and the birthday cake and champagne — but she doesn't know about the *entertainment.*"

"What do you mean, Del?"

"The whole shebang is going to be a Murder Mystery Party."

Carmela was slightly taken aback. "Really?"

"Sure," Del said expansively. "I hired a

114

genuine stage actor to come up with a script and sort of MC the whole thing."

"Okay."

"Anyway, the really big surprise is that some of the guests will have actual roles in the show. That's why I'm calling."

Uh-oh. "Wait. You're saying you want me to play a part in the play?"

"You and Ava. You'll do it, right? I mean, Baby is gonna go bonkers over this. She'll love it. I just know she will."

"Well . . . sure," Carmela said, even though she wasn't really sure at all.

Del laughed uproariously. "I'll send over scripts for you two darlin's, so you can get started memorizing your lines." And with that he hung up.

Carmela stood with the phone in her hand.

"What?" Ava said. "What's up with Del? And why do you look like someone just stole your cookies?"

"Because Baby's birthday party just took a hard left turn."

"What do you mean?"

"Besides shrimp *étouffée,* roast duck with cornbread dressing, cake, and champagne, it's going to be one of those murder mystery parties where all the guests play a role. All the guests meaning you and me."

"Wait," Ava croaked. "We have to say lines?"

"Looks like. Del said he's sending over some scripts."

Dark curls swirled around Ava as she shook her head. "As if we don't have a *real* murder mystery to solve already."

CHAPTER 9

Tuesday morning dawned cool and sunny, with streams of dancing sunbeams filtering through the front windows of Memory Mine. Gabby was fussing with a couple of triptychs that she and Carmela designed — miniature Venetian theatres that were meant to be an inspiration for their customers.

"You think I should put these on display?" Gabby asked. She held up a tiny theatre made of chipboard. It was hand painted, elaborately stenciled, and decorated with gold leaf.

"I think you should do whatever your little heart dictates," Carmela said. "Honestly, Gabby, the window displays you create are always fabulous. I think that's what brings customers in like crazy."

"Really?" Gabby said, obviously pleased. "Well, in that case . . ."

Carmela glanced sideways from where she was restocking paper in their wire bins.

She'd been watching two women out of the corner of her eye. They seemed to be stuck on something.

"Anything I can do to help?" Carmela asked.

"We're hosting a party," said the first woman.

"And want to create our own place mats," said the second.

"But we're kind of stuck," said the first.

"Okay," Carmela said. "But I see that you picked out a lovely rubber stamp."

"A carnation," said the first woman. "But I'm not exactly sure how to make this work."

"You just *stamp* it," said the second woman.

Her friend turned on her. "But, Delia, I want it to be two-tone!"

"Okaaay," Carmela said. "I can show you what to do 'cause it's really pretty simple." She touched the rubber stamp to a mauve ink pad and stamped a carnation onto a white test paper. Then she wiped off what was left of the mauve ink and touched it to a silver ink pad. "Now you stamp over it, but just a smidgeon off to the side. That's how you achieve the lovely two-tone effect you were looking for."

"That's it," said the first woman.

"See, I *told* you," said the second woman.

Carmela winked at Gabby as she came toward the front desk. The two women were still shopping, still arguing a bit, but they hadn't declared outright war on each other yet, so that was probably a good thing.

"Problems?" Gabby said under her breath.

Carmela picked up a roll of dark blue ribbon and spun it in her hands. "Not really. But you should have been with me last night."

Gabby immediately picked up on the tone in Carmela's voice. "What happened?" She planted her elbows firmly on the counter, her chin resting in her palms. "Do tell."

So Carmela gave her a slightly abridged version of the picking-out-the-casket debacle. And, the more Carmela revealed, without having to embroider a single thing, the more the wrinkles in Gabby's forehead deepened.

"No!" she said finally.

"Yes," Carmela said.

"Vesper's really that nasty? And stingy?"

"I think the woman's a viper."

"And Edward really wasn't overcome with grief?" Gabby asked.

"Like I said, he seemed sad at first, but then he started playing footsie with Naomi."

"She of the goofy floofy dog," Gabby said. "Wow. It's crazy to hear what poor Ellie was

119

up against. Lucky you and Ava were . . ."

The phone on the front counter suddenly shrilled, interrupting their conversation.

Gabby quickly picked it up. "Good morning, Memory Mine. How can I help you?" There was a smile in her voice until the caller on the other end spoke, and then the warmth evaporated and was replaced by a glacial coolness. "One moment." She thrust the receiver straight out toward Carmela and made a face. "It's him. The rat."

Carmela came around the desk and took the phone. "Shamus." She knew dang well who the rat in her life was. He might be a handsome, tousle-haired, boyish-grinned rat, but he was still a rat.

"And good morning to you, Little Miss Sunshine," Shamus said. "How are you on this wonderful . . . ?"

"Cut to the chase, Shamus. What do you want?"

"Okay, be that way," Shamus said, his voice hardening. "I was calling to see if you filed that paper yet?"

Carmela's eyes flicked down to the desk and then to a stack of papers that was tucked neatly in one of the side cubbyholes. There it was. A quitclaim deed she hadn't bothered to sign much less file. "Uh . . . what?" she said, stalling.

"Babe, I know you've been putting this off. But it'll take five minutes and cost you like ten bucks. Just walk over to City Hall and do it, okay? Then we're done with this."

Like we'll ever be done, Carmela thought to herself. *No, you keep popping back into my life like one of those creepy, evil clown jack-in-the-boxes.*

She closed her eyes for a moment and drew a deep breath. "Okay," she said. "Okay, Shamus, I'll take care of it."

"Soon?"

"Yes." *Now please go away.*

"You're a peach," Shamus said. He hesitated. "How are the dogs?"

"The dogs are good," Carmela said.

"Don't you think it's about time they enjoyed a sleepover at my place? I've got parental rights, too, you know."

"They can sleep over as long as there aren't any other strays sleeping in your bed," Carmela said.

"You should talk," Shamus snarled. He hung up so quickly his words were barely audible.

"Problem?" Gabby asked.

"Nothing serious. Just typical Shamus stuff." Carmela thumbed through the papers in the desk and pulled out the quitclaim deed. Studied it for a moment. "But I have to run out for a while, okay?"

"Take your time." Gabby waved a hand toward the two women. "I'm going to . . ."

Carmela nodded. Gabby was going to see if *she* could be any help to the women who seemed to be involved in yet another snit fit.

Carmela bounced down the street, thankful for the meager sunlight, enjoying the crisp, cool weather. The French Quarter wasn't its usual buzzy self this morning, and for that she was grateful. It was nice to stroll along and glance in store windows without getting jostled. She stopped in front of Armand's Antiques and studied a gilded clock.

Austrian, perhaps?

Then her eyes caught her own reflection in the glimmering window, and as she tossed back her head, she saw that a few strands of her blond bob (almost a lob — a long bob) kept falling in her eyes. A sure sign she needed a trim.

Okay, let's stop putting this off and get that paper filed. Then we'll make a phone call to Monsieur Gerard's Salon.

During her divorce proceedings, Carmela had wanted to sell any and all joint property, to leave no attachments to her soon-to-be ex. But Shamus, always interested in self above all, wanted to hang on to a rental property they had in hopes that the value would go up. Carmela had offered to deed it to him or sell it, whichever was easier, just to be rid of it, but Shamus had won out. Now, of course, the value had skyrocketed and Shamus was hot to sell. And even though Carmela would have no claim to the profits, she was obliged to file this stupid bit of paper.

Doggone Shamus, this is not what I need right now. I've got other fish to fry.

Carmela stood on the corner of Dauphine Street waiting for a break in the traffic. When it finally came, she darted across. Then it was just another half a block to the city registrar's office.

Carmela's heels clacked against the white marble floor of the cavernous room as she entered. She'd figured the place would be mobbed, but it wasn't. In fact, there were no lines at all.

Maybe I just caught a break.

She scurried up to a window protected by bulletproof glass and metal bars.

"Get a lot of robberies, do you?" she asked as she slid her piece of paper across the countertop.

A middle-aged man who was built like a

fireplug stared back at her. "We have to be careful," he told her. "You never can tell when there's gonna be a big 'mergency."

"You're so right about that," Carmela said.

She watched, feeling a little bored, as the man officiously stamped, notarized, and filed her document.

"That'll be twenty-five dollars," he told her. "Cash or credit cards, no checks accepted."

Carmela handed over her Visa card, and two minutes later, she was on her way. Done and done.

Or was she?

She suddenly realized that, since she was in the neighborhood, she could pop into the district attorney's office where Isabelle had worked.

Within two minutes, she was down the block and walking up the front steps that led into the district attorney's adjoining offices. This was going to be a quick hit, she told herself. Run in, schmooze a couple of the secretaries or former co-workers, and see if she could wheedle some information about Isabelle.

Just when she thought she had the perfect plan, she stopped short. Four uniformed officers were ordering visitors to drop their purses, briefcases, backpacks, and cell phones into gray trays that looked like cast-offs from a high school lunchroom.

Oh crap.

Carmela stepped into line and placed her purse into one of the trays.

A man with a clipboard peered at her and said, "You want to empty your pockets, too?"

Not really.

But she dug into her jacket pocket anyway and tossed a box of Tic Tacs, a single gold earring, and a slightly fuzzy (but unused) Kleenex into the tray.

Then she was through the line and heading for the district attorney's office on the second floor.

The receptionist was a skinny redhead with '80s bouffant hair and '70s granny glasses. "Good morning, how can we help you?" she asked.

"I'm a friend of Isabelle Black," Carmela said.

The receptionist immediately looked stricken. "Oh no, you were one of her friends?"

Carmela nodded. She had been. Kind of. By way of Ellie, anyway.

"We all loved her so much," the receptionist gushed. "We just can't believe what happened. That we'll never *see* her again."

Carmela suddenly flashed on an image of Isabelle lying in a casket and thought, *Well, you actually might see her again. If you come to the viewing tonight.* Then she shook her head to dispel that thought and said, "I've been looking into things for Isabelle's sister. Unofficially, of course."

The receptionist brushed away a tear. "How can I help?"

"I was wondering if I might speak to a couple of Isabelle's co-workers. It's still . . ." She dropped her voice. "It's still a mystery why Isabelle ended up in that cemetery. Or why she was killed."

The receptionist leaned forward in a conspiratorial manner. "And you're trying to . . . ?"

"I'm not really sure," Carmela admitted. "Maybe glean some tiny bit of information? Something that might help in figuring out Isabelle's unsolved murder?"

"Maybe you should talk to . . . oh, Mr. Prejean!" the receptionist cried out, clearly startled as a man suddenly materialized next to Carmela. "I didn't see you come in. I was just talking to . . . well, this young woman can explain it herself."

"I'm Bobby Prejean," the man said to Carmela. "The New Orleans district attorney. What's going on?" He was brisk and

126

businesslike, but his voice was not unkind.

Carmela turned to face him. "I'm Carmela Bertrand. I believe we met once before. At the Children's Art Association benefit?"

Prejean gave her a blank look, and then a slow smile spread across his handsome face. "Carmela. Now I remember you. You and that crazy float builder . . ."

"Jekyl Hardy," said Carmela.

"Jekyl Hardy," Prejean repeated. "You were conducting the charity auction and kept getting the bids all mixed up."

"Sorry about that." Carmela and Jekyl had forgotten their lines, so they'd gone into an impromptu comedy routine.

"Don't be. You two were a stitch," Prejean said. "Joking around like that, singing those crazy little songs. Best auction ever. And you raised a ton of money as I recall."

Carmela smiled at Bobby Prejean. He was tall with dark hair, hazel eyes, and an aristocratic bearing. She could almost picture him wearing an eighteenth-century-style cutaway jacket as he rode a fine walking horse to inspect a plantation up on River Road.

"How can I help you?" Prejean asked.

"Isabelle's sister is a friend of mine," Carmela said. "And I was just . . ."

"Oh my goodness!" Prejean said. "We

127

were all just devastated when we heard that Isabelle had been taken from us. She was one of the brightest attorneys in the office." He made a motion with his hand. "Shall we continue this conversation in my office?"

"Thank you," Carmela said, grateful for his interest and consideration. Prejean led her past a row of desks, then down a corridor lined with offices, and into his private office.

"Sit, dear lady. Sit," Prejean said.

Carmela sat. "I'm guessing your entire office is still in shock over this."

Prejean nodded. "We most certainly are. In this den of . . ." He allowed himself a slight chuckle. "In this den of legal tigers, Isabelle's quiet, unassuming personality stood out. Her star, quite literally, shone the brightest." He shook his head. "Young Edward Baudette must be terribly distraught."

"He is." *Sort of.*

Prejean leaned back in his chair. "So how can I help you?"

Carmela leaned forward. "Do you know if anything — or anyone — had been bothering Isabelle lately?"

Prejean shook his head sadly. "I can't think of anything that had been bothering her. She was . . . like I said, she was one of the most competent people here. Everyone loved her."

Clearly someone had not.

"Anything in her files?" Carmela asked.

"I had two of my best people comb through her files yesterday morning, right after we got a call from the police. But nothing jumped out." He looked sharply at her. "You're looking into this?"

"As a friend and because Detective Babcock and I found her body."

"Ah yes, I did read the story in the *Times-Picayune.*"

"So we feel, I don't know, a certain responsibility?"

"Admirable of you," Prejean said. "With your, um, close association with Detective Babcock, you must be privy to some of the investigation. Do they have any suspects? Or leads, for that matter?"

"Not really. And I'm just checking a few angles on my own."

"Good for you," Prejean said. "In fact, I'm going to give Detective Babcock a call. I want to personally assure him that this office will make every effort to help in the apprehension of her killer. I know Detectives Babcock and Gallant have already spoken with a few people here, but I'm going to go one step further and guarantee that I will personally interview every single person on our staff. Try to determine if they knew of something that might have been going on in her personal life."

"That's very kind of you," Carmela said, just as a harried-looking woman stuck her head into his office.

"Mr. Prejean?" the woman said. She was wearing a black skirt suit and wore her glasses on a pearl chain around her neck.

Prejean looked up. "Yes, Esther?"

"Your Realtor is on the line. Says it's important."

Prejean held up a finger. "One moment."

"Would it be possible for me to talk to some of your people, too?" Carmela asked.

Prejean nodded. "Absolutely, you can. You can do it right now if you have the time. Renee at the front desk can probably steer you in the right direction. She's the one who really runs the show around here." He stood up and Carmela followed suit. Then he grabbed her hand and pumped it enthusiastically. "Will you promise to keep in touch? Let me know what's going on with the investigation, and if I can help in any way?"

"Absolutely," Carmela said. "And thank you."

Renee, the receptionist, turned out to be a godsend. She walked Carmela around the offices, introduced her to several of the other attorneys, and did a credible but not too revealing explanation of why Carmela was here asking questions.

Carmela talked to a couple of assistant district attorneys, one associate, and two young men who were tasked with filing papers for court appearances. They all seemed deeply saddened, concerned about the investigation, but didn't have much to tell her. She wasn't surprised. She didn't really expect a suspect to pop up unexpectedly.

Except for the last person she interviewed. A fidgety-looking man by the name of Hugo Delton. Delton was forty pounds overweight and had the distinctly nervous habit of constantly licking his lips. Which gave Carmela the creeps and made her wonder if he did that when he was in court? Or just when he was alone with women?

"What are you, some kind of detective?" Delton asked her. He'd invited her into his office and was sitting across from her, staring at her intently, giving her a rather thorough once over.

"I'm just a friend," Carmela said. "A curious friend who's taken it upon herself to ask a few questions. See if I can come up with something." She paused. "So . . . you worked fairly closely with Isabelle?"

"I guess," Delton told her. "We mostly saw each other here at work. And, of course, there was the occasional lunch or party together."

"It sounds like the two of you were fairly close friends."

"Mmn, I wish we could have been closer. The girl did love to party." He picked up a yellow pencil and twiddled it. "But it never works out when you date someone you work with, does it?"

"I wouldn't know," Carmela told him. "I mostly work with women."

"Well, there you go."

"Anyway," Carmela said, "since the two of you were close, I'm wondering if Isabelle might have been worried about something?"

"Something or somebody?" Delton asked.

"Probably somebody."

"She hung out with kind of a wild crowd." He rubbed a finger under his nose and made a sniffing sound. "They got their noses into it pretty good."

"Are you talking about drugs?" Carmela asked.

"Hey, I'm just sayin'," Delton said. "No accusations here."

Carmela wondered if Delton was telling the truth or trying to twist the interview. "Anything else you can think of?"

"She worried about some of the lowlifes she helped get convictions on. We all did."

"But she never mentioned anyone or any case specifically? Anything that might have been a little hinky?"

"Nope."

Like you?

But Carmela didn't say that. Instead she stood up and said, "Thank you for your time. If you think of anything, please don't hesitate to call me. I'd be very interested. And I'd for sure pass any information on to the police." She handed him one of her Memory Mine business cards. "Or, obviously, you can contact the police directly."

Delton rubbed her card between his thumb and his forefinger and offered her a flickering crocodile smile. "But that wouldn't be half as fun as seeing you again."

CHAPTER 10

Carmela returned to Memory Mine feeling that much more relieved for finally filing the quitclaim deed, and for her impromptu meeting with Bobby Prejean and company. That had been a stroke of luck. The man was clearly distraught over losing one of his crackerjack attorneys, but still had the presence of mind to throw the full weight of his office behind the investigation. God bless him. As for Hugo Delton . . . well, he'd managed to seriously creep her out. But creepy didn't necessarily mean killer. Still, she decided that she'd keep him on her radar for now. And what were those innuendos about drugs? Isabelle? Really?

As Carmela pushed open the door, she saw that the ever-efficient Gabby was straightening up their bins of discontinued scrapbook items.

"Hi there," Gabby said. Then, "We don't really want to keep these yellow felt daisies, do we? They're kind of . . . way last summer."

"Then toss them into the closeout bin," Carmela said. "I'm sure somebody will love them."

"Everything eventually finds a home, right?"

"Have you been busy?"

"Oh yeah," Gabby said. "But good busy. After you took off there was a tsunami of scrappers. I think everyone's all whipped up because we're closing in on the holidays. They're crafting Thanksgiving place cards and decorations and seriously thinking about Christmas cards and invitations."

"It's that time of year," Carmela said. She was planning to create her own Christmas cards using a midnight blue paper stock that featured a galaxy of stars stamped with metallic ink and dusted with embossing powder.

"But it was nothing I couldn't handle," Gabby said. "Oh, and the mail came. Gobs of stuff, mostly for you. I stacked it all on your desk."

"Great." Carmela started for her office.

"And there are cartons of yogurt in the little fridge, if you're thinking about a healthy lunch today." She grinned. "Hint, hint."

"Thanks," Carmela said. "I guess it doesn't hurt to eat healthy *once* in a while." She pulled open the little refrigerator in the back hallway, grabbed a carton of strawberry yogurt, and ducked into her office.

As she slumped in her chair, Carmela saw that Gabby had stacked the mail into two piles. A small pile of bills and a larger pile of fun stuff. That is, suppliers' catalogs, scrapbook magazines, invitations, and other goodies. She gave the bill pile a cursory glance, dug out a plastic spoon from her desk, and ripped the top off the yogurt.

The fun pile showed promise. Catalogs from Scrapbook Angel, Paper Paradise, and Bagley's Rubber Stamps. Also a small square envelope that held an invitation to a baby shower for Vivienne Poulin's grandniece. Carmela couldn't help wonder why the family had selected a store-bought, fill-in-the-blanks invitation when Vivienne was such a good customer at Memory Mine. For a pittance, she could have put together an invitation that was truly elegant and one of a kind. Oh well.

Carmela sighed and plucked an oversized purple and yellow postcard from the stack. She studied it, frowning at a rather depressing photograph of a woman dressed completely in black, right down to her gloves. She turned the postcard over.

What?

It was an invitation from the New Orleans Art Institute for a costume show opening this weekend called Mourning Cloak.

This is so weird.

Entranced, Carmela studied the postcard. The Mourning Cloak show was being put on by the museum's textile and costume department and was going to highlight clothing worn for funerals and mourning. Focusing primarily on the late 1800s and early 1900s in England and America.

Oh my.

Impulsively, Carmela jumped up and scurried out into the shop. She held the card up high, waving it at Gabby. "Did you see this?"

Gabby gave a slow nod. "I did. Pretty weird, huh?"

"I guess."

Gabby pointed at the card. "Are you thinking what I'm thinking?"

"I don't know," Carmela said. "What are you thinking?"

"What if the lace that . . . you know, was used to strangle Isabelle . . . what if it came from the Art Institute's antique fabric collection?"

Carmela thought that would be way too

strange. On the other hand . . .

She turned the postcard back to the invitation side. "It says here the show opens this Saturday."

Gabby gave her a cat-who-swallowed-the-canary look. "But I happen to know there's a private party for big-buck donors this Thursday evening. Black tie."

"Really?"

"Maybe you should go," Gabby said.

"I don't think that . . ." Carmela hesitated. "Well, maybe I should. Let me noodle it around."

Back in her office, Carmela sat down at her desk and stared at the wall. It held all manner of sketches and photos and snippets of ideas. Her concept wall, she called it. *I should just let this costume thing go and work on . . .*

She reached for the phone.

Her friend Angela Boynton, a curator at the New Orleans Art Institute, picked up on the second ring.

"Carmela?" she said. "I was just thinking about you. We need to get together and have lunch. How about Tipitina's? My treat."

"I'll take you up on that," Carmela said. "But first I have a favor to ask."

"So ask."

"I received this invitation in the mail

today. For your Mourning Cloak exhibition."

"Not my exhibition," Angela said. "But the lady who shares an office with me is one of the curators."

"The thing is," Carmela said, "I'd love it if you could get me an invitation to your Thursday night reception."

"I had no idea you were so interested in costumes and couture," Angela said. "But, sure, it's no problem at all. I'll put your name on our VIP list."

"And a guest, too?"

"I'm guessing that would be the ever-hunky Detective Babcock?"

"You got it," Carmela said.

"No, *you* got it," Angela said. "Oh, and if it's not too much trouble, I need another packet of those oversized brass paper clips with the typewriter keys stuck on the end."

"I'll bring it with me Thursday night."

Carmela clicked the phone off and then immediately called Babcock. The minute he came on the line, she said, "How would you like to go to an art opening this Thursday night?"

"Paintings or photography?" Babcock asked. "And remember, I'm not a modern art guy. And I really dislike graffiti art. It reminds me of bad prison tattoos."

"What a lovely thought," Carmela said. "But what if I told you this was a costume show that's going to showcase all sorts of funeral and mourning clothing?"

"Is there such a thing? Because it sounds very weird."

"I think it's right up our alley."

"Carmela . . . you're not supposed to be investigating."

"I know that. But you said I should keep checking on the lace . . ." When Babcock didn't respond right away, she continued. "And I know this is a long shot, but there's a possibility that we might gather some more information about that hunk of lace."

"Okay, you win. I'll go, but only for a short time. Just long enough to give my brain a rest from all the messes we're trying to juggle here."

"That bad?" Carmela asked.

"Oh, you know. Besides Isabelle's murder we've got a bunch of South American smugglers and some bold smash-and-grab guys that are hell-bent on hitting our high-networth citizens. And then there's Peter Jarreau."

"Who's Peter Jarreau?"

"He's our new media liaison hired by the police commissioner. To, you know, liaison with the media. Such as it is."

"And Jarreau's not doing his job?" Carmela asked.

"Just the opposite. He's poking his fool head in my office every five minutes."

"Liaisoning," said Carmela.

"I guess."

"Look on the bright side. You get to play dress-up and go to a fancy party with me."

"Mmn, how fancy?" Babcock asked.

"Well, it's black tie, so you do have to dress appropriately."

"You mean I have to wear a high-button collar and a cutaway coat à la the eighteenth century?"

"Why don't you skip the coat," Carmela said. "And just wear the collar."

"Just the collar?" Babcock said. There was a long pause. "Wait a minute!" He sounded both shocked and amused. "That sounds suspiciously like you want me to dress like a *Chippendale.*"

Carmela cackled into the phone. "Only if you've got the right moves, cupcake."

Gabby set a stack of white tagboard on the craft table and heaved a sigh. "Carmela, it still feels funny to be doing this. I mean, isn't it awful that about-to-be-bride Isabelle hasn't even been buried yet and we're holding a wedding workshop?"

141

The latest issue of *Martha Stewart Weddings* slid off the top of a thick stack of magazines that Carmela was carrying. She grabbed it before it hit the floor, and she looked at Gabby.

"I totally understand how you feel," Carmela said. "In fact, I have the same trepidation, like it's somehow bad karma. But the people who are coming today probably don't even *know* about Isabelle. So if we canceled at the last minute it would just be to assuage our own feelings."

Gabby fingered one of the magazines. "I guess you're right."

"But it does feel weird," Carmela said.

Still, Gabby seemed reluctant to let the issue go. "Tonight is the visitation at the funeral home?"

"From seven to nine," Carmela said. "And I've got my fingers crossed that none of those lunatic relatives will throw a hissy fit. It would be nice to see some decency and decorum for a change."

Before Gabby had a chance to comment, the front door blew open and Tandy Bliss burst through. Skinny as a model, with her cap of hennaed red hair, Tandy had all the exuberance and energy of a Tasmanian devil. Except she was so much nicer and sweeter. And she had her young cousin in tow.

"Are we early?" Tandy blared as her head swiveled around. "Where is everybody? The wedding workshop is today, right?" Tandy was never soft-spoken, and her booming questions were no exception.

Carmela chuckled. "You're the only ones who signed up, I'm afraid."

That stopped Tandy dead in her tracks. "What? And I even brought along a pan of my famous shortbread bars." Then she peered at Carmela, who was barely suppressing a smile, and said, "Oh you. I bet there's gonna be a stampede of women any second."

"There is," Gabby said. "So watch your toes." She was busy setting up a third table, wedging it into the aisle where the paper bins were located. "Maybe you two had better grab a seat."

"Yeah, yeah," Tandy said. "C'mon Rae Anne, let's take a load off." When she and Rae Anne had established a beachhead at the main table, she added, "You all remember my cousin, Rae Anne, right?"

"Sure," Carmela said.

"Great to see you again," Gabby said.

"She's finally gettin' hitched!" Tandy proclaimed. "She's a blushing bride-to-be."

"That's wonderful, Rae Anne," Carmela said. "Have you set a date?"

Rae Anne nodded. "May tenth. But that's all I've figured out so far. I haven't made any other plans at all. In fact, I barely know where to begin."

"That's why we're here," Tandy said. "So Rae Anne can start figuring out all the really important stuff. Like colors and flowers and invitations and, well, I guess you guys are gonna tell her what all is involved."

The bell over the front door *da-dinged* as two more women rushed in. Then it continued its cheery but relentless ringing as another dozen women streamed in.

"We've got a packed house," Gabby murmured to Carmela, as the women filtered in and, amidst loud exclamations, a few shrieks, and multiple air kisses, found places around the various tables.

"Am I ever ready for this," a young woman named Wendy announced. "I'm in a preplanning tizzy."

"Which is why we're here to help," Carmela said, taking her place at the head of the large table. "We're going to help you get a nice big jump start on your wedding plans." She held up a large sheet of tagboard. "This may look like a blank canvas right now, but by the end of this class you'll have created your very own inspiration board. And if you're lucky, you'll have figured out your concept, theme, signature colors, invitations, place cards, favors, and maybe even table settings."

"How on earth are we ever gonna do that?" asked a small blond woman in skinny jeans and a patchwork military jacket that was most definitely of the designer variety rather than that handed out by a supply sergeant.

"What's your name?" Carmela asked.

"Penny," the woman said.

"Lieutenant Penny," Carmela joked, "please don't be nervous. You and all the other ladies here have already taken care of the most important item — finding the perfect groom."

There was loud laughter at that and everyone seemed to relax.

"But now you need to make a few decisions that will help reflect your very own personal style," Carmela continued. "She held up one of the magazines. "Browse through a few magazines, see if you can't find an invitation or table setting that you really love. Maybe even a wedding dress or a bridal bouquet. Cut out the photos and paste them on your board. Then browse the shop, too. Pick out a snippet of ribbon that might work on your bridal bouquet, some paper samples that might be perfect for your wedding invitations, or even a stencil or embellishment that you could incorporate into your designs. And remember, more and more brides are crafting their own invitations these days, using rubber stamps, collage techniques, and embossing powder to make them one of a kind."

"I love it!" Penny said.

"And don't be afraid to experiment," Carmela said. "That's how you'll begin to explore your taste and narrow down your choices."

"Explain, please," Rae Anne said.

"Oh," Carmela said. "Maybe the paper you thought would be perfect for your invitations turns out to be more suited for your dinner menu. By putting everything together on a concept board, you'll be able to make some decisions and winnow your choices down." She smiled. "The thing about what we do here — the scrapbooking, journaling, rubber stamping, and crafting — is that you get to go on your own artistic journey."

"What about wedding albums?" a woman asked. "Or am I getting ahead of things?"

"Not at all," Carmela said. "We offer a good supply of albums, many of which are just waiting for a would-be bride to apply her own special touch. Imagine adding your own lace or pressed flowers, or strand of pearls with tiny charms."

Their guests were nodding now, murmuring to one another, and beginning to page through magazines. Two women had gotten up and were eagerly pulling out paper samples.

"Okay," Carmela said. She nodded to Gabby and they each grabbed a stack of tagboard and began passing sheets around.

Carmela had thought her crafters would need a fair amount of guidance, and she was happily proved wrong. Indeed, paper was being snipped, glue was being applied, and the concept boards were starting to take shape.

One young woman's concept board looked as if it was going to be all ruffles and romance, with vellum paper, snips of lace, and a packet of seed pearls. Two African American women, Darnella Rashad and Justine Coulter, had veered into more contemporary territory. They'd chosen Japanese washi paper, rubber stamps with Picasso-style hearts, and stamp pads with rich purple and red pigments.

"Could you ever put sealing wax on your invitation?" Darnella asked Carmela.

"I think that would be spectacular," Carmela told her.

Acacia Jones, who lived just a block from Carmela's apartment, and was engaged to a professor at Tulane, said, "Wish tags. I really do want to have wish tags."

Darnella shook back a head full of white wooden beads and said, "What on earth are wish tags?"

"They're very popular right now," Carmela explained. "You make them using small squares or rectangles of really fine paper stock. At the top of each wish tag is printed, *My wish for you.* Then, during your wedding reception, each guest fills out what they wish for the happy bride and groom. Your maid of honor collects them all, and when you return from your honeymoon, the wish tags are presented to you."

"I love the idea," Penny said. She'd been hanging on Carmela's every word.

"Me, too," Darnella said. She jumped from her chair and headed for the paper bins.

Carmela circled back to the main table where Tandy and Rae Anne were working away diligently. Tandy had assembled a collage of floral bouquets that Rae Anne was poring over.

"I think I'm more of a traditional bride

than I thought I was," Rae Anne said to Carmela. "I had all these ideas about carrying just a single flower instead of a big bouquet, or maybe even wearing a blush pink wedding gown, but when it comes right down to it, I think I still subscribe to the old adage of 'Something old, something new, something borrowed, something blue.' "

"There's certainly nothing wrong with that," Carmela told her. But as she moved around the table, that particular wedding ditty seemed to stick in her brain. Hmm. *Had Isabelle been a traditional bride?* she wondered. Was she going to wear "something old, something new"? And, if so, what would that have been?

As Carmela moved to the next table, she decided to ask Ellie tonight at the viewing.

"Wherever did you get the idea for concept boards?" asked one of the women. She held a glue stick in one hand and a pair of scissors in the other, and her concept board was already half finished.

"I make them all the time," Carmela said. "They work just great for anything you're trying to figure out. Holiday plans, a Halloween party, really almost any occasion. I even know one woman who created a concept board to help plan a business."

"No!" the woman cried.

"You know Ink Drop, that cute earring kiosk over at Riverwalk?" Carmela asked.

This time all the ladies at the table nodded.

"My friend put together a concept board to help her figure out her kiosk design, her audience, her choices in merchandise, and her marketing tactics."

"Carmela!"

Carmela glanced up. Gabby was calling to her, waving frantically at her from the front counter. "Excuse me." She hurried up there.

"Do you know if we have any more of this silver gossamer ribbon?" Gabby asked. She held an empty cardboard spool in her hand.

"I guess it's been popular?" Carmela asked.

"We're out."

"Let me look in the storeroom."

Gabby's mouth twisted into a grin. "We don't have a storeroom."

"Sure we do," Carmela said. "It's that box of junk that's sitting on top of my filing cabinet."

"Then you'd better say a prayer to St. Jude, patron saint of lost causes," Gabby remarked. "Because once it's been tossed in there it's gone for . . . Oh my!"

The very flamboyant Countess Saint-

Marche knocked on the front display window, disappeared for a few seconds, and then suddenly rushed through their front door. Gold jewelry jangling, rings sparkling from every finger, the countess was resplendent in a hot pink tweed jacket and matching skirt. And wouldn't you know it, she was wearing hot pink stilettos to match.

Could this be classified as a legitimate hot pink mess? Carmela wondered. Then, adopting a friendly smile, she greeted the woman with, "Fancy seeing you here." Because fancy was certainly what the countess was, the only one who could outdo Ava when it came to high drama.

"Carmela, *darling*," said the countess. "I've just acquired the most *fascinating* ring and I thought of you instantly." The countess owned Lucrezia, a high-end jewelry store located right next door to Memory Mine. She specialized in vintage jewelry, though Carmela harbored a secret suspicion that the woman might also be a receiver of stolen goods.

"Let's see it!" Gabby exclaimed. She never could resist an eye-catching bauble.

The countess extended her right hand and fluttered her fingers, letting the ring catch the light. "It's expensive, but oh so worth it."

"Spectacular," Carmela said. The ring was a ginormous sapphire set in an intricately braided gold band. "The design looks very medieval."

"From Vincenza," the countess proclaimed. She never just talked; every word was a grand proclamation. Alert the drummers, cue the bagpipers. Then she glanced about the shop and, with a mischievous gleam in her eyes, said, "And what do we have going on here?"

When Gabby quickly explained about the wedding workshop, the countess was over-the-top delighted.

"Brides-to-be!" she exclaimed. "And might they still be in the market for a ring?"

"You never know," Carmela said, knowing full well what was coming next.

The countess dipped a hand into her Gucci handbag and pulled out a stack of business cards. "Carmela, do you mind? We have so many exquisite rings on hand. Even a collection of old mine-cut diamonds from the late 1800s."

"Go ahead," Carmela said. "Go ahead and pass out your cards if you want."

"Mon ange," she purred. *"Merci beaucoup."* Then she air kissed Carmela and disappeared into the fray, leaving behind only a faint trail of L'Air du Temps.

CHAPTER 11

"That's what you're wearing?" Carmela asked. She'd just opened her front door to find Ava lounging there, looking like a refugee from an old MTV video. She had on a pair of thigh-high boots, a red leather miniskirt, and a black off-the-shoulder T-shirt. Even Boo and Poobah seemed startled.

"What?" Ava asked. "This isn't dressy enough?"

"Oh, it's dressy," Carmela said. "If you're a backup dancer for MC Hammer."

Ava pulled her face into a pucker. "You think my outfit's too over-the-top?"

"Wait a minute," Carmela said, taking a step back. "Let's see. Leather skirt? Check. Spring-loaded bra? Check. Four-inch-high Lady Gaga boots? Check." She cocked her head. "No, you're just perfect, honey. I wouldn't change a darned thing."

"That's what I thought," Ava said as she

sashayed past Carmela and headed for the dining room. She sank into a chair and said, "Really, Carmela, when are you going to have these seats re-caned? My tushy is practically touching the floor."

Carmela just smiled. "It's on my to-do list. Right up there with putting new shelf liners in all my kitchen cupboards, getting my tires rotated, and winning the lottery."

"So . . . like, not?"

"Let's just say that task is off somewhere in the distant and foggy future. Now, would you like some leftover Big Easy chicken or do you want to keep complaining?"

"Chicken?" Ava brightened. "And what else?"

"Mmn, I've got some sweet potato casserole here, too."

"Sold," Ava declared. "It sure beats eating leftover Halloween candy." She moved to a seat that was a little less saggy and gave Boo and Poobah some much-requested pets.

"I thought so," Carmela said. While the chicken and sweet potatoes heated, she put some French rolls into the oven to warm. Then, five minutes later, she put everything onto plates and put the plates on a tray. She added the basket full of crusty French rolls and carried everything to the table.

"There's French bread, too?" Ava said.

"Petit pain," Carmela said. "From the Merci Beaucoup Bakery."

"My heart tells me to go for the French bread, but my skirt is like, 'Hey, lady, you should munch a carrot stick instead.' "

"Want to do a master cleanse instead? Enjoy a nasty little cocktail of maple syrup and cayenne pepper?"

"Ooh. Pass," Ava said. "In fact, pass me that bread."

"Besides, you're thin as a rail."

"You think? Well, I am a size six." Ava sniggered. "Or maybe that's my shoe size."

Carmela suddenly jumped up from the table. "Forgot something."

"There's more?" Ava asked.

"Honey butter," Carmela said, returning with a small dish.

"Be still my heart," Ava said. "Now I'm gonna have to have *two* rolls. Just hopefully not around my waist."

As Carmela dug into her chicken, she said, "Guess what turned up in my e-mail this afternoon?"

"I don't know," Ava said. "One of those crazy messages that promises there's eighty million dollars waiting for you in a Liberian bank?"

"Noooo," Carmela said. "Del sent me the script for Baby's Murder Mystery Party."

"Do I have a nice, juicy part? Maybe even the starring role?"

"I don't know yet. I printed out two copies but haven't had a chance to look at them."

"A Murder Mystery Party," Ava mused. "Who'd have thought we'd get involved in something like that?"

"Are you kidding?" Carmela said. "I feel like that's all we ever do. And now, tonight, we've got Isabelle's viewing. It feels very strange, very coincidental."

"I think it's totally fitting that we're going to a funeral home tonight," Ava said. "Since I'm in mourning over my recent breakup."

"Who'd you break up with now?" Carmela could barely keep track of all Ava's dates, boyfriends, and paramours.

"Teddy Binger and I have parted ways. Sob."

"What went wrong?" Carmela asked. "The poor guy didn't have enough Roman numerals after his name?" Ava did enjoy her romps with trust fund babies.

"No, no, we just weren't all that compatible."

"Remind me. How long had you two been seeing each other?"

Ava lifted her shoulders and stretched languidly. "Um . . . five days."

Carmela smiled. "And they said it wouldn't last."

Bothell brothers funeral home didn't look all that different tonight than it had last night. Except there were a lot more cars parked out front.

"Looks like there's a real crowd," Ava said as they climbed the front steps.

"That would be nice," Carmela said. "Comforting for Ellie, anyway."

"Especially since it was just the two of them."

Inside the front door, gloom pervaded and the same creepy music emanated from the speakers.

"Isn't that the theme song from *A Nightmare on Elm Street*?" Ava asked.

"Shhh," Carmela said. "Just be polite and sign the guest book."

"You think people really save these stupid books so they can page through them later and look at all the signatures?" Ava looked puzzled. "Or do you have to write thank-you cards to people who showed up?" She looked around and her eyes landed on a young, three-piece-suit-wearing funeral director. "Now *he's* better looking than that stiff who showed us caskets last night. And he's more in my age range, too."

Noticing Ava noticing him, the funeral director approached them with a polite, contained smile. "May I help you, ladies?" he asked.

Ava's eyelashes began batting at a hundred beats per minute. "We're here for the Isabelle Black visitation," she said.

He stuck out an arm. "I'd be pleased to escort you."

Ava dimpled. "And you are . . . ?"

"Billy Bothell."

"Oh, Carmela, dear," Ava said. "This handsome young gentleman has offered to escort us to visit poor Isabelle. Isn't that kind of him?"

Linking arms with Ava, Billy Bothell led the way to Slumber Room Two.

"And you'll be around?" Ava asked as her eyelashes continued to flutter like windshield wipers. "In case we need you?"

"Count on it," Billy Bothell told her.

"Come on," Carmela said, plucking at Ava's sleeve. "Get over yourself and let's get this done, okay?"

"I know, I know," Ava said. "But I'm nervous. You know me. I'm no good when it comes to looking at dead people. I mean, I can barely watch *Weekend at Bernie's* without getting creeped out."

"Just follow me and you'll do fine."

158

They edged through the crowd and headed for the casket. Halfway there, they caught a quick peek of Isabelle lying in her casket.

"Oh no!" Ava said, horrified. "Are you seeing what I'm seeing?"

Carmela never considered herself squeamish. But what she saw gave her a true case of the willies. Isabelle was lying in her casket outfitted in her long white wedding dress!

They were both struck silent for a moment. Then Ava said, "I hate to say this, but she kind of reminds me of Evita Peron."

"Was she buried in her wedding gown?" Carmela asked.

"I know it was some kind of long, flowy gown. I think I saw pictures of her in an old *Life* magazine."

They took two steps closer. Pillar candles flickered, and a sweep of white lilies surrounded the casket.

"It *is* a pretty dress," Ava said. "I particularly like that sweetheart neckline. It's very . . . demure."

"And seed pearls," Carmela gulped. She wondered if the undertaker had slit the dress up the back, like all those horrible funeral suits you hear about. "Who doesn't love seed pearls?"

Ellie suddenly caught sight of them and rushed over, a look of relief sweeping across her face. "Thank goodness, you're here. Now I at least know *some*one."

"Of course you do, honey," Ava said, putting an arm around her.

"Most of the people here are friends of Edward and Vesper Baudette," Ellie said. "Or Isabelle's friends from work." A tear trickled down her cheek as she turned to look at the coffin. "Isn't it awful? I cringe every time I look at my own sister. It's bad enough to see her like this, but to have her wearing her wedding gown . . ." Ellie shuddered.

"Why on earth . . . ?" Carmela began.

"It was Edward's wish," Ellie said. "He wanted to see his bride in her wedding gown."

"I guess that's kinda sweet after all," Ava said.

"You've been a saint," Carmela told Ellie. "Putting up with so much from these people."

"And you've been a good friend," Ellie said. She moved a step closer to Carmela. "Are you still, you know, looking into things?"

"Yes, I am," Carmela said. "I've talked to quite a few people about this."

"Anything yet?" The look on Ellie's face was pleading.

"No, but I know something will turn up," Carmela said. She glanced at Edward and Vesper, who were sitting off to the side of the coffin. "I suppose we should go over and pay our respects."

"Be careful," Ellie warned. "Vesper's in a horrible mood."

They stood in front of Isabelle's coffin for the requisite ten seconds. Ava made the sign of the cross while Carmela bowed her head. Then they stepped over to talk to Edward and Vesper.

"Edward," Carmela said, extending a hand. "My heartfelt sympathies."

"Thank you, thank you so much," Edward said. He was duded up in a sleek-looking black suit, but looked a little dazed, as if he might have leveled himself out on Xanax. In fact, Carmela wasn't even sure that Edward remembered her from last night.

Whatever. She moved on to Vesper.

"My sympathies," Carmela murmured.

Vesper stared at her through bleary eyes. "Yesh, thankth for coming," she said. "Sush a tragedy, hmm?"

Uh-oh, Carmela thought. Vesper wasn't goggle-eyed from crying. Vesper Baudette had clearly been nipping at a bottle before she came here. Or, heck, maybe the woman had a flask tucked in her panty girdle?

Carmela and Ava ducked behind a bank of white gladiolas interspersed with pink carnations.

"Has she been drinking?" Carmela asked Ava. She was steamed. For Vesper to be three sheets to the wind was just plain disrespectful. "I mean, who turns up at a wake half drunk?"

"You would if it was a good old-fashioned Irish wake," Ava said.

They both craned their necks to stare at Vesper. Now the woman just seemed bored. She fidgeted in her chair, then opened her clutch purse, pulled out a mirror, and proceeded to study her eyebrows.

"She's a crazy lady," Carmela said. "I get the feeling she doesn't much care about Isabelle. And that she's bored stiff being here."

"Huh," Ava said. "You think her shoes match her broom?"

"Doggone it, now I really feel bad for Ellie."

"Me, too. In fact, I . . . Say, who's the good lookin' guy over there who's talking to Ellie?"

Carmela glanced around and saw Bobby Prejean standing close to Ellie. He was murmuring something to her, and his hand rested gently on her shoulder. From the look on Ellie's face, his words seemed to be offering enormous comfort.

Carmela's heart warmed to this. Here was a guy, a politico, at that, with a very busy schedule. Yet he had offered both investigative help and had taken the time to come to the visitation. The world would be better off with a few more guys like Bobby Prejean. She glanced around the room. Now she was beginning to recognize a few more people. There was Naomi Rattler, the former maid of honor, and Julian Drake, the former best man. She noted that as Bobby Prejean bid good-bye to Ellie, Drake immediately rushed to Ellie's side to offer his own words of comfort. This was the first time she'd seen Drake since he was pulled sweating and struggling into her presence at the cemetery, and now she was starting to form a new opinion of him.

"Let's go talk to Julian Drake," Carmela said to Ava. "I haven't seen him since . . . well, you know."

"Okay."

Ellie was nodding at Drake, even managing a faint smile, when Carmela and Ava joined them.

Carmela introduced Ava to Drake, and then said, "I haven't seen you since that awful night. I hope the police weren't too rough on you."

Drake looked thoughtful for a moment. "I was understandably upset at first, but now I can see where they were coming from. They were chasing all over the place looking for some kind of deranged killer. And then they stumbled onto me."

"You actually don't look that deranged," Ava said.

Drake fixed her with a goofy, menacing look, and then broke into a smile. "I don't? Well, shucks."

Ellie gave Drake a grateful look. "Mr. Drake has been so kind. He called yesterday to see how I was doing and has been my shoulder to cry on tonight."

"Oh, sweetie," Drake said to her.

"No, really," Ellie said. "You've been just wonderful. Running interference for me with Edward and Vesper."

"I just wish I could have been here last night," Drake said. "I heard it was pretty awful."

"Oh well." Ellie waved a hand. She seemed to be coping much better now. Carmela figured she was processing through the different stages of grief . . . denial, anger, bargaining, acceptance . . .

"Edward's a good guy," Drake was telling

them. "It's his mother that's completely animal crackers. But he knows it, so he takes all her antics with a grain of salt."

Really? Carmela wondered. *Does he really?*

"I understand you're in the casino business," Carmela said to Drake.

"I am," Drake said.

"He's being way too modest," Ellie said. "He's the VP in charge of development for Consolidated Gaming."

"Is that right?" Ava said. "What exactly does that entail?"

Drake smiled. "Right now I'm spearheading the effort to tear down the old Enchantment Amusement Park and build a sleek, new casino on that acreage."

"Wow," Ava said.

"The new Elysian Fields Casino will feature slots, table games, a bingo parlor, and a state-of-the-art thousand-seat dinner theatre," Drake said, clearly eager to talk about his pet project.

"That's going to be a real boon to the local economy," Carmela said. She'd just noticed Naomi Rattler ghosting past.

"Good for state revenue, too," Drake said. "By the time we're up and running we'll be adding millions of dollars to Louisiana's coffers."

"I like the sound of that," Ava said.

"You know," Drake said to Carmela, "we're having an Elysian Fields Casino gala this coming Saturday. To celebrate the groundbreaking and all that. I tried to get Ellie to come, but she said no. But if you'd like to come as my guest. You . . ." His eyes traveled to Ava. "You and your friend would be most welcome."

"We'd love to come," Ava said, jumping at the invite. "Wouldn't we, Carmela?"

"It sounds like fun," Carmela said. She decided it might be a good way to keep an eye on Julian Drake. He was being supportive and sweet to Ellie, and he certainly acted like he had a pure and innocent heart. But . . . you never know. He *had* been near the cemetery that night.

"Then it's all settled," Drake said.

Carmela glanced around, looking for Naomi, but the girl had seemingly disappeared. Then her eyes settled on Edward Baudette. He was making his way through the crowded room, shaking hands, looking appropriately sad, and . . . headed her way.

"Excuse me," Carmela said, pulling herself away from the group and making a beeline for Edward. When she reached him, she grasped him by the upper arm and said, "Edward, how are you doing?"

166

He gazed at her, that same strange, almost absent expression on his face, and said, "It's Carmen, right?"

CHAPTER 12

Carmela smiled tolerantly. "It's Carmela. Carmela Bertrand. You remember, Ellie works at my friend Ava's shop?"

"Oh, that's right."

"I talked to you a few minutes ago? I was here last night?" *What an idiot.*

Edward nodded. "The coffin thing. Sure."

"How are you holding up?" Carmela asked.

"Okay, I guess." Edward glanced around. "This is all so horrible. So nightmarishly different from the way it should have been."

"Well . . . yes," Carmela said.

Edward's eyes sought out Isabelle lying in her casket. "But she does look beautiful, doesn't she? So beatific and peaceful."

"I suppose so."

A tear rolled down Edward's cheek. "Still, this is just so wrong. Isabelle should be walking down the aisle in that dress holding a bouquet, not lying in a crappy coffin with a rosary entwined through her fingers."

"I'm so sorry for you," Carmela said. "Though I must say she does look exquisite."

"I'll always remember her just like this."

Really?

"I take it Isabelle was a traditional bride?" Carmela asked. It was a quasi question-statement.

"Yes, she was," Edward said. "Naomi — you know her dear friend Naomi Rattler — she was always trying to convince Isabelle to wear a white lace jumpsuit or something super trendy. Or carry some kind of crazy bouquet made up of herbs and moss. But Isabelle wanted to wear a ball gown–style dress and a long veil and carry a bouquet of tea roses."

"So I'm guessing Isabelle was a girl who subscribed to the notion of 'something old, something new, something borrowed, something blue'?" Now Carmela was fishing, feeling things out.

"I suppose you could say that," Edward said.

"Do you recall what her 'something old' was?"

Edward shook his head. "I don't think so."

"Isabelle never said anything to you about this?"

"Not that I recall. Anyway, it's almost too painful to think about with her lying here in a coffin."

"I know it is," Carmela said. "And I feel horrible asking about this. But, please, see if you can remember anything. Anything at all."

Edward looked at her sideways. "It's important?"

"It could be," Carmela said.

A few moments went by, and then something seemed to click in Edward's brain. "You're trying to solve her murder, aren't you?" He sounded guarded, maybe even a little nervous.

"No," Carmela said, backpedaling like crazy and trying to put a different spin on her words. "I'm just trying to be proactive. If I come up with anything, and I do mean anything, I intend to turn it over to the police."

"That so?" He looked like he wanted to believe her. Or not.

"So, please, just try to think about this a little bit."

Edward squeezed his eyes shut and sighed deeply. He was quiet for such a long time that Carmela thought maybe he had fallen asleep. Then his eyes popped open.

"I guess there was one thing," he said.

"Funny, I thought of it just now, because you were kind of pushing me."

Carmela leaned in close to him. "What's that?"

"When you bring up the 'something old, something new' bit, I remember now that Naomi had offered to help Isabelle with that."

"Naomi told you this?"

"No," Edward said. His eyes closed again. "Isabelle did."

"What exactly did Isabelle say?"

"It was just, like, a throwaway remark," Edward said. "We were talking about her diamond ring, how we'd finally gotten it sized correctly."

"Okay," Carmela said.

"Then Isabelle said something to the effect of 'That's the new.' And when I said, 'What do you mean?' she said, 'Oh, you know, like that old wedding adage.' Only I don't think she used the word *adage,* more like *wedding poem* or something."

"Sure," Carmela said. Edward seemed to be remembering more and more.

"Then Isabelle said that Naomi was going to take care of the old." Edward stopped and his brows bunched together. "At the time, I thought she was talking about old friends, but it could have been something

171

else, because now that I *really* think about it, now that you're pressing me about this, Isabelle also said something about Naomi buying something at Dulcimer Antiques." He blew out a glut of air and said, "That's all I can think of. At the moment, anyway."

"That was good," Carmela said. "You did real good."

As Edward tottered off to rejoin his mother, Carmela glanced around for Ava. But instead of finding her friend, her eyes landed on a good-looking dark-haired man with steel blue eyes who had just entered the room as quietly and surreptitiously as possible. He wore a black leather jacket and faded blue jeans, and he sported longish hair that was pulled back in a low ponytail. He glanced about with guarded eyes and then crept slowly toward the bier that held Isabelle's casket. He gazed at her for a moment, and then he bent solemnly and eased himself down onto the kneeler that was directly in front of the casket. Head bowed and hands clasped, he seemed lost in deep reflection.

Ava came up alongside Carmela and prodded her with an elbow. "Who's the hottie-patottie who just came skulking in?"

"No idea."

"Well, somebody's going to have to introduce us." She raised an eyebrow at Carmela. When Carmela didn't respond, Ava said, "Shoot, looks like I'm going to have to take matters into my own hands."

Ava whisked across the room and knelt down next to the new mourner. Within five seconds Ava was chatting amiably with him.

Carmela was amazed. The girl had set a new land speed record for flirting. And in a funeral home at that. Just inches from an open casket.

But Ava wasn't the only one who had an eye on the newcomer. As Ava laid a gentle flirt on him, Edward Baudette came storming up.

"What are you doing here? How dare you!" Edward cried.

The crowd hushed, with all attention suddenly focused on Edward and the new arrival.

Ava was stunned, but the dark-haired man wasn't. He stood up and faced Edward toe-to-toe. "This is a public venue," the man declared, a slight menace coloring his voice. "I can certainly come in and mourn my old love."

The word *love* rippled through the room.

"You're not welcome here," Edward seethed.

As if in answer, the man turned and gazed at Isabelle. "Look at what you did," he said to Edward in a low, accusing tone.

"What *I* did?" Edward screamed. His eyes bulged and his face turned bright red. "Security! We need security here!"

Carmela eased closer to see what the fuss was about. A mysterious stranger, perhaps even an old lover? She wanted to know more.

For some reason, Edward suddenly turned his attention on Ava. "You know who this is?" he cried.

"My date for tomorrow night?" Ava said. She adored being cutesy.

"This is Oliver Slade, Isabelle's old boyfriend," Edward raged. "The one she dumped for *me.* The one who felt so betrayed by Isabelle that he stalked her incessantly."

"You're a liar," Slade cried. "I *never* stalked her."

"You most certainly did!" Edward shouted back.

"Edward!" Now Vesper's voice joined in the fray. "Edward, what's going on?"

"Nothing, Mother. Stay out of this."

"Mmn," Ava murmured. "The plot thickens."

"Wait a minute," Carmela said, suddenly

cutting in. "Roll that tape backward for a moment. You said *stalked*?"

"Yes, he did," Edward insisted loudly. "As in calling Isabelle at all hours, sending her notes, and following her home at night."

"You're a filthy liar!" Slade screamed.

Carmela reached out and grabbed Ava by the arm, trying to pull her away. "Ava, come on, you don't want to get involved with this guy."

But Ava wasn't so sure. "I don't?"

Ellie was at their side in an instant. "You really don't, Ava. Come on, listen to Edward, listen to Carmela."

"Unrequited love," Ava murmured. But she let Carmela and Ellie pull her away all the same.

Edward put his hands on Slade's chest and gave a shove. "Listen, you creep. You better get out of here before I *throw* you out."

Slade's response was loud and filled with anger. "You can't make me leave."

Billy Bothell and another funeral home employee suddenly arrived at the scene of the squabble and tried to muscle their way between Edward and Slade. Billy was quiet, but firm. "That's enough, gentlemen. Please, do not make us eject you from the premises."

That seemed to get through to the two men. Edward took a deep breath and stepped back. Slade seemed to dial his anger down a notch.

"Sir," Billy Bothell continued, addressing Oliver Slade, "this might be an opportune time for you to leave."

Slade hesitated a moment. He turned, took one last, lingering gaze at Isabelle, and then stalked out of the room. Carmela almost expected him to stop in the doorway and say, "I'll be back," à la *The Terminator*.

The incident was over, but Ellie was shaking. "Why did he have to come here tonight?" she whimpered.

Carmela and Ava led Ellie over to a sofa in the corner and handed her a packet of tissues.

"After Isabelle and that Slade character broke up, I figured I'd never see him again," Ellie cried. She dabbed at her eyes with a tissue. "Now Isabelle is dead and he *still* comes around."

"Who is he anyway?" Carmela asked.

"He's Chef Oliver Slade, *the* Chef Oliver Slade who is head chef at Le Fougasse, that hot new restaurant over on Magazine Street. The same chef who was written up in *Food & Wine* and cited by *Food Lovers Magazine* as one of the ten hottest chefs in the country."

"Wow," Ava said. "Good-looking, famous, and he can cook. That's a trifecta any woman would love."

"Maybe," Ellie said. "But he had too much ego for my sister to handle. Plus he had a hard time letting her go." She started to cry softly.

"It sounds like he *didn't* let her go," Carmela said.

"Yeah, it sounds like he still loved Isabelle," Ava said as she eased herself down on the sofa. She slid a hand behind her back and said, "Ouch."

"What's wrong with you?" Carmela asked.

"Ah, I think I threw my back out while I was trying to hold my stomach in," Ava said.

That made Ellie laugh a little.

"See," Ava said, "you're feeling better already."

Ellie nodded. "I guess. Thanks to you two." She wiped her nose and managed a half smile. "Thanks for coming tonight. It means a lot to me."

"And this has given me lots to think about," Carmela said. She took Ellie's hand and said, "I hate to ask this, but I have to. Was Isabelle ever involved in drugs?"

Ellie looked shocked. "No. Why?"

"Someone she worked with dropped some

not-so-subtle innuendos," Carmela said.

"Isabelle didn't. She wouldn't."

"You word is good enough for me," Carmela said. She stood up and smoothed her skirt.

Ava leaned in and gave Ellie a hug, then stood up, too. "We'll see you at the funeral tomorrow. You want us to stop by and pick you up?"

"No, it's okay," Ellie said. "Edward promised to give me a ride."

"Okay then," Carmela said. "You take care."

"What a crazy evening," Ava said, as they headed for the exit. "Here I thought it would be all calm and sedate and it was like an episode of *Jerry Springer.*"

"At least nobody threw a folding chair," Carmela said. She held up a hand as they stepped into the lobby. "Whoa, wait a minute. There's Naomi. I gotta talk to her." She waved a hand. "Naomi. Hold up a minute."

Naomi Rattler, who was just about ready to step outside, turned to see who was calling her name. When she saw Carmela, she pursed her lips in an unhappy grimace.

I'm not happy to see you, either, Carmela thought to herself.

"What's up?" Naomi asked. Then, "This

has been a difficult night for me. Whatever you want, please make it quick."

"I think it's been a difficult night for everyone," Carmela said. "But I need to ask you a quick question."

"What's that?"

"Edward told me that you were helping Isabelle put together the 'something old, something new' part of her wedding trousseau."

Naomi waved a hand dismissively. "Oh that. It was nothing."

"It had to be something," Carmela said.

"Not really. I mean, it's not going to happen now, so . . ." She shrugged.

"Edward told me you were quite involved."

Naomi looked upset. "He did? Edward told you that?"

Carmela nodded. "He said you bought something or were going to buy something at Dulcimer Antiques?"

Naomi pulled a petulant face. "If you must know, it was an antique veil. I bought it for Isabelle because she asked me to. That's what she wanted for her 'something old.' "

Carmela's eyes opened wide. "A *lace* veil?"

Now Naomi was just plain snippy. "Last

179

time I looked most veils were made of lace."

"I suppose you're right. Where is it now? I'd love to take a look at it. Antique lace is always so beautiful."

"I have no idea," Naomi said. "Besides, what does it matter? And why are you bothering me?" And with that, Naomi turned and darted out the door.

Ava sidled up next to her. "Friendly sort, isn't she?"

"Naomi is like fingernails on chalkboard."

"You know what?" Ava said. "We should go have ourselves a nice refreshing cocktail."

Carmela sighed. "We've got a funeral to attend tomorrow."

Ava nodded. "Which is exactly *why* we need a cocktail."

CHAPTER 13

Wouldn't you know it? As Carmela and Ava hurried across St. Charles Avenue on the way to Isabelle's funeral, Ava got her four-inch-high heel caught in the streetcar track.

"Help!" Ava cried, just as Carmela realized that her friend was no longer striding alongside her.

Carmela whirled about to find her friend windmilling her arms and hopping up and down on one foot.

"What'd you do?" Carmela cried. They were so close, just a hundred yards from the church. She could practically smell the incense and flowers.

"I'm stuck," Ava cried. "My heel's wedged."

"A wedgie . . . what?"

"No, my *heel* is wedged," Ava said. "My mock croc stiletto's jammed in the tracks." She made frantic motions again. "C'mere and give me a tug."

Carmela turned back to help her. "Here, twist toward me."

"I'm trying, but my skirt's too tight."

"Like it's airbrushed on," Carmela said under her breath. "Okay then, wiggle your foot. Your ankle."

"I tried, but it's not working."

"Then slip out of your shoe."

"I'll lose it," Ava moaned.

"It's a train track, not a sinkhole," Carmela said. "Besides, you're gonna lose your entire leg if a streetcar comes chugging along." But like a good BFF, she got down on her hands and knees and crawled around so she could give the shoe a firm quarter-turn tug. Two seconds later Ava's foot popped loose.

"Thank you," Ava said as she limped across the street and then up the steps of the gray stone church. "You saved my life."

"Or at least your sole."

Ava grinned, then pulled a black mantilla from her bag and slipped it over her head and shoulders.

"What's going on now?" Carmela hissed as they paused at the back of the darkened church. "Why are you suddenly covering yourself up like a Sicilian widow?"

"I'm just devout," Ava said. "I prefer a veil on my head."

"But what about covering up your . . . um . . ." Carmela stared pointedly at the black spaghetti strap bustier Ava was wearing. It was tightly ruched with touches of purple peekaboo lace, and left nothing, absolutely nothing, to the imagination.

"Not to worry," Ava said as they tiptoed down the aisle.

Okay. Whatever.

Carmela hesitated at the fifth row of pews from the back. "How's this?"

"Nobody's going to see us all the way back here," Ava said.

"I think it's more important that we see them," Carmela said as she slid in.

The interior of the church was quiet and cool as mourners slowly filed in. Two Altar Society ladies worked quickly to arrange the area around the altar, which was no easy job since there were dozens of huge bouquets and sprays of white flowers in enormous vases.

"Edward must have traveled to Baton Rouge and back to round up that many white lilies," Ava whispered. "The altar looks like it's decorated with twenty years' worth of Easter flowers."

"White roses, too," Carmela said. She settled back in her pew and looked around. Shafts of sunlight streamed in through tall stained glass windows, and flickers of color shone on a half dozen pews up front. A faint rainbow arched across the vaulted ceiling. It was a stark contrast to the mourners who continually filed in, dressed in black like packs of roving crows.

Ava glanced at her watch. "Almost time."

As if on cue, Oliver Slade strode past them down the aisle. He was dressed in a black mourning coat and dove gray slacks. He wore a black satin armband tightly around his upper right arm and had a white rose pinned to his lapel.

"What on earth?" Ava whispered. "Have you ever seen such a . . . ?"

"Costume?" Carmela said. "No, I haven't. It's like he's harking back to the '20s or something."

"Or a bad drawing room comedy," Ava said. "And what's with the white rose?" She grasped Carmela's arm. "Ooh, do you think he's the one responsible for all those long-stemmed beauties up there on the altar?"

"If he is," Carmela said, "Edward Baudette will probably throw a fit."

In the choir loft above them, the organist riffed a few beginning notes, paused briefly, and then plunged into the sweet, comforting notes of Pachelbel's Canon in D.

"Why do they always play this particular

piece of music in church?" Ava asked.

"Probably because it's one of the most soothing pieces ever written," Carmela said. "There's a reason people select it for weddings and funerals."

"An all-purpose hymn," Ava mused. "Except I read somewhere, maybe in *Star Whacker* magazine, that the most popular funeral song is still Frank Sinatra's "My Way.""

"I can believe it," Carmela said. "Even though nobody *really* does it their way." Her head canted sideways as Naomi and Vesper walked past. Naomi looked trim and fashionable in a black cashmere skirt suit with a matching cloche. She had one arm firmly around Vesper Baudette's ample waist and seemed to be supporting her heavily as she led the woman down the aisle. Vesper lurched sideways once or twice, but Naomi gamely steered her forward.

Julian Drake followed closely on their heels. Maybe he'd been elected to bat cleanup, just in case Vesper actually fell down. Whatever, the three of them finally tottered to the front of the church and settled in the first pew.

Carmela, feeling vaguely emotional now, thought it sad that, instead of fulfilling their wedding duties as maid of honor and best man, the two of them were in charge of the miserable woman who never considered Isabelle as being good enough for her son.

Ava leaned sideways. "I hope they leave room up there for Ellie."

"Don't worry. If they dare to leave Ellie stranded, we'll just march right up the center aisle and carve out a place for her."

"Sounds right to me," Ava said. She glanced toward the back of the church, nervously awaiting the coffin's arrival, then whispered, "Hello, handsome, come to mama."

Carmela lifted an eyebrow at Ava, and then turned to look herself. Ava was focused on Bobby Prejean and a number of people from his office. Prejean, looking businesslike but debonair in a blue suit and black-striped tie, was leading his contingent up the aisle.

Carmela's heart swelled. Everyone from the district attorney's office had turned out to honor Isabelle. God bless them. Then Carmela took a second look to see if Hugo Delton was with them. He was. But she didn't think that he'd seen her.

"If Mr. Prejean is as upset as he looks," Ava said, "I wouldn't mind offering a little warmth and comfort."

"Haven't you hit your weekly hustle

quotient yet?"

"I'm just warming up."

"And, yes," Carmela said, "Bobby Prejean *is* upset. Isabelle was one of his most promising attorneys, so he's vowed to throw the entire weight of his office behind the investigation."

"Speaking of investigations," Ava said, "do you think Babcock will show up today?"

Carmela started to say something and then paused. Would he? Hmm, that was an interesting thought. And could he possibly be here right now, keeping one eye on her and an eagle eye on his various suspects?

That prompted Carmela to crane her neck and look around. Babcock obviously wasn't up front or she would have noticed him by now. But maybe he was sitting on the side aisle? She stole a couple more glances around. Nope, no sign of him there. In the back of the church, then? Hiding behind a statue or a potted plant? No, she didn't see him there, either. Finally, when she'd just about given up, she spotted him. Babcock was crouched in the doorway leading to the choir loft. Well, not exactly crouched, but he was standing absolutely stock-still.

Relying on the old trick that if there isn't a speck of movement, the predator won't spot you? Maybe.

187

Just as Carmela and Babcock locked eyes, there was a click-clack of wheels, and Carmela knew that Isabelle's coffin had arrived.

Oh dear.

She reached over and clutched Ava's hand, and then the two of them, holding their breath, watched the heart-wrenching procession.

Edward and Ellie came first. They each carried a small bouquet of flowers as they walked slowly down the center aisle.

"Ooh." Ava let loose a little gasp and clasped Carmela's hand even tighter.

Then Isabelle's coffin rolled down the aisle. It was the walnut one that Ellie had selected. Only today it was closed and topped with a spectacular spray of white orchids.

Now the organ burst into a prelude and the entire congregation rose to their feet. The choir (Carmela hadn't even realized there was a choir) broke into the opening lines of "On Eagle's Wings."

Carmela figured there wasn't a dry eye in the house as the processional rolled slowly toward the front of the church.

"This is so sad," Ava whispered.

Carmela could only nod as, above her, voices rose together singing, ". . . And hold you in the palm of His hand."

At the front of the church, the coffin was gently seesawed into place, and then Ellie and Edward moved toward the front pew.

But the drama wasn't over yet. Because just as Edward tried to guide Ellie into her seat, Naomi jumped up and shook her head fiercely.

Ava half stood. "I'll smack that little priss upside her head if she tries to exclude Ellie," she hissed.

But Naomi didn't. She just preferred that Edward slide in and sit next to her. Leaving Ellie on the end.

"Grrrrr," Ava growled.

The minister, looking very somber in his dark suit and stark white collar, strode to the altar and motioned for everyone to please sit down. Then he opened his prayer book and began. "Let not your hearts be troubled . . ."

Carmela tried to follow along, she really did, but she seemed to have developed a severe attention deficit this morning.

Or maybe I'm just edgy about everything that's happened.

Yes, that had to be it. Not only that, if Babcock was attending this service, studying everyone with his cool law enforcement eyes, didn't that mean that he suspected the killer might be here, too?

A terrible thought. But one that intrigued Carmela nevertheless.

So who?

Had Oliver Slade really stalked Isabelle? Was his anger less about unrequited love and more about revenge?

Had Edward been locked into wedding plans that had scared the crap out of him? Had he decided that murdering Isabelle was the only way to extract himself?

And what about Vesper Baudette? Mama bears were fierce and known to kill for their cubs. Had Vesper killed for her precious Edward? Had she thought that by killing Isabelle she would free him? It seemed like madness to think that a family could commit murder against one of their own.

And then there was Naomi Rattler and Julian Drake. And Hugo Delton from Isabelle's office. They all might have had ample opportunity. But did they have motive? She needed to find out.

As a soloist sang "I Will Always Love You," Carmela pondered all of this. She felt helpless, though Ellie had asked for her help. Begged for it, really. Which meant she needed to redouble her efforts, search around, ask more probing questions. Get to the bottom of this murder.

As the last notes of the song faded away, the minister beckoned Edward to the lectern. He rose from his pew and then walked up the few steps with a heavy, measured gait. He turned, looked sadly down at the casket, and then gazed out over the mourners.

Finally, Edward spoke. "Friends, family, colleagues. Thank you all for joining us today to pay your respects and bid farewell to our dear Isabelle." He paused for a moment, and then went on. "Yesterday, for the very first time, I saw my bride-to-be in her wedding gown."

There was a sharp intake of breath among all the mourners as they hung on his every word.

"I looked forward to watching Isabelle walk down this very aisle and meet me here at the altar." Edward glanced back at the minister. "I looked forward to Reverend Dufraine giving us his blessing and joining us together in holy matrimony. But it was not to be. I expected a good long life with Isabelle steadfastly at my side. But it was not to be." Now he was sobbing openly as he held out both hands in pleading supplication to her coffin. "Please, dear Lord, bless her and keep her. For she is in your hands now."

One of the ushers rushed to give a sobbing Edward a hand down the steps, but he was shaken off as Edward stumbled back to his pew. Then the minister beckoned Ellie to take her turn at the lectern.

"Poor Ellie," Ava said. "I hope she can get through this okay."

But Carmela's attention was elsewhere. While everyone in church was focused on Ellie as she walked to the lectern, Carmela was watching Naomi grab Edward with both arms. She pulled him to her and they seemed to collapse together. Carmela wished she could have seen what was probably a very satisfied look on Naomi's face. But now she had to focus on Ellie.

Ellie was remarkably poised as she stood facing the mourners. She waited until she had everyone's attention, and then began.

"Isabelle was the finest sister anyone could ever hope to have. When our parents passed away, she was already on her own at Columbia Law School in New York. I was still a minor. Rather than let me go into foster care, Isabelle changed her plans, moved back to New Orleans, and took care of me while going to law school at Tulane." She paused. "I owe her everything. When we were children, she protected me. If someone bullied me, she put them in their place. But now Isabelle has been struck down by a coldhearted killer, and it's my turn to find that killer and put him in his place." She looked out over the mourners with a cold, hard grimace on her face. "And that place would be the Louisiana State Penitentiary."

Across the expanse of three dozen rows of church pews, Ellie's eyes locked on to Carmela's. Her eyes blazed with a cold, hard determination that Carmela felt within her own heart. Then, just like that, Ellie was back to being normal Ellie again. She thanked everyone for coming to honor her sister, then walked back to her pew, head held high.

"Cher," Ava said. "Did you hear what Ellie said? She was basically issuing a challenge."

"She sure was," Carmela said.

"Is Ellie up for it? Are you?"

Carmela tightened her jaw. "We'll find out, won't we?"

There was one more hymn to be sung, and then the little procession repeated itself. Only this time it was the casket that went first, with Edward, Vesper, Ellie, Naomi, and Julian Drake following behind it.

When the church was mostly empty and it was time to join the recession, Carmela realized that Edgar Babcock was no longer skulking in the back doorway.

"Where'd he run off to?" Carmela wondered.

"Dunno," Ava said. "He must be outside already."

They hustled outside and there he was, standing by himself against a metal railing, watching the coffin get loaded into a long black hearse.

"Looking for suspects?" Carmela asked.

"Looking anyway," Babcock said.

"Did you get a chance to check out all the people from the cake tasting? All seven of them?"

"Only three of them actually left Commander's Palace. The other four stayed to drink."

"And the three were . . . ?"

"Edward Baudette, Naomi Rattler, and Julian Drake."

"Hmm."

Babcock continued to stare at the hearse. "Are you going to the cemetery?"

Carmela shook her head. "No cemetery service. Just a funeral luncheon."

"Ah, that's right. At the restaurant your old boyfriend owns." He was referring, of course, to Quigg Brevard's restaurant, Mumbo Gumbo.

"He was *never* my old boyfriend,"

194

Carmela told him. "You of all people should know that." Then, "I need to talk to you about something."

Babcock stuck his hands in his pants pockets and jingled loose change. "You're going to ask me if I spotted the killer?"

"No. But did you?"

"You think I'd tell you that?"

"Probably not. But I uncovered something that might be useful."

"What's that?"

"Turns out Isabelle was a very traditional bride. You know, 'something old, something new . . .' "

"Yeah, yeah," Babcock said, gesturing for her to hurry it up.

"Naomi Rattler, the maid of honor, apparently bought Isabelle an antique veil for her 'something old.' "

Babcock's eyes searched hers. "An antique veil made of . . . lace?"

"That was my understanding," Carmela said. "From a local antique shop."

"Do we know which one?" Babcock asked.

"Dulcimer Antiques, the one that Devon Dowling owns."

"He's the starchy little guy who's always carrying around that chubby pug dog?"

"That's right."

Babcock rubbed his chin. His mind was

obviously hard at work, cataloging this new piece of information. "Do you know where the veil is now?"

Carmela shook her head. "No idea."

Babcock practically winced when he spoke his next words. "Maybe you could . . . ask around?"

That was exactly what Carmela had hoped to hear. Babcock giving his blessing, asking for her help. "Okay, I can do that for sure." She paused. "You think there's some kind of connection? I mean concerning the lace?"

"I don't know. But, Carmela, when I say ask, I mean just a few innocent questions. Do *not* investigate. That's my job and I don't want you stepping on any toes."

Especially yours, Carmela thought.

"Okay, I can do that," Carmela said. When Babcock furrowed his brow instead of answering her, she said, "You've really taken this case to heart, haven't you?"

Babcock squinted over the crowd. "It's the politics that's driving me crazy."

"How so?"

"Because Isabelle was attached to the D.A.'s office, she's basically one of our own. So the mayor's office, even though His Honor is out of town, is pressuring us like crazy to solve this crime."

"You mean solve it fast," said Carmela.

Babcock nodded. "As in lightning round." He watched as Bobby Prejean stepped away from a group of people and headed toward him. "Incoming," he said under his breath.

"Detective Babcock," Prejean said, shaking Babcock's hand vigorously. "Good to see you again." Then he nodded at Carmela. "Carmela."

"It was a lovely service, wasn't it?" Carmela said. She was afraid Prejean would say something about her dropping by his office yesterday. But Prejean had other things on his mind.

"I know you're working hard on this case," Prejean said to Babcock. "But I'm begging you to pull out all the stops. If there's anything — and I do mean anything — that I or my office can do to help, don't hesitate to ask."

Babcock nodded. "Of course. Thank you."

Prejean gave an appreciative nod, then moved off to shake more hands.

"He's a real mover and a shaker," Carmela observed.

"The way that guy operates, I'd say he's going all the way to the statehouse. Maybe even higher."

Carmela gazed at him. "And that's a bad thing?"

"Oh, heck no," Babcock said. "He's a

good guy. Hardworking and smart. I just don't want him using my case to springboard himself up the ladder."

"Ah. So . . . you're going back to work?"

"Yeah." Babcock nodded toward a skinny guy in an even skinnier cut European suit who was standing some twenty feet away. "Police chief wants me to huddle with Jarreau over there. Our media liaison." He said it like he'd been ordered to drink a cup of hemlock.

"So you don't have time to stop by the funeral luncheon?"

Babcock shook his head. "No. How about you? Are you going?"

Carmela was still undecided. But as the funeral hearse pulled away from the curb, she noticed Naomi standing next to Edward, her shoulder bumping up against his, their fingers entwined.

"Yes," Carmela said, making a snap decision. "I think I will go after all. See if anything interesting shakes out."

CHAPTER 14

Mumbo Gumbo was the pluperfect French Quarter restaurant. Cozy and quaint, located in a former art gallery, with crumbling brickwork that crept halfway up the interior walls to give it a rustic, European feel.

At the very front, businessmen luxuriated over dry martinis at the glossy eggplant-colored bar. Farther back, in the darkened restaurant, were large black bumper car-sized booths. Haunting Cajun ballads played over the music system, while potted palm trees and slowly turning wicker fans added to the exotic atmosphere.

Quigg Brevard, the owner, spotted Carmela and Ava immediately and hustled over to greet them.

"Mmn," Ava purred. "Here comes Mr. Luscious."

All broad shoulders in a sleekly tailored sharkskin suit, Quigg was indeed luscious and slightly dangerous looking with his dark eyes, olive complexion, and full, sensuous mouth.

"Hello there," Quigg said to Carmela, as if she were the only person in his rarified universe.

"Hi," Carmela said back. She'd dated him once or twice, and things hadn't really clicked between them. Now that she was hot and heavy with Babcock, Quigg always acted like she was a prize to be wooed and captured.

"I take it you're here for the funeral luncheon?" Quigg asked.

"That's right," Carmela said.

Ava smiled demurely. "But if you've got something else in mind . . ."

Quigg just gazed at Carmela, as if they shared some private amusement. "Let me escort you ladies." He held out a hand for Carmela. "My dear?"

Quigg led them through the dining room and into a large private banquet room. The room was painted an elegant raspberry red and hung with oil paintings (with plenty of crackle glaze) that depicted the French Quarter as it had been in the 1800s.

"Here you are," Quigg said, flashing his trademark grin. "If you need anything — anything at all — be sure to let me know."

"Oh, we will," Ava said.

Carmela glanced about the room. A buffet table with silver chafing dishes and three-tiered serving trays was set up against the right-hand wall. To the left of it was the seating area, an assortment of round tables covered in starched white tablecloths. At the back of the room a long mahogany bar seemed to be the focal point for the mourners, its glass shelves glittering with bottles.

"This looks more like a party than a funeral luncheon," Ava said, noting that all the mourners were either bellied up to the bar or milling around, sipping tumblers of whiskey or glasses of wine.

Vesper Baudette sat at what appeared to be the head table, a large cut glass tumbler in front of her. It was less than half full with clear liquid, and Carmela wondered if it was water or vodka.

Who are you kidding? Of course it's vodka.

A few seats away from Vesper, Naomi Rattler cradled little Bing Bing in her arms, feeding her tidbits of food that presumably came from the buffet.

"Do you see that?" Ava stage-whispered. "Naomi brought her *dog.* She didn't have that critter with her in church, did she?"

"Not that I noticed," Carmela said.

"Would you bring Boo and Poobah here?"

"Only if they were invited."

"Then why bring . . . ?"

But Ava was quickly interrupted by Ellie, who came scurrying over to greet them.

"Carmela! Ava! I'm so glad you could make the luncheon."

"We wouldn't miss it for the world," Ava said.

"Is this Edward's doing?" Carmela asked.

"He said he'd handle the planning, so I suppose so," Ellie said. "Do you really think Vesper would have popped for a fancy buffet and an open bar?"

"Well, maybe the open bar," Ava snorted.

Ellie rolled her eyes. "You're probably right about that."

Carmela gripped Ellie's hand. "Your eulogy this morning was just beautiful, honey. You honored your sister with a very heartfelt speech."

Ellie gazed at her. "Even the revenge part?"

"Especially the revenge part," Carmela said.

Ellie's voice grew quiet. "I need her killer brought to justice. I firmly believe that Isabelle won't rest until that happens."

"Babcock is working as hard as he can," Carmela assured her. "He was even at the church earlier. Did you see him?"

"No," Ellie said. "But I have to say I'm heartened that he showed up."

"And Bobby Prejean's office is offering their full support."

"He told me that," Ellie said. "In fact he's here." She looked around the room, which was getting more and more crowded with every passing minute. "Well . . . I know he's here somewhere."

"Don't worry, I'll track down that hunky D.A.," Ava said.

"Maybe you two should hit the buffet table first," Ellie suggested. "Get a jump on the crowd." She gave a little wave accompanied by a wan smile. "I'll talk to you later."

"Let's definitely hit the buffet," Ava said. "I could use some good vittles, now that you mention it."

The chafing dishes were filled with the best Mumbo Gumbo had to offer. Crawfish *étouffée*, shrimp gumbo, jambalaya, trout *meunière*, apple fritters, creamy rice pudding, and, of course, red rice and beans.

"This is fantastic," Ava said as she sped through the line and began loading her plate.

"You can always count on Quigg's head chef to lay out a fine spread," Carmela said.

"I'm gonna drop my plate over there," Ava

203

said, pointing to a table. "And then hit up the bar for a couple glasses of fancy French wine."

"Sounds good," Carmela said. "Just let me grab a couple of these cocktail sausages." She took two, debated over the pan of green mussels, and then scooped three mussels out of their creamy, garlicky broth. She was just about to find her table, when Bobby Prejean cut in next to her.

"We meet again," Prejean said.

"Say, thanks for not revealing the fact that I stopped by your office yesterday," Carmela said. "Babcock gets a little territorial if he thinks I'm investigating behind his back."

"No problem. In fact, I'm glad you're asking so many questions. I wish more people would. We . . ." He shook his head. "Everyone at our office just loved Isabelle. She was such a rising star. She was really going places."

"That's so interesting," Carmela said, "because that's what I heard about you."

"Me?" Prejean looked surprised. "Nah, I'm just a humble public servant."

"No aspirations to the statehouse?"

"Well . . . maybe someday. But definitely not for a few years."

"You know," Carmela said, "Babcock really is working like crazy on this case. He's got his assistant Bobby Gallant chasing down leads, too. They're both tenacious as all get-out."

"And thank goodness for that," Prejean said. As he took a scoop of crawfish ravioli, peals of laughter broke out nearby and he and Carmela both glanced toward one of the tables.

Julian Drake was sitting there, sipping a glass of bourbon and flirting with a skinny blond woman who was picking at a plate of food. Drake looked confident, happy, and mildly in lust.

"Julian Drake," Prejean whispered to Carmela. "That's who Babcock should be taking a good, hard look at."

"I think he already did," Carmela said. "I mean, Drake was questioned immediately after Isabelle's murder, right then and there in the cemetery. And the next day, too." Carmela worried her upper teeth against her lower lip, and then said, "You seem very suspicious of him. Is there something I should know?"

Prejean pulled Carmela out of line and over to an omelet station that had been momentarily deserted by its chef. "The thing is, our office has recently begun to take a hard look at Drake and some of his casino buddies."

Carmela's eyebrows shot up. "Why is that?"

"Moving under the radar, they've managed to arrange land swaps, received permission from certain state officials to bypass construction ordinances, and personally bought up some of the land adjacent to the new Elysian Fields Casino."

"And this is all illegal?"

"Yes and no," Prejean told her. "We know there has been a fair amount of bribes, payoffs, and good old-fashioned cronyism. Trouble is, we can't make anything stick. And everybody, from the city council to the local ward bosses, wants that old amusement park cleaned up. It's basically been a pile of junk for over ten years."

"So in their eyes the casino project is a good thing," Carmela said.

"It is in mine, too, but only if it's done legally."

Carmela's radar was suddenly pinging like crazy. "And you're investigating this."

"Trying to."

"Was Isabelle working on this, too?"

"She was," Prejean said.

"Whoa," Carmela said, her heart skipping a beat. "That adds a whole new perspective. I mean, what if Isabelle had stumbled upon something!"

"You mean some information that led to her getting killed?" Prejean said. "I thought about that. I even talked it over with Babcock, but we couldn't find any connection."

"But if Julian Drake was going to be the best man in her wedding, maybe *that* was the connection!"

"If she'd uncovered some impropriety, I'm positive she would have told me. I mean, we worked together very closely and I trusted her. Trusted her completely."

But for Carmela, this new information put Drake squarely at the top of her suspects list.

"There you are," Ava said when Carmela finally joined her. "You've been a busy girl, flirting with that cute D.A." She gave a slow wink. "I was worried that he might sweep you off your feet."

"Hardly," Carmela said.

"Then I'm going to have to go over and flirt with him, since Chef Oliver hasn't turned up yet."

"I don't think he will. And you keep your distance from that chef if you see him again. The last thing you need is to get cozy with some kind of stalker guy."

"Some girls would kill to have a guy that

crazy over them," Ava said.

"And some girls get killed because of it," Carmela told her.

"Okay, okay, I get it." Ava glanced around. "Who's the guy in the Sansabelt slacks making goo-goo eyes at you?"

"Don't encourage him," Carmela said. "That's Hugo Delton. He works in the D.A.'s office and he's a creep."

"You do tend to attract that type. Hey!" Ava said, as Edward Baudette strolled past their table. "How are you holding up?"

Even though he looked tired and a little grim, he greeted them politely.

"Thanks for coming," Edward said. His eyes were still red, and he had purple hollows under them from lack of sleep.

"You gave a lovely eulogy this morning," Carmela told him.

Edward slipped into the chair across from her. "Thank you." He managed a wan smile then tried to stifle the yawn that followed. "Sorry, I'm just so tired."

"I can imagine," Ava said.

"How's Naomi holding up?" Carmela asked. Naomi's emotional involvement with Edward seemed to run way beyond being warmhearted and friendly. She looked like she was lining him up for a permanent position. As her boyfriend, and then, after a suitable period of time . . . her fiancé?

"Naomi's holding up okay, I guess. She's certainly been incredibly supportive to me."

"We noticed," Carmela said.

But Edward remained moody and just plain bummed. "Look at this," he said. "All of the people that are here today were supposed to be our wedding guests. But they ended up as funeral guests."

"I'm so sorry about that," Carmela said. Was she? Didn't she still harbor a few suspicions against Edward? Oh yes, she did. She was still trying to figure out if he was legitimately grief stricken or was a greatly relieved fiancé pulling off an Academy Award–caliber performance.

"But the funeral was beautiful," put in Ava. "The flowers were to die . . . uh, I mean they were lovely."

"Yes, Naomi handled most of the details. Besides being a fashion blogger, she's also a highly sought after event planner."

"Imagine that," Carmela said.

"I had no idea," Ava said.

"I spoke to Naomi last night," Carmela said. "About Isabelle's antique veil."

"Oh?" Edward said.

"Because Ava and I were wondering if we could get a look at it," Carmela said. "We're both so very fond of antique lace."

209

"We really are," Ava said, trying to look interested.

Edward shook his head. "I really couldn't say where it was. Probably at the apartment Isabelle shared with Ellie. So I guess you'll have to ask her."

"I'll do that," Carmela said.

Five minutes later, with Ava on the hunt for Bobby Prejean, Carmela tracked down Ellie. But when asked about an antique veil, Ellie just shook her head.

"What?" she said. "An antique lace veil?" She looked disturbed. "Dear Lord, is it anything like the lace Isabelle was strangled with?"

"I really don't know," Carmela said. "That's why I'm trying to track it down."

"Well, this is the first I've heard about it," Ellie said.

"So it's not at your apartment?"

"If it is, I haven't got a clue where it would be."

"Do you think the veil could be at Vesper's house?" Carmela asked.

"You could ask her," Ellie said. "But trying to talk to her is like trying to get an audience with the pope."

Carmela was determined, however, and when she saw Vesper shaking hands with an older couple, a couple she recognized as being denizens of the Garden District as well, she swooped in for the kill.

"Vesper," Carmela said, sounding positively chirpy.

Vesper stared at her with heavy-lidded eyes. "Who are you?"

Carmela touched a hand to her chest. "Carmela. Ellie's friend, remember? I was there when you picked out the coffin, and at the visitation, and then at . . ."

"No. I don't remember."

"Listen," Carmela went on breezily, as if nothing could deter her. "I was wondering when I could stop by and pick up Isabelle's veil?"

That question shook Vesper to her core.

"What!" she shrieked. "Why on earth would you want to do that?"

Now Carmela employed a little white lie. "Because Ellie would love to have her sister's veil as a memento. You certainly wouldn't begrudge her that, would you?"

"She wants the veil," Vesper said. She spoke slowly, as if she were just learning English as a second language.

Carmela kept a friendly smile on her face, even though she wanted to smack this woman. "That's right. And I know you're frightfully busy, so I'd be happy to stop by your home and pick it up myself."

"My home," Vesper repeated.

"Yes. How would tomorrow afternoon work for you? Let's say two o'clock?"

"Well, I don't . . ."

"That's just perfect," Carmela said. "I'll see you then."

When Carmela was finally able to round up Ava, she was sipping a mimosa cocktail.

"You're having another drink? Don't you have to get back to your shop?"

"Miguel is taking care of things," Ava said. "Besides, where else can I get my vitamin C with bubbles?" She gave a pussycat grin. "And I'm celebrating."

"Celebrating what?" Carmela asked.

"I'm officially in love."

"Again? Who's the lucky gent?"

Ava dimpled prettily. "You know who. That hunky D.A."

"I wish you two all the happiness in the world. However, the man does strike me as a bit of a hardworking, upstanding public servant. Not the kind of guy who wants to bask in your limelight."

"You're worried I might lead him astray?" Ava asked.

"No, but you could sidetrack his political career."

"Still," Ava said, "he is rather gorgeous. A girl can dream, can't she?"

"That she can."

"So what was your big confab with Old Stone Face all about?"

"I'm trying to weasel Isabelle's antique lace veil away from Vesper."

"She has it?"

Carmela nodded.

"And you think that antique lace veil might somehow lead to the antique lace murder weapon?"

"I don't know," Carmela said. "But I'm sure going to try and jam a few puzzle pieces together."

"Good girl," Ava said. "Smart girl."

"We'll see about that."

Ava took another sip of her drink. "Can you believe that little gold digger Naomi is also an event planner?"

Carmela glanced at the buffet table. "Huh. They've already run out of sweet potato casserole and they were skimpy on the shrimp gumbo. If Naomi was my event planner I'd fire her."

"Yeah," Ava snorted. "Out of a cannon."

CHAPTER 15

It was almost two o'clock by the time Carmela arrived at Memory Mine, only minutes before she was scheduled to teach a charm bracelet class.

"There you are!" Gabby exclaimed. "I was wondering when you'd turn up. How was the funeral?"

"Sad. Strange."

"They usually are," Gabby said. "Did you learn anything new? Did any new clues shake out?"

Carmela told Gabby about tracking down Isabelle's lace veil. And how she was going to talk to Devon Dowling, who'd sold it to Naomi. And then pick up the veil at Vesper's house tomorrow.

"And what about all those other suspects that have been buzzing around in your head?"

"Mostly they're still buzzing," Carmela said.

"Oh dear, and I know you made a very big promise to Ellie."

"A promise I'm going to try my best to keep," Carmela said. She picked up a packet of charms and balanced it in her hand. "Bobby Prejean, Isabelle's boss, thinks we should be looking hard at Julian Drake."

Gabby looked startled. "I thought the police had already eliminated him as a suspect."

"They did, but I think Drake deserves another look. Apparently he's been involved in some political maneuvering over at that new Elysian Fields Casino. I got it straight from the horse's mouth, from the district attorney himself, that his office has been watching the negotiations very carefully."

"Holy smokes, does that mean Isabelle was involved, too?"

Carmela nodded. "I'm afraid so."

Gabby winced and held up an index finger. "Which means you'd better be careful, Miss Carmela. You get too close to the killer and your head's going to end up on the chopping block."

"Then you'd have to run the shop yourself."

"Oh no you don't," Gabby said. "Don't try to get cute about this and deflect my warning. Murder is serious business. I know

215

you want to help Ellie, but you need to take care of yourself, too." She hesitated. "I've got a bad feeling about this."

"So do I," Carmela said.

Thank goodness, Gabby had already arranged an assortment of link bracelets, charms, fittings, and findings on the back craft table.

You're my saving grace, Gabby, Carmela thought as she quickly perused the supplies. Gabby had also put out small bags of jump rings and small plastic trays filled with charms in the shapes of keys, butterflies, letters, numbers, feathers, ballerinas, birds, and stars. Carmela pulled open a drawer and pulled out clear bags that held tiny picture frames, hearts, ovals, and squares. These were designed to hold small pictures and photos and were always very popular.

Six ladies showed up for the class today. Three of her regulars and three newbies, two of whom were redheaded sisters visiting from Amarillo, Texas.

"I'd sure like to make a New Orleans–inspired charm bracelet," said Molly, the talkier of the two sisters. She pronounced it New Or-*leens,* not the typical N'awlins as natives preferred.

"Then you'll need some special charms,"

Carmela told her. She pulled out a small box filled with silver charms that depicted tiny magnolias, riverboats, Andrew Jackson statues, gumbo pots, Mardi Gras masks, streetcars, tombstones, lampposts, and fleur-de-lis.

"And we attach them to these pretty little silver chain bracelets?" said one of the women.

"Using jump rings," Carmela said. "Here, I'll show you how." She took her small needle-nose jewelry pliers and gently bent open a small jump ring. "Once you've worked your jump ring open, you can slide on your charm, and then attach it to your bracelet. Just be sure to gently squeeze your jump ring closed again so your charm hangs on tight."

"Easy-peasy," Molly said.

"Right," said her sister.

"Now what about these little frames?" one of the women asked.

"You can slide a little photo into those," Carmela said.

"Like a locket," another woman said.

"That's right. Then you can put your photo frame on your charm bracelet or string it on a nice ribbon and wear it like a necklace."

"Ribbon," said Molly. "I'm going to need ribbon."

Once the ladies were completely consumed with designing their bracelets, Carmela slipped into her office and called Babcock.

"Okay," she said to him, "I tracked down that veil."

"Good girl," he said. "Where is it? I'd like to have my forensic team take a look at it."

"Vesper Baudette has it at her house. I'm going to run over there tomorrow afternoon and pick it up."

"Not until tomorrow, huh?"

"If you're so hot to take a look at it, why don't you just get a court order and send a car over there, all lights and screaming sirens?"

"Because then they'd see me coming."

Carmela thought about that for a few moments. "Do you really think Edward or Vesper had something to do with Isabelle's death?" She certainly did, but she wanted to know where Babcock's mind was on this.

"Maybe. We're still following up with interviews and several other things. Nothing's really congealed yet."

"I need to tell you about something else," Carmela said.

"Okay, shoot."

"I had a conversation with Bobby Prejean at the luncheon. About how the D.A.'s office was looking into some sort of impropriety surrounding the new Elysian Fields Casino."

"Yes," Babcock said. "I already know about that."

"What?" Carmela was surprised and a little disappointed that she wasn't the one to spring it on him. "You let me go on and on and you already knew about this?"

"I was trying to see how much you knew. And, just off the bat, I'd have to say it's too much for comfort. My comfort."

"You can't ask me to investigate some things and not others," Carmela said. "It's a package deal."

"That's not how I see it."

"Have you had a chance to talk to that creepy Hugo Delton yet? He was throwing fish eyes at me again at the luncheon. He strikes me as a stalker type."

"No, that would be Oliver Slade."

"Maybe we've got two stalkers," Carmela said.

"Carmela . . ." Babcock's tone was vaguely threatening. "I'm looking into all of this. Enough said."

Carmela could tell when she was pushing Babcock too hard. It was her cue to back off and go underground. What he didn't know wouldn't hurt him. "Okay, will I see you tonight?"

"Can't, sorry. A detective's work is never done. But on the bright side, we've got your museum thing tomorrow night. So we'll spend a lovely evening together. I can hardly wait, I so love museum events."

"I'm going to ignore your dripping sarcasm for now. Just be sure to wear a tux."

"That's really necessary?"

"No, you can wear ratty jeans and a concert T-shirt if you want. Of course you have to wear a tux. It's a black-tie event, for goodness' sake. There'll be big-buck donors there."

Babcock sighed loudly. "The things you talk me into."

"Honey, you ain't seen nothin' yet."

Carmela popped back out to the craft table.

"How's everybody doing with their charm bracelets?"

She was answered with two distracted nods and a grunt. The women were all leaning over their workstations with great intensity, clipping on charms, chattering about themes (a Parisian theme seemed to be the table favorite), and picking out photo frames.

They don't even need me anymore.

But Carmela knew this was how it should be. Once you got a crafter started on a project, their excitement and enthusiasm kicked in big-time. Which meant their minds were whirling and their fingers were twirling.

"Gabby," Carmela said, in a low voice, "can you take it from here? I want to run over to Dulcimer Antiques."

"Talk to him about that wedding veil?" Gabby asked.

Carmela nodded.

"Go," Gabby urged. "But be careful."

Devon Dowling, the owner of Dulcimer Antiques, was chubby, semi-balding with a scrawny pigtail that hung halfway down his back, and the biggest gossip in the French Quarter.

When Carmela walked into his shop, he grinned like the Cheshire cat and said, "Did you hear that Burt Cannedy got busted for selling a hot Guanyin statue?"

"On purpose?" Carmela asked. She didn't know exactly what a hot Guanyin statue was, but it sounded vaguely Asian.

Her question seemed to take some of the wind out of Dowling's sails. "Well, no. Burt didn't actually *know* the statue was stolen

221

goods, but when the original owners tracked it down and got it back, Burt was left holding the bag."

"That's never good." Carmela glanced around Dulcimer Antiques and wondered how many of his pieces were of questionable origin. The French Quarter, with its almost fifty antique shops, was always a hotbed of buying, selling, and trading. Combine that with a bunch of old families who were often selling off family art and antiques under the noses of close relatives and you had yourself a hopping art market.

"I have something to show you," Dowling said. "I know you're a nut for bronze dogs."

"I am." Carmela had started a collection of antique bronze dogs several years ago, and it had since grown into quite a lovely kennel of canines.

"Take a gander at this," Dowling said. "Nineteenth century." He handed her a dog caught in an elegant stretch, its head slightly lower than its back haunches and curling tail.

"It's gorgeous," she said, just as his pug, Mimi, sauntered out of the back office to see what was going on. Mimi was the canine clone of Dowling, compact and chubby. With a shorter pigtail.

"For the right price, you could make that

puppy yours," he said.

"And what's the right price?"

Dowling paused and brushed a finger across his lips. "I could easily get five hundred for this. But for you, let's bring it on down to . . . four?"

Mimi stared at Carmela with her hard, bright eyes, as if daring her to go for it.

"I love the dog," Carmela said. "But I'm afraid it's not in the budget this month."

Dowling took the dog back from her and set it gently on a stone mantelpiece. "Maybe next month, then. We'll put it here for safekeeping."

"What I really came to ask you about," Carmela said, "is a lace veil. You apparently purchased some vintage clothing a while ago?"

"Yes," Dowling said. "I rarely handle items of that ilk, but I happened upon an odd lot at an auction over in Gramercy. I always get excited about auctions along the River Road because of all the enormous plantations that used to be out that way. I think maybe three hundred and fifty at one time? So you can usually find something that's old and tasty."

"And you bought . . . ?"

"Let's see." Dowling waggled his fingers along the side of his cheek. "Along with a set of Limoges china and a set of Buccellati flatware, I purchased that small lot of vintage clothing. A couple of wedding gowns, lace parasols, high-button shoes, kid gloves . . ."

"And a lace veil."

"Yes, and a veil," Dowling said.

"And then you sold the veil to a woman by the name of Naomi Rattler?"

Now Dowling just looked confused. "Maybe. I really can't remember exactly who purchased it. To tell you the truth, Mimi and I have been so frantically busy lately my brain is pretty much fried."

Carmela looked around the shop. It was empty save for her and Dowling. And, of course, Mimi.

"This is kind of important," Carmela told him. "It was purchased for a friend of mine who just passed away."

"Oh dear. *That's* not good."

"Is there any way we could confirm this particular sale? Perhaps you could go through your sales records?"

"My records. Yes, I suppose I could do that."

"They're on your computer?" Carmela prompted.

As Dowling laughed, his belly actually jiggled along in unison. "Computer? Oh my, no. I do business the old-fashioned way. I keep *books.*"

Dowling wasn't kidding. He actually hauled out an old-school black ledger and began paging through it. Carmela half expected a quill pen to go along with it.

"It wouldn't have been all that long ago," Carmela said. Really, how many antiques had the man even sold in the last month or so? Thirty? Forty at most? After all, he had oodles of competition.

Dowling ran his finger down the page as his lips moved in silent accompaniment. Then he said, "Okay, this must be it. Who did you say the buyer was?"

"Naomi Rattler."

"The fashion blogger?"

"I guess she is," Carmela said. "But I understand she does event planning, too."

"Okay, yes. I've got it right here. Purchased three weeks ago by N. Rattler. You want her address?"

"No, that's okay. And you say the lace veil was old?"

Dowling thought for a few moments. "Mmn, I'd have to say at least a hundred years. But in very fine condition. No rips or tears, not even a hint of discoloration."

"Was it French lace or Belgian lace? Do you remember?"

Dowling waved a hand. "Honey, I only

know the difference between French toast and Belgian waffles. Lace is so not my thing."

CHAPTER 16

Boo and Poobah were always delighted to have company. Especially when it was Aunt Ava who came for dinner (again!) and brought them bite-sized liver treats.

"These are one hundred percent organic free-range treats," Ava said, as she popped a bite into each dog's mouth.

"Beef liver?" Carmela asked. She was standing at the stove stirring a pot of shrimp gumbo.

"That's right."

"Then wouldn't free range be, like, from out on the plains somewhere?"

"I guess," Ava said. She wandered into the kitchen and picked up an already open bottle of wine. She tilted it toward Carmela and said, "May I?"

"Yes, you may."

Ava poured herself a glass. "You want some, too?"

"No thanks."

Ava wandered back into the living room and plopped down on the leather sofa. She unfurled a fashion magazine she'd brought along and started paging through it.

"Have you seen those new swimsuits for guys?" Ava asked. "They're like a Speedo, only half a Speedo. There's just a tiny piece of knit fabric that wraps around one leg and another small piece that holds all the important bits together."

"Kind of like a slingshot," Carmela said. Honestly, where did Ava come up with this stuff?

"Exactly. I find the whole idea rather intriguing. Very continental. Very Saint-Tropez."

"Maybe you can talk Naomi into highlighting one of those things on her fashion blog. If she even really writes one."

Ava cackled merrily and slapped her leg. "For sure."

"Okay," Carmela said. "Dinner is served." She carried the bowls of gumbo to the table and said, "Nothing fancy."

"We had fancy for lunch," Ava said. "And look where it got us."

"A case of heartburn?"

Ava nodded. "A little. Or it could've come from that third serving of peach cobbler I wolfed down."

"Or all those cocktails."

They dug into the spicy gumbo while Ava made appreciative murmurs. Then she said, "Oh," and dug in her handbag. "I brought along a petition for you to sign."

"What's it for?" Carmela asked. The last time she'd signed one of Ava's petitions she'd almost ended up on Homeland Security's watch list.

"You'll like it. There's this woman named Danielle who wants to set up feral cat feeding stations all over the city."

"That's a nice idea," Carmela said. "Very kind."

"Isn't it? Of course, it wouldn't work if something else got to them first."

"Like what?"

Ava shrugged. "I don't know. Raccoons? The homeless? Tourists?"

Carmela poked her spoon toward Ava. "You make a good point there, lady."

"Oh," Ava said. "And I took a look at that blog that Naomi writes. *Haute to Trot?*"

"How is it?"

Ava grabbed her phone, fiddled with it, and held it up for Carmela to see. "Pretty dang awful. Take a look at her latest post. It's all about trends."

Carmela squinted at Ava's phone and read out loud. "Says here, and I quote, 'Oversized bows are destined to make a huge comeback next Spring.' "

"Gag me," Ava said.

Carmela went on. "She also thinks that some designer named Stanislaw Efron is the new up-and-coming designer and that sports leggings will be worn instead of pants."

"Not if you have a fat butt," Ava said.

Carmela handed the phone back to Ava. "This is pretty awful stuff."

"It's gibberish."

"I don't think Naomi knows her Gucci from her Pucci."

"Ya got that right," Ava said.

It wasn't until after Ava had finished her dinner — and her second glass of wine — that she narrowed her eyes and said, "I want to pitch you something."

Carmela was immediately suspicious. "What are you talking about?"

"I think we should go back to that cemetery. I mean tonight. Right now."

Carmela's eyes widened. "Oh no. Bad idea."

"Hang on just a gol-dang minute," Ava said. "Before you dismiss this idea entirely, please hear me out. You know that Ellie is more than a little psychic, right?"

"C'mon, really?" Carmela said. "I figured all that hoodoo-voodoo card reading and I Ching forecasting was just for the benefit of all those eager, lookin'-for-a-good-time tourists."

"Absolutely not. Juju Voodoo is a totally legit operation and Ellie is a seriously gifted psychic." Ava took another sip of wine as if to convince herself.

"Okay," Carmela said. "But where exactly is this conversation going? Because I'm *not* psychic."

"I just told you. I think we should go back to that cemetery."

"Whaaa . . . ?"

Ava held up a hand. "Don't go all postal. I already broached this idea to Ellie at the funeral luncheon and she's gung ho in favor of it."

"All gung ho for what? Please define exactly what we're talking about."

"She's in favor of going back to the *exact* spot where Isabelle was murdered to see if she can pick up any auras or strange vibrations."

Carmela was shaking her head. "I doubt we'll pick anything up, but we're likely to get our pocket picked. That place is seriously dangerous at night." *As poor Isabelle found out.*

But Ava refused to be deterred. "What harm can there be? We'll just let Ellie stand at the scene of her sister's death for a few minutes. Maybe she'll sense something and be able to divine a clue. If not, we'll come home. Quick and simple. Easy in, easy out."

"Not so easy . . ."

"You do still want to help, don't you? I mean, Ellie is counting on you."

"You don't have to guilt me, Ava. You know I want to help."

"Well . . . then we should do it."

They batted the idea back and forth for a few more minutes, but in the end, Carmela finally (and reluctantly) agreed to make a return trip to Lafayette Cemetery.

"You won't regret this," Ava said. She grabbed her cell phone, quickly called Ellie, and said, "It's a go. We'll pick you up in front of your apartment."

"Why do I feel like I was just set up?" Carmela asked as she pulled on her denim jacket.

Ava grinned. "Probably because you were."

"Remember, this wasn't my idea," Carmela said to the two women as they stood at the cemetery's front gate. Darkness had descended all around them, and there was a hint of dampness wafting in from the nearby Mississippi. She flicked her flashlight on and aimed the glossy circle of light at an uneven walkway.

"It is scary in here," Ellie admitted. Then she lifted her chin and said, "But it's for a good cause."

"Atta girl," Ava said.

Tentatively, as if they were starting down the yellow brick road to find the wizard, the three women walked into the cemetery. A chill night wind rustled the leaves overhead, somewhere off in the distance an owl hooted, and gravel crunched like dry bones beneath their feet.

"Ellie, stay close," Carmela cautioned. "This is exactly how the cemetery felt the night that . . . um, the last time I was here." She waved the flashlight back and forth and then bounced the beam off graves and markers that stood directly in their path.

"This is awful," Ellie whispered. "I didn't think it would be so scary."

Marble tombs loomed at them from out of the darkness, and the scrolled wrought-iron fences that enclosed many of the old family crypts seemed to elongate and reach out to them.

They scrabbled along slowly for another three or four minutes and then Carmela said, "We're pretty near the spot where Isabelle's body was found. Ellie, are you positive you want to go through with this?" Carmela feared that the site would be so emotionally charged that Ellie might make herself sick.

"I can do it," Ellie said. But her voice sounded tentative and strained.

Carmela flashed her light ahead, letting it land on a rounded marble tombstone. "There. That's it. The exact spot."

Ava reached out to hold hands with Ellie, but Ellie just brushed her away and stepped forward. Then she knelt down on one knee and touched the ground with her right hand. She bent her head forward, closed her eyes tightly, and went completely motionless, as if in a deep trance.

Ava gave a nervous sideways glance at Carmela.

Carmela tilted her head as if to say, "Hey, this was your crazy idea."

Two minutes passed. Then five. Carmela was about to say something to break the silence when Ellie's face suddenly crumpled and tears streamed down her cheeks.

"Not tonight," Ellie said. "It's just not working. Isabelle will not speak to me tonight."

Ava gaped at her. "Wait a minute. You're

telling us you got through to her?"

"I could feel her presence, yes," Ellie said. "I'm positive it was her. But it's like something was holding her back."

"She can't rest," Ava gasped. "She'll never rest until her killer is found and brought to justice."

"I don't think any of us will rest," Carmela said, "until that happens."

"But you could feel her?" Ava pressed. "She was right here with us?"

Ellie nodded. "I think . . . yes."

"Imagine that," Ava said. "It was practically a séance."

But Carmela couldn't share the positivity of the encounter, if that's what you could call it. "We should get back. It's cold and dangerous here."

"Sure," Ava said. "Okay. But I'm really glad we came. Aren't you, Ellie?"

"Getting a fleeting glimpse of Isabelle's spirit has renewed my desire to find her killer," Ellie said.

"Mine, too," Ava said, as Carmela walked on ahead. "Hey, wait up!"

But Carmela was suddenly on her own mission. "I need to make another stop."

"Huh?" Ava said.

"Where?" Ellie asked.

Carmela led them along a narrow path

that threaded its way past dozens of dark, tippy gravestones. "Over this way, I think." She was mentally retracing her steps from the other night.

"What are we looking for?" Ava asked.

Carmela pointed into the darkness. "Right there. That's the mausoleum where someone knocked me in the head with the gate. I want to take a closer look."

"Be careful," Ellie said.

But Carmela was already in front of the large mausoleum and inspecting the gate. "Look at this," she said. "The hasp on the lock is broken. That's how someone — maybe even Isabelle's killer — got inside and hid out."

"Holy crumb cake," Ava said. "Does Babcock know about this?"

Carmela frowned. "I told him that somebody clunked me in the head with a gate, but I'm afraid he kind of brushed it off. There was so much going on that night. Finding Isabelle's body . . . and then Julian Drake was dragged in kicking and screaming as a possible suspect."

"But other than the broken hasp, there's not much to see," Ava said, inspecting it for herself. "There's not really a clue, per se."

But Carmela wasn't ready to settle for defeat. Not by a long shot. She shone her flashlight up and down the walls of the mausoleum and along the ground. Then she crept up close to a dusty stained glass window that, during the day, allowed a modicum of light to filter into the mausoleum. She stood on her tiptoes and shone her flashlight inside.

"You're not going to go in there, are you?" Ellie asked. She sounded scared.

"No, I'm just taking a look," Carmela said. She cranked her wrist and continued to shine her flashlight inside the mausoleum. All she saw were two wooden coffins with about an inch of dust on top of them. *Eeeyew. Awful.*

"We really should go," Ava said. Now she was the one who sounded jittery. She took six steps in the direction of the front gate, with Ellie following her.

Carmela stood there and nodded. Yes, she supposed it was time to go. Pity they weren't more productive.

She made one last flick of her flashlight beam and suddenly noticed a glimmer of something.

What's that?

She reached down and touched a small scrap of paper that was stuck just under the edge of the mausoleum door. She picked it up and rubbed it between her fingers. It felt thick and rich. Expensive, maybe, like good parchment paper.

Ava turned. "What have you got there?"

"I don't know yet," Carmela said. *But I'm going to find out.*

Once Ellie was dropped back at her apartment and Ava given a hug good night, Carmela retreated tiredly to her own apartment.

Boo and Poobah were already curled up and snoring gently on their overpriced monogrammed dog beds, and Carmela's comfy queen-sized bed beckoned as well.

She shucked off her clothes and pulled a cozy flannel nightgown over her head. All she had to do was brush her teeth and . . .

Knock, knock, knock.

Somebody was knocking insistently at Carmela's front door.

What on earth? Ava? She should be snuggled in with her cat Isis by now.

Carmela threw on her quilted bathrobe and hustled to the front door.

"Ava?" she called out, without opening the door.

"It's me," came a man's voice.

Who's me?

Was it Babcock? Carmela wondered. But no, it didn't sound like him at all.

238

"I'm sorry to disturb you," came the male voice.

This time Carmela cracked open the door, but kept the heavy-duty security chain on. "Hello?" she said.

Hugo Delton peered at her through the narrow opening. "Carmela," he said. "Hello there."

Carmela stared at him. "It's a little late, isn't it?" *And a little creepy for you to just show up on my doorstep unannounced.*

"I was in the neighborhood and thought I'd stop by."

Creeping up behind Carmela now, Poobah let loose a low, throaty growl.

Delton frowned. "You have a dog?"

"I have two dogs." Carmela's heart was hammering inside her chest. "Guard dogs."

Delton stood a step back. "You're not going to let them out, are you?"

"It depends," Carmela said. *Good, he's afraid of dogs. That makes me feel a little better about opening the door to this strange night visitor. Which I will never, ever again do.*

Delton made a hand gesture with his fingers splayed out. "I'm just trying to be friendly here."

And I just wish you'd go away.

Delton offered her a garish smile. "I didn't mean to scare you, Carmela."

"You didn't," Carmela said. *Show no fear. Don't let him see that your hands are shaking.*

Delton cocked his head. "But I startled you."

Carmela wondered where exactly this line of conversation was going. And then she had a sudden, mind-blowing thought. Had Delton followed her to the cemetery tonight? Had he been spying on the three of them? Had he been lurking and smirking among the tombstones? And if so, why? Oh dear. Was Hugo Delton Isabelle's killer?

"You'll have to leave now," Carmela said stiffly. Her cell phone was sitting on the dining room table. She wished she had it in her hand right now so she could punch in 911. Summon help.

Delton gave a low chuckle. "I'm sorry, Carmela. I'll leave now. I see my little intrusion has made you a bit paranoid."

Carmela closed the door without bothering to answer him and turned the latch firmly. Then she stood there, one ear pressed against the wooden door (the good, strong wooden door), and listened as his footsteps retreated across the courtyard.

No, she thought as she gathered her bathrobe up around her chin, she wasn't paranoid at all. She was freaked-out.

CHAPTER 17

Thursday morning dawned sunny and filled with promise. And Carmela had almost forgotten about the little scrap of paper she'd picked up from the cemetery the night before — as well as her creepy late-night visitor.

Customers had been streaming into Memory Mine ever since they'd unlocked the front door, and Gabby was hard at it, manning the front desk, greeting customers with a friendly hello. In fact, Gabby's heroic ability to multitask, to juggle any number of problems, reminded Carmela of the flair bartenders had who worked in the nightclubs over on Bourbon Street. The ones who created special signature cocktails by tossing alcohol, ice cubes, cherries, and orange slices high into the air, then spinning around, keeping time with the music, and catching everything in a glass with nary a spill nor splotch.

Carmela located a packet of brass brads for one customer and three pieces of military-inspired scrapbook paper for another. Then she hustled over to help Jill, one of her regular scrapbookers. Jill had just returned from a trip to the Holy Land and was interested in assembling her one hundred plus photographs in a heartfelt and meaningful way.

Carmela led her back to the paper racks and pulled out a number of sheets that featured motifs of vintage bibles, stained glass windows, tranquil waters, and inspirational quotes.

"These are great," Jill said. "But what about embellishments?"

"We've got that covered, too," Carmela said. She showed Jill their assortment of faith stickers and foil cross stickers. "Plus, we've got tons of angel stickers and tiny brass angels if you'd like to adhere them to your album cover."

"Okay," Jill said. "Now I have to sit down and do some planning."

"Absolutely," Carmela said. "And in case you need more supplies, we carry the entire Grateful Heart line, too."

Carmela worked with another woman named Abby, who was trying to figure out an Asian-themed travel scrapbook. For this

Carmela pulled a handful of Japanese rice paper, some Asian-inspired decals, and some blue and white beads. As an afterthought, she dug out two small pieces of Japanese ephemera, one reminiscent of a Japanese woodblock print and the other featuring Mount Fuji.

It wasn't until late morning that the pace slowed and Carmela remembered the little scrap of paper that she'd plucked from the ground last night. She pulled it from her pocket, set it on the front counter, and studied it carefully. The paper definitely looked like parchment. But what was it from? And could it have been dropped by her assailant — Isabelle's killer — on Sunday night? Had the little scrap just been lying on the ground these last four days?

"Whatcha got?" Gabby asked when there was a break in the action.

When Carmela told her about the foray back into the cemetery last night, Gabby looked aghast.

"Are you serious?" Gabby asked. "What were you three ladies *think*ing?" When Carmela didn't answer, she said, "This going-out-on-a-limb investigation has got to stop."

"I know. And it will stop."

"You'll stop when you've got Isabelle's

murder all figured out, is what you're really saying," Gabby huffed. "But what if you . . . ?" Her face carried a pained expression.

"I won't," Carmela said. "I'll be careful."

That quieted Gabby for all of two seconds. Then curiosity flickered in her eyes and she touched a manicured fingertip to the bit of paper. "It's parchment paper, right?"

"That's my hunch, too," Carmela said. "In fact, I was wondering if it matched any of our parchment paper."

"If it does, then you might be able to trace it back to one of our local suppliers."

"That's pretty much what I was thinking."

Gabby hesitated. She wasn't willing to jump in feetfirst, but she was certainly willing to dabble a toe. "Okay, I suppose it wouldn't hurt to take a look."

"I was hoping you'd say that."

Gabby searched their rack of parchment paper and pulled out a half dozen sheets. She brought them back to the counter and spread them out. Then they both studied her selections.

"Your paper scrap seems to be a much heavier stock than what we carry," Gabby said.

"In other words, no match," Carmela said.

Gabby touched the scrap again. "It's definitely a heavier stock. It has that important look. Do you think it might have been torn off a fancy invitation of some sort?"

"Maybe."

"Are you going to hand this over to Babcock? I mean, finding it in the cemetery like that, right where you got clunked with the gate . . . well, it seems like a legitimate clue."

"I don't know. It could be nothing."

But Gabby wasn't buying it. "And it could be something important." She shook a finger at Carmela. "You'd better be careful."

The phone rang and Carmela figured she'd been saved by the bell. But nothing was further from the truth. Ellie was on the phone and she was babbling like crazy, basically in a blind panic.

"What? What?" Carmela said to her. "Slow down so I can understand you."

"I think somebody broke into my apartment last night!" Ellie cried.

"What? Last night while you were sleeping?"

"No, no, I think it happened when we were at the cemetery. But I just noticed it now."

"You noticed what?"

"That my window was unlocked. And

there's, like, a tiny pry mark."

"And you're sure you're alone? That nobody's hiding in some nook or cranny?"

"I'm sure," Ellie said. "I just grabbed a great big kitchen knife and walked through my entire apartment with it clutched in my hand. Looked in my closet, under the bed . . . you know, the usual places where a potential maniac would hide."

"Did you call the police?"

"No, I called you. I kind of hit the old panic button."

"Is anything missing from your apartment?" Carmela asked.

"That's the weird part," Ellie said. "Nothing's gone, but it feels like somebody came in and took a look around. Things are like . . . disturbed. Not a lot but a little. Do you know what I mean? Am I making any sense?"

"I know what you mean," Carmela said. She hesitated. "Okay, you need to do a couple of things."

"Like what?"

"You have to call Detective Babcock and report this immediately. I don't know, he might send a squad out to investigate, or maybe some of the crime-scene guys. If he does, great. If not, call me back and I'll beat him on the head. Also, you need to contact your landlord right away and have the locks changed. Can you do all that?"

"I can do that," Ellie said. "And thank you. Thank you for always being there."

"Okay, take care. Talk to you later." Carmela hung up the phone and gazed at Gabby.

"Now what?" she said.

So Carmela told her about the maybe-sorta break-in.

"And nothing was missing?"

"That's what she said."

"Weird," Gabby said. "Why would somebody break in but not take anything? *Who* would break in?"

"I don't know," Carmela said as a thought flickered into her brain. Hugo Delton had hinted about drugs. Had someone been searching for Isabelle's drugs, or had he just been full of hot air?

She also wondered if Edward had snuck in to take a final look around. Or could it have been Chef Slade doing one final stalk? Whoever this strange predator had been, it certainly seemed as if they wanted one last sniff.

Carmela felt jittery for the rest of the morning. Even after she knocked back a tuna fish sandwich on a mini French baguette, bag of chips, and Diet Coke from Pirate's Alley Deli, she still felt queasy. Plus, it was getting close to the time when she was supposed to pay a visit to Vesper Baudette. Just the thought of confronting that rather formidable opponent made her slightly woozy. Because even though Vesper might be eccentric or even crazy, she was rich, well-connected crazy. And in New Orleans, rich and well connected trumped everything else.

Carmela shook her head, trying to clear her thoughts. But they circled around and came back again. She thought for a moment and then dialed the number for the district attorney's office and asked for Bobby Prejean.

He came on the phone sounding harried and busy. But when Carmela told him about the break-in at Ellie's apartment and asked about the possibility that Isabelle had been involved in drugs, he got both quiet and serious.

"Are you kidding?" Prejean said. "Isabelle was as straight as an arrow. She'd never use drugs. Heck, she was a health nut. She used to run across the street to Toby's Juice Bar and get wheatgrass shooters. Stuff looked like swamp water but she loved 'em."

"The thing is," Carmela said, "Hugo Delton said that Isabelle might have been involved with drugs."

"Delton's an idiot," Prejean snapped. "He's already on notice. Problem is, it's almost impossible to get rid of a city employee. You've got to run it past three boards and a mediator, and then they always get a state rep to defend them. Impossible situation."

"Thank you," Carmela said. "You just made me feel a whole lot better." *Except for the fact that he came to call on me. That he knows where I live.*

"If I could only figure out how to get rid of Delton," Prejean grumped.

Carmela was about to edge out the door when Baby Fontaine came bouncing in. Petite, fifty-ish, with a distinct patrician air and dressed in one of her trademark Chanel jackets paired with slim blue jeans, Baby was one of her dearest friends.

Carmela hoped Baby wasn't there to ask her about the party on Friday night, since Del explicitly wanted it to be a surprise to her.

But Baby was there on another mission. She wanted to grab a bunch of scrapbook supplies.

"I promised my garden club that I'd help

get a scrapbook started," Baby said. "Everyone took beaucoup snaps of their gardens and boulevards this summer, and they all want to assemble it into a scrapbook." She shrugged. "I guess it's the digital equivalent of pressing flowers."

Carmela immediately thought of the felt daisies, and then dismissed them. They were too cheesy for an upscale Garden District scrapbook. But she had lots of other gorgeous items that would work.

"You've already selected an album?" Carmela asked.

Baby nodded. "It's the white one with the floral cover that I bought from you last month."

"Then you're probably going to need some floral paper to match."

"Exactly what I thought."

Carmela cruised past her paper bins, grabbing at least a dozen different sheets of paper. Some were alive with blossom and bloom designs; some were handmade papers with subtle bits of flower petals embedded in the fibers.

"Oh," Baby said. "The handmade paper, for sure."

Carmela pulled out a sheet of cream-colored paper. "This is one of the best ones we carry. Handmade in Thailand and embedded with yellow galanda petals."

"Then that's the one we should go with."

"Let's see," Carmela said, grabbing a few more items. "You're going to need gossamer ribbon, some silk petals, fusible fibers, and maybe a few bird and dragonfly embellishments."

Baby grinned. "Load me up, girlfriend."

Carmela grabbed two rubber stamps and added them to the mix. "Let me ask you something."

"Mm hm." Baby was busy perusing the display of stencils.

"How well do you know Vesper Baudette?"

"Just well enough to say hi to," Baby said. Then her head snapped up and she suddenly went cross-eyed. "Wait a minute, does this have anything to do with the murder of Edward Baudette's fiancée?"

"Yes, it does."

"I read about that in the paper," Baby said, scrunching up her face.

"The thing is," Carmela said, "the murdered woman, Isabelle, is the sister of Ellie Black."

"Ava's Ellie? The one in the purple skirt who tells fortunes and reads cards?"

"That's the one."

Now Baby was extremely interested.

"Mmn . . . and let me guess, you're investigating?"

"Only because Ellie begged me to."

"And because you've got an insatiable curiosity."

"There's that," Carmela admitted. "So . . . what do you really know about Vesper Baudette?"

"Well, she's a neighbor of sorts, since she lives a few blocks from me in the Garden District."

"What else?"

Baby thought for a few moments. "I'd have to say that Vesper's not all that friendly. I mean, she's a member of the garden club and all. And was supposed to have her garden open for visitors during our annual Garden Club Ramble. Only she didn't. She gave us some runaround about how she was way too busy."

"Do you think she really was?" Carmela asked.

"No," Baby said. "I think Vesper's just cranky and antisocial."

Carmela carried all of Baby's scrapbook supplies up to the front counter so Gabby could begin ringing her up. "The reason I ask is that I'm supposed to be at Vesper's house in about . . ." She glanced at her watch. "About fifteen minutes."

"Then you'd better get going," Baby said.

"You go on," Gabby added. "I can take care of things here."

"Okay," Carmela said. "Thanks. I'll catch you guys later."

"See you Friday night." Baby gave a big wink. "At the party."

"That's supposed to be a surprise!" Carmela cried, just as she was halfway out the door.

Baby laughed. "I'm a pretty good actress. So I'll be sure to act surprised."

Vesper Baudette's home was located on Prytania Street, barely two blocks from Lafayette Cemetery. As Carmela homed in on it, she felt like she was constantly being pulled back to this part of town. The murder last Sunday, their creepy-crawl last night, now she was passing by it again today. Could this just be a crazy coincidence or was something else at work here?

Carmela wasn't a big believer in fate or destiny, but it sure felt like something had been preordained.

She was also noodling around the idea that Vesper might have been the one who lured Isabelle into the cemetery and strangled her that fateful night. Vesper was a strong, stocky woman, so she could have managed it. Then, living as close as she did, it would have been easy for her to make a quick getaway.

But wait — then Vesper had to have been the one who smacked me with the gate. Could that have been Vesper? Was that my first encounter with her? Is that why she always pretends not to know me?

Carmela also thought it possible that Vesper could have snuck into Ellie's apartment last night. Vesper was unfriendly, confrontational, and a bit irrational. So she could have easily decided to root through Ellie's belongings.

Looking for what? To steal something Edward had given to Isabelle? Maybe. Possibly. She'd have to think about that.

Carmela pulled her car up in front of Vesper's home. She gazed at the place, giving it the once-over, and immediately felt intimidated.

The place was enormous. A two-story brick mansion with a double-pitched hipped roof, surrounded by sumptuous grounds and an elegant wrought-iron fence. There was a front veranda that ran the width of the entire house and a magnificent covered side portico where a brick driveway no doubt led to a carriage house. The last time she'd paged through *Delta Living* magazine, a couple of these white elephants had been for sale with astronomical asking prices that topped two million. Amazing. Just amazing that a house could cost so much. Because how much did one person need, really? She had a one-bedroom apartment that held all her worldly possessions just fine. Ava lived in a studio. Of course, her closets were jam-packed with party clothes and she stored most of her shoes and boots in the oven.

Carmela strolled up the front walk, stood poised on the veranda, and rang the doorbell. She could hear its chimes echoing deep within the house. Bing, bang, bong. Minutes later, an unsmiling maid opened the door partway.

"Yes?" the maid said. She was of an indeterminate age and wore no makeup. The word *plain* would have been kind.

"Carmela Bertrand to see Mrs. Baudette."

The maid hesitated momentarily, no doubt thinking that perhaps Carmela should have used the service entry. Then she opened the door and allowed her in.

"This way, please." The maid led Carmela through a large, dimly lit entry that was paneled in dark wood — possibly teak — and then down a hallway. Halfway down, she stopped, pointed, and said, "You may wait in there."

Carmela walked into what had probably been an impressive library at one time, but was now a quasi library–sitting room. That is, there were books on some of the floor-to-ceiling shelves, but not on all of them. The shelves not occupied by books held a mishmash of things — statuary, framed photos, small needlepoints under glass, ceramic cherubs, and a few antique plates.

The furniture was heavy and slightly depressing, a wine-colored sofa and two chairs that looked like they could use a good steam cleaning. Still, Vesper was rich, and rich people often lived quirky lives.

The one painting that hung over the fireplace, a portrait of a man standing on a dock in front of a three-masted schooner, was the crowning glory of the room. It was dark and moody, but managed to have touches of light in all the right places. This painting wasn't just your garden-variety portrait, either. This one had been created by a seriously talented artist who knew exactly what he was doing.

"You like the painting?" Vesper asked. She was suddenly standing in the doorway, staring at Carmela.

"Very much," Carmela said.

"It's my grandfather. Colonel Josiah B. Wilkerson. He was one of the early sugar plantation owners. From up the River Road near Darrow."

Carmela gave a faint smile. "Very impressive."

"I really don't know why you're here," Vesper said.

"The veil."

"I *know* you're here about the veil. I just don't know *why* you want it."

Carmela kept a respectful expression on her face, all the while wishing somebody would drop a house on Vesper, *Wizard of Oz* style.

"I'm here for Ellie's sake. Because it would be a grand gesture on your part to let her have her sister's veil."

Vesper sighed heavily, and then swept an arm toward a low table that was pushed up against a wall. Carmela hadn't noticed the blue box sitting on top of it. Now she moved toward it. "This is it?"

Vesper nodded.

Gently, carefully, Carmela removed the top of the box and set it aside. Then she reached in, through a dozen layers of tissue paper, and a drift of lace fluttered out.

"My goodness," Carmela said. "This is exquisite. It's hard to believe this veil is one hundred years old."

"Yes," Vesper said. "It's a gorgeous

heirloom. Naomi Rattler may be a bit of a self-involved simpleton, but the girl does have a certain degree of taste. She chose well."

Carmela examined the veil carefully. It was a cascading two-tier cathedral veil made from ivory-colored silk net tulle. It was probably Edwardian or Victorian or maybe could have been worn by one of the women of *Downton Abbey*. The veil was trimmed in exquisite lace and looked completely intact. In other words, it didn't look as if a hunk of lace had been stripped from it to be used as a garrote.

"This is an amazing find," Carmela said. "Naomi was lucky that she was able to source it."

"Yes, trust Naomi to be a clever little kitty."

There was something about the way Vesper said Naomi's name that tripped Carmela's radar.

"How long have you known Naomi?" Carmela asked.

"As long as Edward has known her," Vesper said. Her eyes seemed to dance with a little something extra. Was it mirth? "You realize," Vesper continued, "that Edward and Naomi used to be inseparable. In fact, I thought for sure that the two of them would get married."

"But then Edward fell in love with Isabelle," Carmela said.

Vesper sighed. "Yes, he did."

"It seems to me Edward and Naomi are still awfully close."

Vesper gave a garish wink. "You never know. They could always rekindle the old flame."

Carmela decided that's exactly what Naomi had already done. Yes, this was definitely Naomi's second chance. The first time she'd set her sights on Edward, Isabelle had come along and dashed her hopes.

But not to be deterred, had Naomi hatched a fiendishly clever plan? Had Naomi gotten incredibly tight with Isabelle with only one thing in mind — that being to kill her?

It was an awful, dark, twisted thought. But Carmela knew it was one that just might carry a grain of truth.

"Thank you," Carmela said abruptly. She suddenly wanted to get as far away from Vesper as possible.

"You're going to have to tell Naomi that you took the veil," Vesper said. "She's going to want to know, since she's the one who bought it."

"I'll tell her," Carmela said. But to herself

she thought, *I'll tell her when I'm good and ready.*

CHAPTER 18

When Carmela's doorbell rang, Boo and Poobah rushed the door like a crowd of teenage girls rushing the stage at a One Direction concert. But when the door opened and Babcock stepped in, their ears drooped and they immediately lost interest. Babcock was a party pooper. He never brought doggy treats.

"You're a little early," Carmela said breathlessly. "I'm still getting ready."

Babcock gave Carmela a slow, admiring once-over. Her black-on-black lace bodice fit snuggly over a black silk ruched skirt. A black satin belt with an emerald buckle cinched her waist, and she was jacked up a good three inches in a pair of Manolo Blahnik high heels.

"Don't you look tasty and glam," Babcock said. "Makes me almost glad I wore my tux."

Carmela smiled back at him. "And you

look very dashing," she said, just as his hand went up to fuss with his bow tie.

"Darned thing."

"Here, let me." Carmela reached up and made the necessary adjustments. Which gave Babcock ample opportunity to grab her by the waist and give her a light kiss.

"If you'd rather stay home . . ." he said in a coaxing tone.

Carmela pulled away. "Can't," she said. "This costume show is important."

"Speaking of which, did you pick up the veil from Vesper?"

"I got it, but it wasn't easy."

"Fighting crime never is."

Carmela gazed at him. "Is the veil connected to Isabelle's murder? Do you think it might really be a clue?"

"You never know. Why don't we take a look at it?"

Carmela took Babcock by the hand and led him to the breakfront in the dining room where the blue box was sitting. She opened the box and carefully removed the veil, shaking it out gently and letting it unfold and tumble to the floor. "Isn't it lovely?"

Babcock wasn't interested in the veil's appearance until Carmela handed him the small piece of lace that he'd cut from the ligature that had strangled Isabelle. He held the lace fragment up to the veil for a few seconds and frowned.

"It's not even close," he said. "But I guess we didn't think there'd be an exact match."

Carmela didn't want to give up quite so easily.

"But it's the same era. So there could be some connection. Maybe the veil and the piece of lace came from the same purchase lot that Devon Dowling bought at auction."

"Maybe," Babcock said. "But probably not." He sighed. "Look, I'd love to agree with you and claw our way closer to solving Isabelle's murder, but I think tracking bits of lace isn't the way to do it."

"I hate that we're giving up on this so easily."

"Okay then, we won't."

Carmela eyed him carefully. "What do you mean?"

"Can you drop this veil off at the crime lab tomorrow?"

She smiled. "Of course. You trust me to do that?"

"Only if you know where it is."

"Yes, I know where the crime lab is."

He bent forward and kissed the top of her head. "Good. Thank you. We'll have them take a look at it and render an expert opinion."

Carmela gently gathered up the veil to repackage it. "What happened with the break-in at Ellie's apartment? Did you go over or send someone else?"

"I sent Bobby Gallant over."

"And?"

"It was pretty much what Ellie told me on the phone. A few things had been moved and there were pry marks on the window."

"Who do you think went creeping in there?" Carmela asked.

"We don't know. We dusted for prints, but didn't get anything substantial."

"No fingerprints from Edward Baudette or Naomi Rattler or Chef Oliver Slade or . . ."

"Whoa. You think everybody's a suspect?"

"Guilty until proven innocent," Carmela said. "Napoleonic law." She was about to say more when there was a sudden *tippy-tapping* at her door. "Oh, that'll be Ava."

Carmela ran to the door, pulled it open, and found Ava standing there. She was wrapped head to toe in a black velvet shawl.

"Okay," Carmela said, tapping a toe. "Let's see it."

"Huh?" Ava said, but she was grinning madly from ear to ear.

"Yeah," Babcock seconded. "Let's see the outfit."

Ava slowly dropped her wrap to reveal a black strapless bustier over a semi-sheer, ankle-length skirt that was slit all the way up her left thigh. Black fishnet stockings and four-inch stilettos completed her vampy look.

Carmela inhaled. "You do know we're going to the Mourning Cloak opening gala, don't you? To celebrate a collection of Victorian and Edwardian mourning clothes?"

"Of course," Ava said. "That's why I'm dressed head to toe in black."

"Are you ever," Babcock said.

Without a glance over her shoulder, Carmela's elbow flew back and jabbed him in the ribs.

"Oof," came his singular reply.

The three-story-high foyer of the New Orleans Art Institute was ablaze with lights from the enormous French crystal chandelier that dangled overhead. The marble entry fluttered and hummed with dozens of well-heeled couples dressed to the nines in elegant tuxedos, gowns, and cocktail dresses.

"Ooh, fancy," Ava said as she looked around.

"Black tie," Carmela replied.

"That really means snooty, doesn't it?"

"Not necessarily," Carmela said.

"Sure it does," Babcock said. He nudged Carmela. "But you fit right in with this crowd."

"I *know* some of them because I was married to Shamus for one brief moment in time."

"And to all that Meechum money," Babcock said.

"Which I hardly saw a penny of," Carmela said.

"Any regrets?"

Carmela took his arm and snuggled close. "Not in the least."

They swooped down the main corridor, all three of them, looking youthful and handsome and crackling with energy.

As they passed a Cezanne, Carmela said, "That was donated compliments of the Meechum Family Foundation."

"Did Shamus pick it out?" Ava asked.

"No," Carmela said. "I did. At an auction at Crispin's in New York."

"Impressive," Babcock said.

"Wait a minute," Ava said. "And would that be a Picasso?" She pointed to another abstract painting shaded in blue and framed in stark wood.

"It's by Marcel Duchamp," Carmela said.

266

"Girl," Ava said. "You really know your artists. You're like a walking encyclopedia." She pointed to another painting. "Who's that one by?"

Carmela leaned in to get a closer look. "I think that might be a Balthus."

They were admiring the painting when Zoe Carmichael, one of the young television reporters from KBEZ-TV, came sauntering along. She was cute and bouncy, had heaps of reddish-blond hair that complimented her pale complexion, and was always eager to grab a sound bite. Following in her wake was Raleigh, her cameraman.

"Carmela," Zoe chirped. "You're just the kind of person I was hoping to see." Then she turned her high beams on Babcock. "And the illustrious Detective Babcock as well. Are you here to solve a one-hundred-and-fifty-year-old murder?" Zoe would kick anybody to the curb if she thought she could score a story.

Babcock laughed politely and drifted away.

Zoe immediately turned her attention back to Carmela. "Care to say a few words for the camera? Give us your impression of this crazy Mourning Cloak show?"

"I'm afraid I haven't seen it yet," Carmela said. Plus she really wasn't hot to offer up an opinion. Those things often came back to bite you.

"The show is utterly divine," Ava squealed. "I mean, who doesn't love a nice stiff corset and a black mourning dress?"

Zoe churned a hand, signaling for Raleigh to step forward. He was a middle-aged man wearing saggy khaki slacks and a photojournalist vest. He immediately hefted the camera to his shoulder and aimed it directly at Ava.

"One more time," Zoe coached Ava. "One more time for the camera."

So Ava happily burbled her line again. When they had the take they wanted, she asked, "So . . . will I be on the news tonight?"

"Film at eleven," Zoe told her. "Or maybe on a segment during our *Morning Alive Show* tomorrow." She grinned and said, "*Morning Alive.* That's pretty funny considering we're shooting footage about a mourning show with dead people's clothes."

"Hysterical," Carmela agreed.

As they entered the large gallery where the Mourning Cloak show was being held, Ava gave an excited shudder.

"They should have timed this exhibit more in line with Halloween," she said. "Look at the acres of black fabric. And the faces on some of the mannequins are covered with crepe veils."

"Kind of creepy," Carmela said. Dozens of displays created a sea of perpetual darkness while Gabriel Fauré's "Requiem" played as background music.

"I wonder how a woman in mourning could even see with that awful thing splotched across her face. How she could walk down the street?" Ava asked.

"I think that was the point. I think they were supposed to stay home."

"Bummer," Ava said.

They stopped in front of an exhibit marked *Widow's Mourning Garb,* where every outfit included a billowing floor-length skirt with a long-sleeved black top. The mannequins were additionally covered with black shawls and wore long black gloves. The ladies' bonnets were stiff and severe, anchoring long pieces of crepe fabric, which either covered the face or hung down the back.

Ava puckered her brow. "I wonder what the symbolism is. Why do some veils completely cover the face and others don't?"

"I can answer that." Angela Boynton, one of the museum curators, suddenly popped up behind them.

"Angela!" Carmela exclaimed.

"Hey, sweetie," Ava said. "Long time no see."

"I'm so glad you both could make it here tonight for the opening of the show," Angela said. She gazed around quickly. "We seem to be enjoying a record turnout."

"It's a fascinating subject," Carmela said, though she was far more interested in getting a look at some antique lace.

"Seems like Victorian dresses were kind of a tricky deal," Ava said.

"I'll say," Angela agreed. She gestured at a bonnet with a heavy veil. "But these crepe veils were only used when a woman was in full mourning. After the first year, a widow moved into half mourning where the rules weren't as strict."

"You mean she could start dating again?" Ava asked.

Angela chuckled. "Not quite."

"And what's with the ribbons?" Carmela asked.

"Those are called love ribbons," Angela told them. "They could be in either black or white, though most mothers preferred white if they were mourning a child. We have a complete display of them just past the jewelry exhibit."

"Jewelry!" Ava was enthusiastic. "We don't want to miss that."

"And is there lace?" Carmela asked.

"Should be," Angela said. "But you'll have more fun if you wander around and explore all the different displays by yourselves. Meanwhile, I've got to go make nice with some of our gold circle patrons."

"By all means," Carmela said.

Angela leaned in. "You know who the major underwriter for this show is, don't you?"

Carmela shook her head. Why would that matter? "No," she said. "Who?"

"Crescent City Bank."

"Uh-oh," Ava said. "Does this mean Carmela's ex-husband is lurking around?"

Angela nodded. "I'm afraid so. The Crescent City Bank Foundation contributed a sizable amount of money, so Shamus and his sister, Glory Meechum, are our honored guests tonight."

"Oh goody," Carmela said. Though she really didn't mean it.

"Forget about mean old Shamus," Ava told Carmela as they strolled up to the jewelry display.

"I try to every day," Carmela said.

"If we run into him we'll just snub him." Ava pressed her nose against a glass display case. "Oh, bless me. Will you look at this jewelry?"

Carmela peered in. "Mourning jewelry."

"Yes, but isn't it spectacular?"

"Mmn," Carmela said.

"I particularly like that brooch with the onyx beads and the skeleton etching." Ava tilted her head. "What do the words say?"

"I think it says, *Not lost but gone before.*"

"And look at that ring," Ava said. "Jet. What is jet, anyway?"

"What does that little white placard say?"

"Oh. Let's see . . . it says here that jet is fossilized coal that was primarily found near Whitby, England."

"And that locket next to it is made from bog oak," Carmela said.

"That doesn't sound very appealing."

"And there's a ring with a braided lock of hair in it."

"Carmela, would you wear a ring with *my* hair in it?"

"Sure. Why not?"

"And look at all the urn and weeping willow motifs," Ava said.

"Better than all the skeleton images."

"Still," Ava said. "If I could get reproductions of these skeleton head rings, I bet I could sell them at Juju Voodoo."

"Niche marketing to the macabre-minded."

"Oh you," Ava said. She grabbed Carmela's arm. "C'mon, I see a waiter in a black vest bearing down on us with a silver tray. My instincts tell me it's gonna be food!"

It was food. Delicious food, in fact.

"What is this?" Ava asked as she crunched away.

"Cucumber and cream cheese on brown bread," the waiter said. "And Old English crumb cake bites."

"Wonderful," Ava pronounced. "Kind of like tea party food." She took a second small sandwich and glanced around, practically sniffing the air. "And I see an entire *table* full of appetizers over there. I think it's time to stage the Great Appetizer Raid. Are you with me, Carmela?"

"Absolutely."

Carmela and Ava steamrolled up to the appetizer table where a chef, flanked by two assistants, was setting out dainty appetizers.

"Grab a plate, grab a plate," Ava cried, just as a white-coated assistant placed a delicate cookie on her plate. She immediately popped it in her mouth and chewed appreciatively. "Mmn, now this is tasty."

The head chef turned toward her and smiled. "I see we have a fan for our Victorian

273

funeral biscuits."

"Funeral biscuits?" Ava said, almost choking.

But it was Carmela who did the double take. Because she suddenly realized that the chef, in his pristine white jacket and tall hat, was Chef Oliver Slade!

CHAPTER 19

"What are *you* doing here?" Carmela cried.

Chef Slade swiveled to face her. There was a flash of recognition and then a self-satisfied smile oozed across his face.

He waved the tip of his knife, a long, wicked-looking blade, at Carmela and said, "You're the lady who was at the viewing the other night. The one who was rooting for Edward Baudette to punch my lights out."

"Hey," Ava said. "I was there, too."

"I remember," Slade said. "You were the nice one." He brandished his knife again. "And you're cute, too."

Ava fixed him with a dazzling smile.

"Ava . . ." Carmela's voice carried a warning tone. "Don't."

"Don't what?" Ava asked.

"Get friendly."

Slade rolled his eyes. "What? You're afraid of the Big Bad Wolf?"

"Maybe I am," Carmela said. "Or should

be, anyway. I understand that Isabelle was afraid of you."

"That's not true," Slade said harshly. "Don't you dare say that."

Carmela gazed at him. "What are you doing here, anyway?"

"I get tapped for almost all the Art Institute's high-end parties." He deftly sliced the crusts off a crab salad sandwich and then cut it into four small pieces. "I'm one of their premier caterers."

"So you do catering and you're the head chef at Le Fougasse?"

"The *chef de cuisine.*"

"But you say you do most of the catering here?"

"That's right."

Carmela was beginning to get an uneasy feeling. "So you've been involved in the Mourning Cloak show from the very beginning?"

Slade shrugged. "Obviously. In fact, I was asked to come up with appetizers that actually fit into the Victorian and Edwardian mourning themes." He pointed at a tray of food. "My broiled oysters with peach and paprika are right out of merry old England. Likewise my Victorian jewels, which are basically miniature fruitcakes."

Carmela's brain was in a whirl now. "So I

imagine you were privy to this collection while it was being curated?"

"Sure. A chef needs to understand the flavor of an exhibit before he can match it with the appropriate food." Slade gave her an odd look. "Why exactly are you drilling me with all these questions?"

Carmela plunged ahead. "You do know that Isabelle was strangled with a piece of antique lace, don't you?"

Slade drew back as if slapped. "Why would you say something like that? Why would you go and upset me like that?"

"Because there's an awful lot of old lace right here."

Slade's eyes seemed to pop out of his head. "Whaaa . . ."

"I thought you might be interested in knowing the facts, harsh as they are," Carmela said.

Now Slade's dark eyes bore into her with real anger. "Excuse me, are you trying to pin Isabelle's murder on *me*?"

"According to the New Orleans Police Department, you're one of the prime suspects."

"I certainly am not," Slade cried.

"I'm afraid you are," Ava put in. She hunched her shoulders up. "Sorry."

Slade's lip curled and his fists bunched as

he glared at Carmela. His voice rose in a thunderous roar. "Listen you stupid woman, how dare . . ."

Like a deus ex machina from a Greek play, Shamus Allan Meechum suddenly descended upon the scene. Brown eyes flashing, a look of consternation on his handsome face, he said, "What's the problem here?" Then he slid a protective arm around Carmela's waist and said, "Are you okay, honey?"

Carmela nodded. She was okay. Kind of. And shocked that Shamus had not only come to her rescue but had also called her *honey*.

Shamus focused a furious glare on Oliver Slade. "Did I hear you *threatening* Carmela?"

"Stay out of this," Slade warned. He flicked his fingers toward Shamus as if shooing a fly. "Our private conversation isn't any of your business."

Shamus folded his arms and struck an imperious pose. "It most certainly is my business, since Carmela is my special guest tonight."

Slade stepped out from behind the table and advanced toward Shamus. When he was standing just a foot away, he said, "Maybe you better move along, fella. Stop mouthing off at me."

Shamus's jaw tightened and his eyes blazed. "Maybe *you're* the one who should move along. Seeing as how my bank financed most of this little soiree, I can pretty much hire and fire personnel at will." He smiled at Carmela and Ava. "Are we really in need of this guy's services?"

Slade inhaled sharply and turned bright red. "Excuse me, I didn't . . ." His words trailed off in a low mumble.

"No, you didn't," Shamus said. He was rolling now, pleased with himself, happy he could intimidate someone in front of Carmela and Ava.

Carmela rested a hand on Shamus's arm. "Shamus, that's enough. It's over." She half dragged him away from Chef Slade and the appetizer table.

"But that jerk was threatening you," Shamus grumped.

"And you came to my rescue," Carmela said. "Thank you, Shamus. You did good."

"Hey!" a loud, authoritative voice rang out. "What's the problem here?"

Carmela, Shamus, and Ava all spun about to find Edgar Babcock bearing down on them like a cruise missile, armed and dangerous.

Carmela held up a hand to ward him off. "It's over. No harm done."

But Babcock was not to be deterred. He glanced over at Chef Slade and said, "Was that guy yelling at you?" Then *he* did a double take and said, "Holy Christmas, it's Oliver Slade!"

Carmela nodded tiredly. "That's right, one of your suspects."

"He's a suspect?" Shamus screeched. "Suspect in what?"

"In a murder," Ava added helpfully.

"Then you better go arrest him," Shamus said to Babcock. "Like right now."

Babcock shook his head. "I can't do that. He's a suspect in an ongoing investigation, yes. But I don't have enough *evidence* to charge him. Making that kind of move would gum up everything right now."

Shamus leaned toward Babcock and glowered. "Are you taking care of her?" He hooked a thumb and pointed at Carmela. "I mean really taking care of her?"

Babcock was starting to lose patience. "Of course I am."

"But you let that insolent twerp . . . that *murder* suspect verbally attack Carmela. What kind of escort are you? Why would you leave her all alone and vulnerable?"

"What am I?" Ava asked. "Chopped liver?

Who's taking care of me?"

"I think you've pretty much demonstrated that you can take care of yourself," Carmela said.

"I'm warning you," Shamus continued. He was stuck on the Carmela-Slade predicament like a burr under a saddle blanket. "You'd better be watching out for her." He raised his hands as if to give Babcock a shove, but Carmela hastily intervened.

"Enough," Carmela said, easing herself between the two men. "Let it go. I'm fine." She gazed at Ava, who raised a delicate eyebrow. "*We're* fine."

But Shamus was still mumbling and grumbling under his breath. So much so, that Carmela grabbed Ava and left. Just walked away. If Shamus and Babcock wanted to continue their macho standoff, that was fine with her. But she was tired of watching them act like a couple of Neanderthals about to club each other with a woolly mammoth tusk.

"That was exciting," Ava said.

"No, it was tiresome," Carmela said. She glanced into a display case that contained a long black dress and saw by the reflection in the glass that Babcock was ambling over to join her.

"It's a good thing you divorced that

clown," Babcock said.

"He's not all bad," Carmela said. Wait, was she defending Shamus now? Good grief, what was the world coming to?

"He's an idiot," Babcock said.

"And you're coming off way too possessive."

Her words gave Babcock pause. "I thought women liked that."

"Well, they do." Carmela smiled. "Sometimes."

Carmela and Ava circled the gallery, elbowing their way through the crowd of well-heeled art patrons. Ava was having fun, flirting and winking, laughing and drinking, while Carmela was still seriously on the hunt for lace.

Stopping at one of the larger display cases, a case that held three mannequins dressed in mourning clothes, Carmela said, "There's some black lace."

Ava snapped to attention. "Where you at, hon?"

"Lace. Trailing down from that bonnet."

"Oh yeah. And it looks real old, too."

"I wonder if that piece is on loan or if it's in the museum's permanent collection," Carmela said.

"Let's see what the little placard here

says." Ava pressed forward, scanned the description, and said, "Oh. Oh no."

"What?"

"I think you better read it for yourself, *cher.*"

Carmela read the description, wondering what had gotten such a rise out of Ava. Then her eyes hit the bottom line. "What?" Her voice rose in a querulous squawk.

The bottom line said: *Dress and Bonnet on Loan from the Collection of Vesper Baudette.*

"Vesper?" Carmela was stunned beyond belief. "This stuff's on loan from Vesper?"

"From her *collection,*" Ava said. "Go figure."

"I had no idea."

"Holy bat poop," Ava said. "This means . . ." She turned bug eyes on Carmela.

Carmela seized upon Ava's thought. "It means that Vesper really could have owned the lace that strangled Isabelle. That Vesper could have *done* it."

"She's certainly cold enough."

"Ice water runs in that woman's veins," Carmela added. "And she really disliked Isabelle. A lot." She shook her head. "I was just at her house this afternoon. And she said nothing — nothing! — about having a costume collection."

"So what are you gonna do about it?"

"I don't know."

"Tell Babcock?"

Carmela stood like a pillar of salt. "I'm not sure."

Carmela needed a drink. In fact, she needed *two* glasses of wine before she was able to calm down.

"Feeling better now?" Ava asked. They were sitting at a makeshift café that the museum had put together. A place where tea, Pimm's Cup, Chardonnay, and Cabernet seemed to be the specialty of the house.

"Lots better." Now Carmela was sipping a cup of oolong tea. She figured the tea would somehow counteract the two drinks she'd just slugged down.

"May I join you?" a male voice asked. And then, before either of them could answer, Bobby Prejean slid into the chair across from them.

"Bobby," Carmela said. She was glad to see him. Prejean seemed like a voice of reason in what had turned out to be a night of surprises.

"How do," Ava said, fluttering her eyelashes and leaning forward, the better to show off her décolleté.

"Enjoying the evening?" Prejean asked politely.

"It's been a trip and a half," Ava said.

Prejean chuckled. "Dare I ask?"

"We just found out that Vesper Baudette lent some pieces to this show," Carmela said.

Prejean leaned forward. "Excuse me?"

"From her collection of antique clothing," Ava said.

Now they really had his attention.

"She collects antique clothes?" Prejean said. He digested this information for a few moments, blinked, and said, "But that could mean . . ."

"Yes," Carmela said.

"Does Babcock know about this?" he asked.

"I plan to enlighten him," Carmela said.

Prejean shook his head. "Whew. That's kind of crazy. That nobody seemed to know about this."

"And that Edward Baudette never stepped up to inform anyone," Carmela added.

"He's here tonight," Prejean said.

"What?" Carmela said. "Edward is?"

"And Vesper. I just saw them across the room."

"We'll do our best to avoid them," Ava said.

They all sat in silence for a few moments, then Carmela said, "You know, you're pretty much the last person I expected to see here."

"Are you interested in mourning clothes?" Ava asked him.

"Not a bit." Prejean nodded into the crowd. "But if you really want to know why I'm here, it's because I'm interested in him."

Carmela and Ava followed his gaze until they saw Julian Drake standing there in a cluster of people.

"I had no idea he was here, either," Carmela said, a little startled.

Prejean gave a sour chuckle. "Wherever there's money, you'll find Drake."

"You really want to pin something on him, don't you?" Carmela said.

Prejean continued to stare at Drake. "You have no idea. He's nothing but trouble. I'd just as soon run him out of town or convict him of one of many frauds he's trying to perpetrate on the people of New Orleans."

"Besides illegal real estate transactions," Carmela said, "maybe you even like him for Isabelle's murder?"

Prejean sighed. "Well, he certainly strikes me as a viable suspect."

"Probably because he is," Ava said.

"Bobby Prejean! Mr. Prejean!" shouted

an over-caffeinated female voice. Then Zoe Carmichael rushed up to their table. "Excuse me, but, Mr. Prejean . . . could we possibly do a quick interview?"

The district attorney gave a cautious smile. "Of course. Anything for the viewers of KBEZ."

"Great," Zoe said. She motioned for Raleigh to get ready. "Is it true you might toss your hat into the ring for the next governor's race?"

Carmela glanced at Prejean. First she'd heard. "Is it true?" She didn't think it was a bad idea.

"No, no," Prejean demurred gracefully. "It's far too early to even consider the next gubernatorial race. Besides . . ." He glanced at Carmela again. "I have more important business at the moment."

"This guy has become a real media darling," Zoe said to Carmela as she pulled Prejean close to her so Raleigh could get a two-shot. "You can always count on him for a great quip." Then she lifted the microphone to her pink-gelled lips, gazed directly into the camera lens, and smiled broadly.

"And we're rolling," Raleigh said.

CHAPTER 20

Babcock was stuffing his phone in his pocket when Carmela found him.

"Ready to go?" he asked.

"Not exactly," Carmela said. "But I'm guessing you are."

"Hah, we can't get out of here fast enough. You know who I just ran into? Edward and Vesper Baudette."

"I heard they were here." Carmela sucked in a deep breath. She had to tell him. "Did you know that Vesper has a collection of antique clothing?"

He cocked a not-quite-believing eye at her. "What?"

"A couple of the costumes on display here tonight are on loan from her."

Babcock stared at her. "You've got to be joking."

"Hey," Carmela said, "I can't make this stuff up."

"Well, doesn't that . . ." He was glowering

now. "And neither of them ever said a single word to me about antique clothes."

"Something else to look into."

"No kidding. You wait here and I'll grab your opera cape from the coat check." He frowned again. "Wait a minute, weren't there three of us? Where's Ava?"

"She said she'd find her own way home."

"Of course."

While Carmela waited for Babcock, she popped open her beaded clutch bag and grabbed a Kleenex. But just as she was about to dab at what felt like a bit of smudged mascara, Julian Drake sidled up to her.

"Hey," he said, a magnanimous grin lighting his face. "Having a good time?"

"It's been a blast," Carmela said. Had it really? No. Of course not.

"Don't forget about our big Elysian Fields Casino party this Saturday. You're still invited, you know. Your gal pal Ava, too."

"That's very kind of you."

"So you're coming, right?"

"Still planning to." Carmela hoped Babcock didn't see her talking to Drake. "I suppose all the permits have been issued and construction is ready to begin?"

"Pretty much," Drake said. "So we're going to have what you'd call a ceremonial grand opening. You know, silver shovels, hard hats, and dignitaries du jour. We're putting up a huge tent on the site and plan to have a couple of bands, lots of free booze, and the best food New Orleans has to offer."

"I can't wait," Carmela said. Babcock would kill her if he knew she was planning to attend, but she still wanted to keep a watchful eye on Drake. There was something about the man . . .

"Holy crap, there's the deputy mayor," Drake cried. "Gotta go shake hands and make nice with the hoi polloi." And with that he was gone.

"Who was that?" Babcock asked from behind her.

Carmela whirled around to face him. "Hmm?" She wondered if she had a guilty look on her face.

"It looked like Julian Drake," he said.

"It . . . it was." Carmela wished she had the knack for pulling off slick fibs like Ava did.

Babcock frowned. "Let me get this straight. You pitched Drake to me as a possible suspect and now you're making nice with him?"

"I was simply being polite."

"Same thing," Babcock snapped. "Jeez,

Carmela, you're the one who told me Isabelle was investigating him in a clandestine way."

"The man spoke to me; I spoke back. I told you. Polite."

"Your idea of polite is to wrap a man around your little finger until he tells you what you want to hear." He snorted. "I should know."

"You're in a bad mood because you just found out about Vesper's costume collection."

"That and I'm giving you fair warning, Carmela. I want you to steer clear of Julian Drake. No more investigating. That means no wandering into his office, no impromptu lunches, no accidental meetings. Got it?"

"Sure." *Gulp. And what about his big party?*

Babcock wrapped the cape around her shoulders. "Now let's . . ." Something flew out of the cape's inner pocket and went splat on the floor. "What's that?"

"Oh darn," Carmela said. She bent down and picked it up. "These are the brass paper clips Angela asked me to bring along. Do you mind if I take two minutes to run down to her office and give them to her?"

"No, no, that's okay," Babcock said. He suddenly looked worried, as if he knew he'd been too harsh with her. "I'm sorry if I flew

291

off the handle just now. So much is going on and I worry about you."

Carmela kissed him on the cheek. "Apology accepted. Be right back."

Carmela cut back through the lobby and flew down the main corridor, past collections of English silver, a trove of Etruscan vases, and a Greek mosaic. When she hit the Egyptian mummy, she hung a left and sped down a darkened corridor.

Halfway down, her footsteps ringing in her ears, she realized it was *very* dark. Was this the smartest place to be all by her lonesome?

Probably not. But she was almost at Angela's office so . . .

Carmela slid to a stop. She'd just heard what she thought might be footsteps.

Behind me? Yes, behind me.

Heart thumping, she touched a hand to the wall and listened again.

There's nothing there.

She knew that's what everyone told themselves when there was really a big, bad monster in their closet.

Uh-oh, bad simile or analogy or whatever it was.

She listened again and thought she might

have detected a faint shuffle. *That* wasn't good.

Carmela put her back against the wall and slid along in the direction of Angela's office. If the door was unlocked she could creep in there and lock the door behind her. Then she could . . . what?

She'd call Babcock. That's what she'd do. Ask him to come and get her.

It was a good plan; it really was. Except when she got to Angela's office (still creeping along like a ninja in the dark) the door was locked.

Time to execute plan B.

Except there was no plan B. And Carmela was getting more and more frightened. Was someone still there? Or was she just hearing mysterious footsteps in her head?

No. She was pretty sure someone was following her. She knew in her gut that they were.

Carmela clenched her hands reflexively. And was suddenly aware of the packet of oversized clips clutched in her right hand.

Without hesitating, without overthinking it, she stepped into the middle of the corridor, gave a good Roger Clemens windup, and flung the package down the corridor. She heard it whap against the wall, then slap down hard on the floor and slide away.

And, glory be, that's when she heard the pitter-patter of footsteps retreating down the hallway. In fact, she listened to them retreating until they faded into nothing at all.

"Hello?" Carmela called out.

There was nothing. Just a faint echo of her voice.

Carmela started walking down the corridor in the direction from which she'd come. Nobody popped out at her. No ghostly hands reached out to grab her around the neck.

And just as she turned the corner by the Egyptian mummy, just as she stepped into faint light, she felt something catch on her shoe. Something soft.

She stooped down and picked up a soft black cloth. Or was it a cloth?

Turning it over in her hands, there was just enough faint light so she could see it was a mourning veil.

Who on earth would want to scare her that way? Was it Oliver Slade? Or Julian Drake? Could it have been Vesper or Edward?

Who indeed?

"You look a little discombobulated,"

Babcock said as they pulled away from the curb.

"No," Carmela said in a small voice. "I'm okay." But she was really thinking, *Should I tell him? Because if I do and he freaks out, he's going to want to keep me under lock and key like one of those poor ladies in mourning. I'd be a prisoner in my own house.*

Carmela pondered this just as the radio in Babcock's car erupted with static.

"Yeah?" he said.

"This is dispatch," came a voice. "We just got a call from Bobby Prejean that he was involved in a hit-and-run accident."

"Where?" Babcock asked.

"I wouldna called you," the dispatcher continued, "if he wasn't the district attorney."

"Just tell me where," Babcock said in a terse voice.

"Intersection of Rousseau and Felicity," said the dispatcher. "That five corner mash-up near the river."

"On my way," Babcock said. "Send a squad."

"Already did."

Babcock reached down, grabbed a light, and stuck it on his dashboard. "Hang on," he said as the red light began to pulse. Then he punched it hard and his car careened

down Magazine Street. They flew past Arch-
wood Antiques, the Latest Wrinkle, and
H. Galvez Oyster House. Hooking a right at
Philip Street, they careened the six blocks
to Rousseau and turned left. Then it was
just another few blocks to the intersection
of Rousseau and Felicity.

Bobby Prejean's dark blue Audi was
parked way up on the curb, and a squad car
had already arrived. Two uniformed officers
were standing with Prejean, talking to him
as he made jerky, animated gestures.

Babcock was out of his car in a flash,
Carmela scrambling to keep up with him.
"What happened?" he called out. "Anybody
hurt?"

"He's okay," one of the officers said. "Just
shaken up."

"I can't believe it," Prejean sputtered. He
looked pale and nervous. "I was just entering the intersection . . ." He made a vague
directional gesture with one hand. "And this
black SUV came flying out of nowhere.
Suddenly I heard gunshots." He put both
hands on top of his head as if to try to calm
his jumbled thoughts. "I think they were
shooting at me!"

"Slugs recovered? Casings?" Babcock
asked the officers.

"We just gave a cursory look," said the

officer whose name tag read *Bailey.* "Nothing yet."

"Bring in the crime-scene guys. Lock down this area," Babcock said. He turned back to Prejean. "Then what happened?"

"They tried to run me off the road," Prejean said. "It was bizarre. I've never experienced anything like it."

"Did they sideswipe your car?"

"No, thank goodness. Probably because I ran it right up onto the sidewalk. Didn't even think what I was doing. And then I guess they just got nervous and took off." He touched a hand to his chest. "I was scared, that's for sure."

"But you did good," Babcock said. "It sounds like you kept your wits about you."

Carmela stepped forward and gently touched Prejean's arm. "Was it one person in the car or two?"

Prejean shook his head. "I don't know. It was so dark I couldn't tell."

Carmela thought again. "Was the person who shot at you sitting in the driver's seat or the passenger seat?"

"Um . . . maybe the driver's seat?" Prejean said.

"So maybe just one person," Babcock said.

"But like I said, it happened so fast, I'm not one hundred percent sure of anything,"

Prejean stammered out. He shook his head. "You always expect crime victims to be more aware. Until it happens to you."

"So you weren't able to get a plate number?" Babcock asked.

"No," Prejean said. "Sorry."

Carmela looked east where large warehouses blocked a view of the river. "Do you think someone might have followed you from the Art Institute?" she asked.

"I don't know. It's possible," Prejean said. Then, "You don't think this has anything to do with Isabelle's murder, do you?"

"You never know," Babcock said. He was bent down, inspecting the side of the Audi.

Prejean turned to Carmela. "Because if it does, it could mean the killer is after me."

Carmela didn't say anything, but she thought to herself, *Yes, there's a good chance he is.*

CHAPTER 21

First thing Friday morning Carmela was back at Vesper's house, pounding on her front door.

Bam, bam, bam.

She was feeling angry and out of sorts, and ready to demand some answers. After all, when she'd stopped by yesterday to retrieve the veil, Vesper hadn't mentioned a doggone thing about having a collection of antique clothing and fabrics.

And if I hadn't gone to the Mourning Cloak Show last night, I would never have known.

In Carmela's book that meant Vesper must be hiding something.

"Who is it?" came a mumbled voice.

"It's me. Carmela. Open up, please."

The door creaked open a half inch and Vesper peered out. She was wearing a quilted robe, and her hair stuck up in goofy clumps. Pink fuzzy slippers encased her feet. She was bleary-eyed and had obviously just gotten out of bed without the benefit of morning coffee.

"What are you doing here?" Vesper asked. She sounded both hostile and a little shocked that Carmela had dared make a return trip.

"When I was here yesterday you didn't say one word to me about your antique fabric and costume collection. I had to learn about it last night. Reading a lousy placard at the museum."

Vesper glared at her. "And that is your business . . . why?" Then she yawned and said, "Oh, wait a minute, it isn't your business."

Carmela wasn't about to take any crap or back down from this hostile, aggressive woman. "You should have told me. It's important."

"I never said anything because you never asked. And, frankly, my private collection and what I choose to do with it is certainly nothing that concerns you. Now good day to you and please leave."

Vesper tried to close the door but Carmela stuck out her foot and stopped it.

"I need some answers."

Vesper gave a tired nod. "Ah yes. I think I know where your annoying little mind is going. You are an amateur sleuth who is under the delusion that the lace that strangled Isabelle came from my collection."

"Did it?" Carmela said.

"You're so misguided it's ridiculous. I may not have liked Isabelle, and I certainly didn't think she was a suitable match for Edward, but I would never murder her!"

"Somehow I'm not totally convinced."

"Talk to Edward," Vesper said. "He'll tell you how very tolerant I really was."

"In other words," Carmela said, taking a step back, "he'll cover for you."

This time Vesper really did slam the door in her face.

Still feeling out of sorts after her nasty encounter with Vesper, Carmela nevertheless headed for the crime lab. She'd promised Babcock she'd drop the veil off and she intended to do exactly that. Of course, she was also hoping that by committing to this good deed she might cadge a bit of inside information from him, too.

Carmela drove back through the French Quarter and threaded her way along North Peters Street, passing the Café du Monde, the French Market, and the flea market. Tourists were flocking everywhere as music *plinkety-plinked* and the sweet smell of beignets hung in the air. Then she left it all

301

behind and took a left, driving straight toward Lake Pontchartrain via Elysian Fields Avenue.

Twenty minutes later, Carmela arrived at the UNO Research and Technology Park where the NOPD's Crime Lab and Evidence Division was located. Pulling into their parking lot, she decided the place looked more like a cool high-tech company. The sleek building gave the impression of a business that manufactured hubs and routers, not a crime lab that conducted autopsies and investigated strange pieces of evidence using electron microscopes and mass spectrographs.

Still . . . this was where the magic and the breakthroughs happened, so she grabbed the box with the veil in it and carried it inside.

"May I help you?" said the young woman at the front desk. She looked like a pleasant receptionist, trim with a shock of reddish-brown hair, but Carmela had the impression that she'd probably achieved the fitness level of a marine sergeant.

"I'm delivering a piece of evidence for Detective Edgar Babcock," Carmela said.

"Oh yes," the receptionist said. "We've been expecting you."

"He called?"

"First thing this morning." She slid a sheet of paper across the desk and said, "If you could just write a general description of your item and then sign and date it?" When Carmela hesitated, she added, "It's our standard operating procedure for chain of custody."

"Of course," Carmela said. She tapped her pencil. "By any chance is Charlie Preston around?" Charlie was one of the crime-scene techs that she'd gotten to know fairly well. In fact, this particular tech had once had the hots for Ava. If she could talk to Charlie, then maybe she could get a handle on what was going on with the lace that had been used to strangle Isabelle . . .

"Sorry, no," said the receptionist. "Mr. Preston is not here. It's been a very busy day."

Carmela was headed to Memory Mine when she started thinking about the bit of parchment she'd picked up in the cemetery. She hadn't turned it over to Babcock — and she definitely hadn't left it at the crime lab — because she wanted to check it out herself. If she *had* turned it over, Carmela was pretty sure it would have disappeared into a black hole and Babcock would have frozen her out of any and all information.

But Carmela had a germ of an idea, which was why she swung by Cavalier Printing. Cavalier was one of the smaller but higher quality print shops she often used for posters, brochures, and invitations. And, just her luck, Jimmy Bowen, the foreman, was standing at the front desk when she walked in.

"Just the man I wanted to see," Carmela said.

Jimmy turned, recognized her, and smiled. "Uh-oh, we didn't screw up one of your orders, did we?" Jimmy was a chubby African American teddy bear who always wore cool glasses with different colored plastic frames. Today his glasses were teal blue.

"No, but I do have a question for you about paper stock."

"Then come on back to my office," Jimmy said. He led her into the back of the print shop where two small offset presses were humming away like crazy. Sheets of colorful paper flew into metal trays every few seconds, ready to be stacked and boxed. There were bundles of paper stock wedged everywhere, and the place smelled pleasantly of ink and warm paper.

Carmela pulled out her scrap of parchment paper and showed it to Jimmy. "Are you familiar with this particular paper stock?"

Jimmy took it gently in his hands and studied it. "Parchment. Maybe a sixty-five pound cover weight. Good soft feel, fast drying surface. We use a lot of this type of stock."

"I know you do."

"It's especially popular this time of year when people tend to request a nicer stock for invitations and announcements. For holiday menus, too, at some of the fancier restaurants."

Carmela took a deep breath. "I was wondering if this snippet matched up with any of the jobs you might have run recently?"

Jimmy considered her request for a moment and then said, "Well, let me see about that." He went to a large flat file and pulled open the top drawer. The file drawers contained samples of all the jobs he'd run recently.

"I really appreciate this," Carmela said.

Jimmy pulled out four different sample pieces that were printed on a similar type of paper. In fact, to Carmela's eye, they all looked like a perfect match.

"These are some of the more recent pieces we printed on parchment." Jimmy showed her two invitations, a citation, and a small poster. "The parchment that comes closest to your sample, that is."

"This is great," Carmela said. "Any way I could take a few of these samples with me?"

"No problem," Jimmy said. "Knock yourself out."

"What on earth have you got there?" Gabby asked. Carmela was back at Memory Mine and had her four print samples spread out on the back table.

"I'm trying to see if I can match that scrap of parchment I found," Carmela said. "So I stopped at Cavalier Printing and these were four pieces they've printed lately on that same type of parchment."

Intrigued, Gabby moved closer. "Cavalier Printing is also one of the more upscale printers," she said. "Plus they're right in our area."

"Exactly."

"So what have you got? Oh, this big one is a poster for an opening at Click! Gallery."

"A place we know well," Carmela said. The gallery was just a few blocks away from Memory Mine and specialized in photography as well as contemporary prints and paintings. In fact, Shamus had once had a photo exhibit there. His so-so nature photos had consisted of egrets and herons dipping down to grab fish, some turtles sunning themselves on logs, and alligators lurking in dank swamps. In her estimation it was Photography 101, but Shamus represented Crescent City Bank, and Click! Gallery was one of their clients. So the old boy network's quid pro quo had surely been at work.

"Show me that scrap of paper again," Gabby said.

Carmela pulled it from her wallet and handed it to Gabby.

Gabby held the snippet up against all four samples. "They're all close. In fact, they're almost all a perfect match."

"That's what I thought. Only I don't know where any of this leads."

"Let's see," Gabby said. "This piece, this citation, is for someone named Earl Zander. You know who he is?"

"Never heard of him."

"Well, it says here he showed great dedication and zeal in service to the Jaycees."

"Good for him," Carmela said. "But I don't seem him connecting to the Baudettes in any way. Or to Isabelle and Edward's wedding."

"Neither do I," Gabby said. "What about these two invitations? They're for real estate open houses."

"Pretty fancy invites for an open house."

"That's because they're probably fancy houses," Gabby said. She turned her attention to the large poster. "And this one's for a concert of Baroque music at the Old Town Repertory Theatre."

"That doesn't trip anything for me, either," Carmela said. "In fact, nothing seems to relate to my hot list of suspects."

"So maybe the bit of parchment is unrelated?"

"Maybe. Still, I found it lying right there by that mausoleum. It just *feels* like it should mean something."

"Maybe you should be checking obituaries," Gabby said. "Maybe the parchment came from a funeral program for someone who was recently buried nearby."

"Maybe," Carmela said. "Or it could just be a dead end."

Carmela got busy with a customer then, helping a woman named Gail with her newest project.

"Are you going to make another one of your salt box shrines?" Carmela asked her. Gail was famous for taking empty Morton salt boxes, slicing the cylinder open to form a doorway, covering and lining it with pretty paper, and then creating little scenes inside them.

"Yes, I am," Gail said. "I'm focusing on perfume bottles and butterflies for my latest salt box project. I want to cover one with some sort of filmy paper, add an arrangement of paper butterflies and silk flowers, and then put a cluster of three vintage perfume bottles inside."

"That sounds fantastic," Carmela said. "I've also got some small brass bees that might work with your design."

"And I'll need some bits of lace."

"For some reason," Carmela said, "lace has been very popular lately."

Carmela pulled some sheets of floral paper that reminded her of vintage wallpaper, then found some paper that actually had designs of miniature French perfume bottles on them. She was about to grab a butterfly stamp and some embossing ink when the phone rang. Because Gabby was busy helping two other customers, Carmela dipped into her office and grabbed the phone.

"Memory Mine."

"It's me."

"Babcock?" she asked.

He chuckled. "You were expecting another me?"

"No . . . I . . . well, hello." She figured he

was calling to check on her, to see if she'd dropped off the veil like she promised. "I dropped off that veil like I promised."

"Good," Babcock said. "Thank you for doing that."

"You're welcome. Have you spoken to Vesper yet? About her costume collection?" She wasn't about to tell him that she'd stopped by Vesper's house herself to give the old bat a piece of her mind.

"Not yet, because something else has come up."

"What's that?"

"We're going to pick up Chef Oliver Slade and bring him in for questioning."

"What! Why?" This wasn't what she'd expected. "What's going on? You found some sort of evidence against him? Or a witness finally came forward?"

"Nothing that concrete, I'm afraid. But Edward Baudette did come in this morning to hand over Isabelle's cell phone."

"Okay." Carmela was waiting for the big reveal.

"Seems he took a more careful look at Isabelle's cell phone log and discovered a whole batch of calls that came directly from Oliver Slade."

"Wow. Seriously? So Slade really was harassing her?"

"It looks like . . . possibly. But it's all pending the verdict of our tech people. They have to thoroughly check out the phone records."

"Still, does that mean, well . . . do you think Slade could be the killer?"

Babcock made a growly sound. "I didn't *say* that. You realize this is an ongoing investigation so . . ."

"So what?"

"Stay tuned."

"That's it?" Carmela felt like she'd been shortchanged. "Are you gonna let me know what happens after you bring Slade in and sweat him?"

"Probably not."

"But if you find enough evidence to charge him . . . ?"

"Then, my dear, you could be among the first to know."

CHAPTER 22

Carmela was so jazzed by Babcock's call that she decided to run over to Juju Voodoo and tell Ava and Ellie the big news. But first she had to tell Gabby. She smiled at Gail, who was artfully tearing pink and purple tissue paper like crazy, then tiptoed to the front counter where Gabby was testing some new metallic inks.

"Babcock just called with some extraordinary news," Carmela said. "He's bringing in a suspect for questioning."

With eyes growing as round as charger plates at a fancy dinner, Gabby leaned in to hear more.

"It's Chef Oliver Slade, Isabelle's old boyfriend."

Gabby's hand flew to her cheek. "The stalker guy? We should have known."

"Well, he was one of our guesses."

"Now what happens?"

"We have to wait and see how this all

shakes out, whether he's formally charged or not, but I think this news is too juicy to keep to ourselves."

Gabby nodded eagerly. "I guess."

"Can you hold down the fort while I run over to Juju Voodoo and tell Ava and Ellie?"

"Absolutely. Do you think there's enough evidence to charge this guy Slade? Wait a minute, *is* there evidence?"

"Apparently, he left a ton of threatening phone calls on Isabelle's cell phone."

"Wow. Threatening . . . really?"

"I assume that's what they are," Carmela said.

"Run over and tell them," Gabby said. "This is the best news we've heard in days."

When Carmela pushed through the glossy red door of Juju Voodoo, she was delighted to find that she'd popped in between customers. There was the usual array of voodoo dolls, magic spells, saint candles, and scented oils — and Ava bent over the counter arranging some magic poultices in a basket. The sign on the basket said *SALE — 20% OFF* and Carmela wondered how good luck could be sold at a discount, but decided not to ask.

"*Cher,*" Ava said, straightening up and pushing her hair off her face. "You're all huffy and puffy and look like you're bursting with news." She grinned. "Oh my, I bet this is about you and Babcock."

Carmela struggled to catch her breath. "Is Ellie here? I have something to tell you both."

Ava grabbed a pink velvet pouch filled with mystical herbs and flew around the counter. "He finally did it, didn't he? Babcock finally proposed." She thrust the velvet pouch into Carmela's hands. "This is only temporary, until I whip up a stronger charm, but I guarantee it will bring you oodles of joy." Her arms closed around Carmela. "And a long and happy marriage."

"Hold everything," Carmela said. "Babcock did not propose."

Ava's face fell. "Oh, *cher.* He didn't?"

"No, and I don't want him to right now."

Now Ava just looked confused. "Oh. Then . . . what is it?"

"I've got major case news. But I want to tell you and Ellie together."

"She's in the back room," Ava said. "Doing a tarot card reading for one of our special clients."

"But she'll be out soon?"

Ava consulted her watch. It was a fake Rolex she'd bought from a vendor who hung around outside St. Louis Cathedral.

"Any minute now."

As Ava spoke, the door in back opened and a woman dressed all in black came speed-balling out. She wore large dark sunglasses and a felt hat with a brim that dipped down to obscure her face. Carmela figured she must be a local socialite who was sublimely nervous about being recognized.

As the woman scooted out the side door, Ellie emerged from the back room. Dressed in shades of purple and red, her typical fortune telling garb, she had three strings of clacking gold beads strung around her neck.

"Ellie," Ava said. "Our dear Carmela just turned up on our doorstep. And she's brought us some news."

Ellie gazed at Carmela. "Is it good news?"

"It could be," Carmela said.

Ava held up her hands in a flutter. "Wait, wait. Let me fix us a quick pot of tea. I have a new elderberry and chamomile blend that I got from that darling little tea shop in Charleston. The one you recommended, Carmela."

"Okay," Carmela said. "Let's get things brewing."

Ava bustled about for a few minutes, and then carried a steaming pot of tea back to the reading room. Carmela set out cups and saucers and Ava poured.

"This tea is wonderful," Ellie said, taking a sip. "But my heart is in my throat over your news, Carmela."

"Yes, tell us," Ava urged.

"Babcock called me, maybe twenty minutes ago," Carmela said. "Chef Oliver Slade has been brought in for questioning."

Ava dropped her cup into its saucer with a loud *clink*. "Doggone. Now there's a waste of a fine-looking man."

But Ellie had gone so quiet that Carmela feared she might faint. Then she noticed one solitary tear slip down Ellie's face. Within a minute, there was a torrent.

"Oh dear, oh dear," Ava said. She fanned a clutch of paper napkins at Ellie, then peeled one off and handed it to her.

Ellie wiped at her eyes and said, "How did the police decide Oliver Slade was the one? That he killed Isabelle?"

Carmela shook her head. "No, I'm afraid it's not quite that cut-and-dried. They didn't decide anything. What happened is . . . Edward Baudette finally took a look at the telephone log on Isabelle's cell phone. And discovered that Slade had called her a dozen times a day — for weeks on end."

"So he's really just there for questioning?" Ellie asked. "He's not under arrest?"

"That's my understanding," Carmela said. This wasn't going the way she thought it would. Ava seemed disappointed and Ellie was suddenly shaking her head.

"Why are you shaking your head, honey?" Carmela asked.

"I'm confused," Ellie said. "When Isabelle was dating Oliver Slade it wasn't such a big deal."

Ava frowned. "How so?"

"When the two of them were dating it was fairly casual," Ellie said. "They weren't even exclusive."

"Maybe that's why Slade called her so much," Ava said. "Because he *wanted* their relationship to be exclusive."

"Maybe," Carmela said. Suddenly, what felt like a piece of the puzzle clicking into place didn't seem to be clicking at all.

"I hope Detective Babcock and the other investigating officers aren't pinning all their hopes on Oliver Slade," Ellie said. "He's got a massive ego, but . . ."

"There are other things cooking, too," Carmela said.

Ava waggled her fingers. "Explain, please."

"First off," Carmela said, "the forensic people are taking a good hard look at that antique lace veil that Naomi Rattler gave to Isabelle."

"Okay," Ava said.

"And I'm still trying to track down leads on that piece of parchment we picked up in the cemetery," Carmela said.

Ellie sniffled. "How are you going to do that?"

"I took a guess on who the local printer might be and found some posters and invitations that had been printed on the same paper stock."

"Smart," Ava said.

"In fact, I'll probably turn that stuff over to Babcock, too."

"What's going to happen to the veil once the police are done with it?" Ellie asked.

Carmela smiled at her. "Babcock said they'd return it to you."

For the first time Ellie seemed happy at the thought of having a tangible memory of her sister.

"You know," Carmela said to Ellie, "I'm a little shocked that you're not arguing for Oliver Slade as the number one suspect."

"I know," Ellie said, "but somehow he doesn't feel right."

"You gotta go with your gut," Ava said.

Carmela thought for a few moments. "All along Bobby Prejean has been urging us to take a good hard look at Julian Drake."

"I hate to think he's the killer," Ellie said.

"He's been such a good friend. And he was even going to be in Isabelle's wedding!"

Carmela took a sip of tea and pursed her lips. "And then there's Vesper. Her donation of antique fabrics to the museum puts her clearly in the running."

"I told Ellie all about the costume show last night," Ava said. "About how Vesper's stuff was on display." She made a face. "Plus, she's a crank. Cranks are capable of almost anything."

"I just think it's odd that Vesper never came forward about her love of antique lace and fabrics," Carmela said. "If she'd cleared the air right away, admitted she had an entire *collection,* she probably wouldn't be a suspect."

"Is she a suspect?" Ava asked. "In Babcock's eyes?"

"I think she's probably on the B list, but, yes, she's on his watch list."

"It's all very confusing," Ava said.

Ellie's brows knit together. "It is confusing, but I think progress is definitely being made." She reached over and touched Carmela's hand. "Thanks to you."

"I wish I could do more," Carmela said.

"You've been great," Ellie said. "So I hope you do keep on investigating."

"I think I'm running out of leads,"

Carmela said.

"Oh no, you've got to keep going," Ellie cried. "I feel like you're my only hope!" She looked like she was going to start crying again.

Carmela stood up and swept Ellie into her arms. "I don't know how much more I can do, but I'll try. I promise I will."

"You know what we should do?" Ava asked.

Carmela and Ellie both snuffled, then stared at her.

"What?" they asked in unison.

"I think we should ask the Ouija board for answers."

"I'm not sure I want to fool around with that," Ellie said. "It's not technically a divination tool. It's more like a parlor game."

"Come on," Ava pushed. "You never know. If the spirits are willing we could definitely find something out."

Carmela and Ellie exchanged nervous looks while Ava knelt down and pulled a Ouija board out from a hidden cupboard in the wall. She moved the teapot away and set the board in the middle of the table. The brown wooden board was frayed around the edges from years of use, but the ancient-looking letters, numbers, sun and moon, and the words YES, NO, HELLO, and GOOD BYE were still legible.

How many people had tried to contact the spirit world using this board? Carmela wondered. *How many had actually gotten through?*

Ava reached in and placed a small white planchette right in the middle of the board.

"We're really gonna do this?" Carmela asked.

In answer, Ava dimmed the lights. Then she sat down and gave them whispered instructions: "Just rest your fingertips gently on the planchette. Don't push it; just allow the spirits to guide it. If we try to force an answer, we'll go off in the wrong direction and anger the spirits."

"We wouldn't want that," Carmela said.

"Sshh," Ava said.

They sat there, fingers poised, waiting patiently for something to happen. The planchette just sat there in the middle of the board. Not moving an inch.

Ava said, "Perhaps we need a spirit guide."

"A friendly one," Ellie said.

Ava closed her eyes and, in a slightly theatrical voice, called out, "We poor mortals have important questions to ask the universe, and we need a friendly spirit to part the veil between earth and the great beyond to help us find the answers."

As if it was on metal rails, the planchette began to move. Slowly at first, then it picked up speed.

"You're doing that," Carmela said to Ava.

"Me? No way. I tell you, we got something going here! Let me ask . . . are there spirits present?"

The planchette shot to YES.

Ellie started to tremble. "I don't like this. It feels spooky and unfamiliar. This isn't how my readings normally go."

"Spirits," Ava continued. "We implore your help. You have a newly arrived soul in your midst. Our dear, dear Isabelle Black."

Ellie choked out a sob.

"We are trying to find out who murdered her. We are asking those of you on a higher plane if you can give us a name."

The planchette began to move again, slowly cruising along the letters, as if trying to find a place to start.

"Look," Ava said. "I think it's trying to spell something out."

"Dear Lord," Carmela said

The planchette continued to move until it got to the letter C.

"C," Ava said. "It stopped at C. You all see this, right?"

"I guess," Ellie said.

"Please continue," Ava said.

Amazingly, the planchette did. It bobbed along the arc of letters, finally stopping at the letter L.

"Is there more?" Ava asked.

Turns out there was. The planchette continued along to the letter O and then on to the letter W.

"Is it cloud?" an excited Ava cried out. "Is it trying to spell out cloud?"

"I think it stopped on W and not U," Carmela said.

"Are you sure?" Ava said. "So it spelled CLOW?"

"I think so."

"What if the spirits are trying to spell out clove?" Ava said. "You know, like the spice. They could be pointing us toward Chef Oliver Slade!"

"I don't like this," Ellie said. She was jumpy and clearly unhappy.

"But we're making good progress," Ava said. "Okay, let's get this thing fired up again and keep going."

But the planchette refused to move.

"Huh?" Ava said. "What happened?" She glanced around the room. "Spirits? Oh spirits?"

"This is too weird," Ellie said. "I don't like it at all." She lifted her fingers off the planchette and crossed her arms in front of herself, protectively. "In fact, I'd rather not do it anymore."

"Come on, honey," Ava pleaded. "Just give it one more try. I think the spirits work better with you on the board. After all, Isabelle was your sister."

But Ellie was firm. She put her lips together tightly and shook her head.

If pressed, Carmela could easily admit to being just as spooked. But she said nothing.

"Come on, honey, just one more time?" Ava said. "Anybody?" With her friends not in the mood to continue, Ava sighed. "Then I'll just give it a shot myself." She rested her fingertips on the planchette and it immediately began to move, slowly at first, and then it skittered across the board. "Whoa! Look at this."

The planchette circled the sun image, hovered for a moment, and then slowly moved toward the bottom of the board.

But Ava's hopes of any meaningful message were dashed when the planchette stopped for the last time — on the word GOOD BYE.

CHAPTER 23

Gabby looked up from the front counter and said, "Oh, you're back."

"Back to the light," Carmela said. "Run toward the light."

"Pardon?"

Carmela waved a hand. "Nothing. Don't mind me. I've just been communing with the spirit world, such as it is." She cast another glance at Gabby, who suddenly seemed all atwitter and burning with nervous energy. "But what's going on with you? You look like a cross between a cat on a hot tin roof and one that just swallowed the canary."

"Carmela," Gabby said, her words suddenly tumbling out. "I hope you don't mind. But I got curious about those parchment samples, so I made a couple of calls."

"You did?" Carmela thought this was interesting. Gabby was usually incredibly reticent when it came to investigating, while she was the one who generally blazed a trail where angels feared to tread. "Who did you call?"

"One of my calls, the one that really paid off, was to a good friend of mind, Cynthia Mouton, who sits on the board of directors of the Old Town Repertory Theatre."

"The theatre on the poster." Carmela was beginning to get a warm, tingly feeling.

"That's right."

"So . . . ?" Carmela waggled her fingers. She wanted to hear more.

"Anyway," Gabby said, "guess who the event planner was for this particular concert? The concert that's advertised on the poster?"

Carmela stared at Gabby for a few moments until a thought began to fizz inside her brain. "OMG. Was it Naomi Rattler?"

"Bingo."

"You're not serious."

"Yes, I am," Gabby said. "So maybe Naomi's your connection."

"Oh my gosh," Carmela cried. "You are so brave. You are so smart."

"Don't you think it might be a solid lead?" Gabby was practically preening now.

"I think it's a fantastic lead. One that warrants serious investigation."

"So what are you gonna do?"

That question gave Carmela pause. "Well, I honestly . . . Jeez, I hate to say this, Gabby, but I think I have to tell Babcock."

"Really?"

"I don't want to. I mean, I'd love to go cowboying in and pin Naomi's ears to the wall if I could. But this is serious. This is big-time. If she really was the event planner, then maybe she honchoed those posters, too."

"And maybe she's the one who dropped that snippet of parchment in the cemetery," Gabby said.

"Which could point to her as a stone-cold killer," Carmela finished. "Okay." She touched a hand to her chest. "Whew. This is a lot to take in. I'm going to call Babcock right now."

Gabby nodded. "I can't wait to hear what he says!"

It wasn't until Carmela finally got Babcock on the phone that she realized she might have to seriously spill the beans to him. On just about everything.

"I just came across some very important information," Carmela told him. "But first I have to make a full confession."

There was a sharp intake of breath and then Babcock said, "You're in love with somebody else."

"No," Carmela said. "Of course not."

"Then what is it?"

"It's complicated."

"It always is. But try me anyway."

"Well . . . Wednesday night we went back to the cemetery."

"What!" Babcock's voice boomed so loudly in Carmela's ear that she practically winced with pain. "Wait a minute. Who's we?"

So Carmela told him about how Ava, Ellie, and she went back to Lafayette Cemetery to try to commune with Isabelle's spirit.

"You *what*?"

"Do we have a bad connection here?"

"You *communed*?"

"Tried to." Carmela paused. Why had it sounded so logical when Ava explained it and so crazy when she did? Clearly, Babcock was horrified by their foolhardy actions. Oh well, the next thing she was going to tell him would no doubt tip him over the edge.

"And then what?" Babcock demanded.

"And we found something."

"What?" It wasn't so much a question as a shriek of anger.

So Carmela had to tell him about snooping around the mausoleum and coming up with the snippet of parchment.

"You're crazy, you know that? You've really gone off the deep end."

Carmela could tell Babcock was winding up for a nice line drive of indignation, so she interrupted him. "There's more."

This time he squawked like an injured crow.

But when she finally told him about the parchment matching up with the poster for Naomi's event he fell dead silent.

Carmela waited. And waited. And waited some more.

"Edgar," she said, almost whispering. "Are you still there?"

"I'm thinking," he said.

Carmela made a leap of faith. "But it's a good lead, huh?"

His answer surprised her. "It's not terrible."

"Come on, this is really something."

"It could be," Babcock said.

"See, I knew you couldn't stay mad at me."

"Oh, I'm still mad. I'm just thinking-mad."

"I've never heard that expression before," Carmela said.

"Probably because I've never felt that way before. It's going to take some time getting used to."

"But you're for sure going to follow up on Naomi Rattler and the parchment, right? Please tell me you're going to follow up on this."

"I'll look into this on one condition," Babcock said. "You have to promise to stop going off on all these crazy tangents."

"Hmm."

"Was that a yes?"

Carmela crossed her fingers. "Sort of." She was still going to attend the casino party tomorrow because she was determined to keep an eye on Julian Drake. He still held a prominent place on her watch-what-happens list.

"Okay, then," Babcock said.

"Wait a minute," Carmela said. "You have to tell me what happened with Oliver Slade. You brought him in for questioning . . ."

"Oh, that," Babcock said. "Turns out there was a backlog of calls on Isabelle's phone all right, but our tech guy determined it was from many months ago."

"Really? So nothing recent?"

"It would appear not."

"So Slade's not going to be arrested, because he wasn't really harassing Isabelle."

"Let me put it this way," Babcock said.

"Oliver Slade walked out of here an hour ago."

"So you don't see him as a viable suspect?"

"Ah, probably not," Babcock said. "But I want you . . . wait, are you still at your shop?"

"Yes."

"I'm going to send a uniformed officer over to pick up that snippet of parchment. The poster, too, if I can have it."

"Sure. Okay." Carmela paused. "You're not mad at me?"

"I don't know," Babcock said. "I think I'm too dazed by your foolhardy stunts to make any kind of rational assessment right now."

"Okay. Can I ask you one question?"

"What? *What?*"

"Are you coming to Baby's party tonight?"

"Carmela," Babcock moaned. "No."

"What'd Babcock say?" Gabby asked. She'd been darting past the doorway to Carmela's office, not quite eavesdropping but certainly anxious.

"Let's just say he was somewhat taken aback," Carmela said.

"But he's going to keep looking into things? Talk to Naomi Rattler?"

"He said he would."

Gabby frowned. "I guess you had to tell him about going back to the cemetery, huh?"

Carmela rolled her eyes. "Oh yeah."

"How'd he take it?"

"Not very well, I'm afraid."

"He was mad?"

"You know those old-fashioned cartoons where steam pours out of a character's ears?"

Gabby cocked her head. "Yeah?"

Carmela grimaced. "That was Babcock."

Twenty-five minutes later officer Chester Farley arrived at Memory Mine. He was a burly officer with an Inspector Clouseau mustache who came creeping into the shop like he was following a potential suspect down a dark alley. Carmela half expected him to pull out his nightstick and line everyone up against the wall.

"Carmela?" Officer Farley said when he caught sight of her. "Carmela Bertrand?"

"That's me." She would have sworn his hand hovered above the can of pepper spray fixed to his utility belt.

"I'm supposed to pick up some evidence."

"I've got it right back here," Carmela said. Officer Farley followed her to the big craft table where she had it all ready to go.

"This is what kind of store?" he asked.

"We're a scrapbook shop," Carmela said.

"What's that?"

"Oh, you know, arranging photos in albums where the pages have been designed and embellished."

"Sounds real artsy."

"It is," Carmela said. She opened a business-sized envelope and showed him the scrap of paper. "Tell Babcock that this is the snippet of parchment I found in Lafayette Cemetery."

Farley nodded. "Gotcha."

"And this is the poster that matches that particular scrap of parchment. It advertises the concert that Naomi Rattler helped organize."

"Rattler," said the officer. "Interesting name."

Carmela slid the poster into a large manila envelope. "Isn't it?"

"I knew some Rattlers who lived over by Des Allemands. Not very nice people, though. Two of the men were poachers."

"What did they poach?" Carmela asked.

"Alligators, nutria, wild turkeys, you name it," said Officer Farley. "If you could eat it, skin it, or wear it, they wanted it."

Carmela handed him the envelope. "Now there's a lovely thought."

■ ■ ■ ■

One of the crafts Carmela loved working on was gift bags. So when two women came in and asked about them, Carmela was more than happy to give a quick demonstration.

"You're Mandy," Carmela said to one of the women that she recognized. "You've been in before, right?" Mandy had long, folksinger-type hair and wore a flowered top over skinny jeans.

"I bought a bunch of your Halloween paper last month," Mandy said. "To make trick-or-treat bags and some other stuff for my kids. Everything turned out so great that I brought my friend Joanie with me today."

"We're glad you came back," Carmela said.

"And we're hoping you can give us some spiffy ideas for gift bags," Joanie said.

Carmela smiled. "I think we can manage that."

Carmela started with a simple white gift bag, eight inches by ten inches in size, with plain rope handles at the top. Carmela collaged on a sheet of red mango leaf paper, then tore strips of pink Japanese lace paper and glued those on, too. Then she cut out some glossy red hearts in three different sizes, pasted those on, and decided her gift bag still needed embellishing. First, she glued on some gold crinkle paper that she'd torn into random strips. Then she crumpled up a sheet of white paper, daubed it in gold paint, and added a few judicious touches of gold. For the pièce de résistance, she glued on a large gold angel embellishment and replaced the rope handles with filmy gold ribbon.

Her two customers watched in amazement as Carmela deftly turned a basic bag into a work of art.

"Gorgeous," Joanie said. "Just perfect."

"But you're a professional," Mandy sputtered at Carmela. "We . . . I can't do that."

"Of course you can," Carmela said. "Here's what you're going to do. Follow the exact steps that I did, only use a green and gold palette."

"Okay," Mandy said.

"Do the dabbing thing with the gold paint. But, instead of adding an angel, use a different type of charm. Maybe a gold key or some silver mesh leaves."

"I *could* do that," Mandy said.

"And I'm going to make one using a blue and purple palette," Joanie said.

"That's the spirit," Carmela said. "Just look around the shop, especially at all the art papers, and I'm sure you'll pick up lots of ideas."

Carmela wandered back to the front counter where Gabby was experimenting with some new rubber stamps.

"Just look at these," Gabby said. "They're animals and they're all done in a Japanese woodblock style."

Carmela peered at Gabby's random stampings. There were shy-looking deer, cuddly bears, an inquisitive little mouse, and some very cute rabbits.

"These are adorable," Carmela said.

"Plus they're oversized. Even if you just use one of these stamps you can make a great card design."

"I can also see them stamped on velvet throw pillows. Using some permanent gold ink."

"Adorable," Gabby agreed. Then she gazed at Carmela. "You're still thinking about the murder, aren't you?"

"Is it that obvious?"

"No, you're very good at hiding things. But I can tell. You're worried that time is passing and you still don't have an answer."

"I know Babcock is following up, but I worry that we're still not getting close," Carmela said. "There are suspects, but they're all obvious suspects. What if there's

336

somebody out there who's a crazy wild card? Somebody we don't know about or completely overlooked?"

"Scary thought," Gabby said. She glanced over at the door and murmured, "Speaking of crazy, here comes the countess."

That was the countess's cue to burst through the door. Today she was wearing a purple suede jacket with a black peekaboo top, and sleek black slacks tucked into black leather boots. She looked, Carmela thought, like a kinky riding instructor.

"Carmela. Gabby," the Countess Saint-Marche purred. "How are my two most favorite neighbors?"

"We're good," Carmela said. "Just working away."

"Being crafty," Gabby said.

The countess grabbed Carmela by the arm and pulled her aside. "I have something to tell you," she said in a loud whisper.

"Oh really?" Carmela let herself be steered back toward the album display.

Now the countess was practically breathless. "I'm probably not supposed to say anything, but this is news. Big news."

"Okay."

"Your sweetie dropped by my shop this morning."

"Wait. You mean . . . Babcock?"

The countess nodded.

"Really?" Carmela squeaked. "This morning?"

The countess gave an emphatic nod. "First thing. And . . ." She widened her eyes as she paused to add emphasis to the rest of her announcement. "He wanted to look at rings!"

Carmela felt her throat tighten up. "Um . . . uh . . . diamond rings?"

"Sweetie, is there any other kind?"

"Well, sure." *Maybe a nice topaz ring or moonstone for Christmas? But a diamond ring? As in an engagement ring? Yipes.*

"Of course I tried to steer him toward the most expensive diamond!"

Now Carmela just looked terrified. "Did he pick one out?" She was definitely not ready to settle down again. Fact was, she still had a bad taste in her mouth from being married to Shamus.

"No, he did not select one," the countess said. She pursed her lips. "It was kind of a disappointment."

Kind of a relief, Carmela thought. Maybe Babcock had changed his mind. Maybe, after looking at rings — and looking at the hefty price tags — he'd decided to back off. She hoped he had. That would be good. In more ways than one.

"Oh, Carmela," the countess said. "We'll get one of those spendy little baubles on your finger yet."

Carmela hoped not. Because not only was she not ready to settle down, she still hadn't figured out if the countess's title was genuine or not. Or if her merchandise was, either!

Chapter 24

The private party room at Parpadelle, one of the fanciest restaurants in the French Quarter, was aglow for Baby Fontaine's surprise birthday party. Winged brass sconces festooned the elegant rose-colored walls, and crystal-draped chandeliers hung from the ceiling. An enormous dining table was swathed in white linen and surrounded by wingback chairs that were elegantly upholstered in textured gold fabric.

"This is gonna be some wingding," Ava said, as they strolled into the dining room. "And look, it's going to be a sit-down dinner for . . . what? Almost forty guests?"

"It's a banquet all right," Carmela said. She noted that two even more elaborate chairs sat at the head of the table. "A banquet for Queen Baby and her consort."

"Think Baby will be surprised?"

"I'm positive she will." There were twenty revelers already gathered at the party and

Carmela knew most of them. They were either scrapbooking friends or people she'd met at Baby's Garden District home at one or another of her lavish parties.

"Ooh, and there are canapés," Ava squealed as a black-coated waiter approached them and tipped his tray as if to coax them.

"Caviar on toast points or jalapeno popper spread on butter crackers?" he asked.

"One of each," Ava said as they helped themselves.

"Thank you," Carmela said.

"Mmn, this is soooo much better than the food that Slade dude tried to pawn off on us last night," Ava said.

"Better caliber of guests, too."

"And I can't wait for the music to start pumping."

A blue bandstand, set next to a low stage, was emblazoned with silver letters that proclaimed *The Sweet Jazz Quintet.* The musicians were seated there, looking very suave in their matching tuxedos, and playing soft jazz.

"They're all subdued and cool right now," Ava observed. "But see . . . there's a trombone and saxophone leaning against the bandstand. Once they start howling away on those brass instruments this party will really pop."

"Ava," Carmela said. "Did you do something to your hair?" For some reason, Ava's hair seemed to be twice its normal size.

Ava patted her head happily. "Oh, not really."

"Come on, you did something."

"Okay, if you must know, I got a weave today. That manicurist I go to, Bambi, she does Botox and weaves, too."

Carmela studied Ava's massive amount of hair. "So what kind of hair is that?"

"Human, I guess. Or at least half human."

They grabbed glasses of champagne from a passing waiter and stood there, enjoying the scene. As the room filled up, the music began to heat up, too, just as Ava had predicted.

"Carmela! Ava!"

Both women turned and let loose high-pitched shrieks when they caught sight of their dear friend Tandy. They flung their arms around Tandy as she cooed happily and administered air kisses.

"Ooh," Tandy said. "I just knew my honey pies would be here tonight."

"We wouldn't miss it," Carmela told her. She'd slopped half her champagne on the floor. Oh well.

"It's a major event," Ava said.

Tandy, in a black cocktail dress that made her look positively waifish, craned her head around and asked, "Is Baby here yet? I wanna see Baby."

"She's gotta show up pretty soon," Ava said. "After all, she is the guest of honor."

As if on cue, the band suddenly segued from "I Gotta Feeling" by the Black Eyed Peas into "Happy Birthday."

Ava clapped happily. "Ooh, here she is. The girl of the hour!"

The curtains behind the small stage parted, and Baby Fontaine and her dashing husband, Del, suddenly appeared. The guests clapped and cheered as the happy couple waved and blew kisses. Calls of *"Bonne Fête"* mingled with shouts of "Happy Birthday."

"Baby looks radiant," Carmela said. And she really did. Wearing a pink chiffon gown with sequins at the neckline and hem, Baby sparkled like a miniature constellation.

"All those sequins," Ava sighed. "Reminds me of when I was a pageant queen. And look, her nail polish matches her dress perfectly. It's probably something real posh like 'Ooh-la-la Rosebud' or 'French Peony.' I wish I could wear fancy polish like that."

"You can," Carmela laughed. "Just stop

343

wearing those acrylic nails."

"And all that bloodred lacquer," Tandy added.

Ava fluttered her fingers and slashed at the air. "But this color does suit my personality."

Baby and Del pushed their way through the enthusiastic crowd, shaking hands, giving kisses, thanking everyone for coming. When they reached Carmela, Ava, and Tandy it was like old home week. And then when Gabby and Stuart showed up, the hugs and kisses got even more frenzied.

"Were you surprised?" Ava asked Baby.

"Shocked!" Baby said. She really was doing a marvelous job of acting surprised.

Finally, Del pulled Carmela aside. "I hope you and Ava are ready to be big-time stage stars," he said in his trademark Southern lawyer drawl.

"We're sure gonna try," Carmela said. She tapped her handbag. "I've got my script right here."

Del grinned. "Did you enjoy it?"

"It's great." She'd only skimmed the first ten pages. Figured she could speed-read the rest later.

Del chomped down on a cigar. "I'm not exactly Mr. Broadway, so I tapped Howard Garland, one of our local actors and playwrights, to honcho this whole theatrical thing."

"Okay." Carmela had never heard of Howard Garland.

"In fact, you should touch base with him right now. You and Ava."

Without waiting for a reply, Del dragged Carmela and Ava backstage into a small, darkened area. Garland was waiting there, looking tall and gangly, pacing nervously. His hair was parted in the middle and he wore a small mustache.

"Are these my actors?" Garland asked. His voice was slightly quavery.

"Two of them anyway," Del told him. Hasty introductions were made, and Carmela and Ava smiled tolerantly as Garland, sipping a tumbler of clear liquid, his Adam's apple bobbing excitedly, quickly explained the play to them.

"Great," Carmela said. What she really meant was, *Whatever.*

"Got it," Ava said, giving Garland a thumbs-up. Either her ADD had kicked in or her mind was elsewhere.

"This play is filled with both humor and pathos," Garland told them.

"I thought it was a fun little murder mystery," Carmela said. "A one-act play." She decided Garland was trying to write his own rave review.

"It is," Garland said. "But to pull it off, the acting has to be perfect. We only get one chance!"

"That's live theatre for you," Carmela said.

When Garland skittered off to harass the other actors, Ava arched an eyebrow and said, "The man's got a white silk scarf wrapped around his neck and he pronounces it *thee-ate-er.* I'm guessing that means high-strung and temperamental."

Carmela patted Ava's hand. "For Baby's sake we'll just have to muddle through."

"And was that vodka he was guzzling?"

"It was either Grey Goose or paint thinner."

From off in the restaurant came the high, sweet tinkle of a bell being rung.

"I think that's our cue that dinner is being served," Carmela said.

"Excellent," Ava said as they walked back to the table and found their names on the place cards. "By the way, have you read the script?"

"Naw, I just skimmed it."

"Me, too. I was too engrossed in reading the new issue of *Star Whacker* magazine instead. It was their fat issue."

"What's that?"

"Oh," Ava said as they sat down. "It's something I look forward to all year. The magazine features all these awful candid photos of Hollywood stars, mostly lazing at the beach or sitting on a yacht, with their most unflattering jiggly parts showing."

"And you enjoy this . . . why?"

"Makes me feel good about myself," Ava said. "Anyway, I figure I'll read the script just before we go on."

"High five," Carmela said. "That's my plan, too."

Dinner was an elegant sit-down affair that started with an appetizer course of turtle soup and moved on to a second course of trout amandine with mirlitons.

In between the turtle and the trout, Carmela filled Ava in about her hunt for the matching parchment. She told her about stopping at Cavalier Printing and her theory that the snippet could have come from one of Naomi's posters.

"I knew there was something I didn't trust about that little twit," Ava said. "She's a cold-blooded killer, I just know it."

"I'm afraid we don't know anything for sure."

Ava sighed and took a sip of wine. "Where's the bit of parchment now?"

"Babcock's got it."

"Huh. I hope he can make something happen."

"I know," Carmela said. "It feels like this murder case is really dragging on."

"Think how poor Ellie feels."

Just as the dessert course was being served, Garland plucked at Carmela's sleeve. "We're almost ready to start the play," he whispered.

"Now?" She was reluctant to relinquish her pecan pie.

But Garland was insistent. "Come on, you two. Hurry up."

So along with three other hapless guests, Carmela and Ava shuffled backstage, ready to act their little hearts out.

"You're to play the very haughty Esmeralda," Garland told Ava. "And you . . . Carmela, is it? You are to play the visiting cousin Miss Fabian."

Carmela, not wanting to leave this completely to chance, whipped out her script and did a speed-read through the entirety of the play. When she hit page twelve, her eyes goggled and she said, "Wait a minute, *I'm* the killer?"

Garland bobbed his head. "Yes, so as Miss Fabian you're going to have to be your most menacing."

Ava let loose a high-pitched giggle. She thought this was hysterical.

"I'm not menacing," Carmela said. "Look at me. I'm wearing a vintage wrap dress and flats, for goodness' sake. I look like a soccer mom who shops at Macy's and drives a minivan, not some crazy chick thrill killer."

"I know how to make you a lot scarier," Ava said. She reached into her voluminous purse and pulled out a big black metal gun. "Here, use this as a prop."

Carmela was appalled. "You've got a gun?" She accepted it like she was handling a dead rat. "Dear Lord, you're plum crazy, lady. Where on earth did you get a gun?"

"Remember that zombie run we took part in at Halloween? The one that the New Orleans Police Department sponsored?"

Carmela cocked an eye at her. "Yeah?"

"This is the gun I used."

"So you stole it from the police department?"

Ava lifted a shoulder. "More like appropriated it."

"Then you realize this isn't an actual weapon," Carmela said, feeling a little better. "It doesn't fire real bullets. It's a paintball gun."

"That's the beauty of it," Ava said. "You can intimidate people like crazy, but nobody's gonna get their fool head blown off. They'll just get whopped with a big blob of paint."

"I like it," Garland burbled.

"You would," Carmela said.

The play was really a silly little drawing room comedy. A waiter was shanghaied to stumble out with fake blood smeared all over his shirt, lights flipped on and off, and Garland played the role of the rather pompous private investigator.

Carmela felt like an idiot running on and off stage, but their audience — especially Baby — seemed to be enjoying the spectacle immensely. Whether it was the lines that Garland had penned, the frantic pace of the play, or just seeing their friends stumble, flub, and giggle their lines, the crowd clapped, cheered, and even hissed in all the right places.

As the finale approached, Carmela was unmasked and apprehended, and cheap tin handcuffs (surely bought from the Dollar Store) were slapped on her wrists. Then, as the audience clapped wildly, all the actors took a collective bow just as two waiters rolled out an enormous pink five-layer birthday cake. Candles blazed, sparklers sparked, and champagne corks popped. It was a wild combination of New Year's Eve, Mardi Gras, and Bourbon Street on a slow Tuesday. The band struck up "Happy Birthday" yet again, and this time everyone joined in the singing.

Baby jumped to her feet, put both hands to her lips, and flung thank-you kisses at everyone.

"Speech," her husband yelled. "Speech."

Wiping tears from her eyes, Baby leaped onto the stage.

"Thank you, thank you all," she gushed. "I'm thrilled and absolutely *surprised* by this amazing celebration." Her eyes sought out Carmela's and she gave a slow wink. "Thank you all so much for your amazing outpouring of love. This has been the best party a girl could ever wish for on her 'eleventy-twelfth' birthday." She paused. "Now let's cut the cake!"

"We did it," Ava said, grasping Carmela's arm. "We pulled it off."

"Wonderful, just wonderful," Garland gushed. He seemed to have found a new tumbler of clear liquid and was bolting it down like mad.

Carmela held up her hands. "Just get these things off me, okay?"

Ava removed Carmela's handcuffs and

then patted her hair. In the heat and humidity, Ava's hair seemed to have increased tenfold in volume. "How do I look?" she asked.

Carmela gazed at her friend. "You want the truth?"

"Ooh, I guess."

"It looks big. Like . . . *really* big."

"Uh-oh. And how's my mascara?"

Carmela didn't want to say it had morphed into a tarantula, so she just made a tiny little grimace.

That sent Ava into a paroxysm of worry. "I better freshen up."

"Not a bad idea," Carmela said. She was dying to get a breath of fresh air herself. And to get away from Howard Garland, who was now trying to embrace all the female actors and give them big wet smooches.

They ducked out of the party room and strolled through the back half of Parpadelle's dining room. It was dark and moody here, with lots of potted palms and red leather booths. Waiters spoke in hushed tones and swished back and forth on Oriental carpeting. It was the kind of quiet, private dining room where one could have an assignation.

As they slid behind a potted palm tree,

Ava said, "Cripes. Do you see who's sitting up front?"

Carmela's head swung around. "Who?"

Then she spotted the two of them for herself. Vesper and Edward Baudette. Seated at a table just opposite the bar. Two wine bottles rested in silver wine buckets, and they were surrounded by various silver trays. It would appear they were enjoying a rather elaborate dinner.

"It doesn't look like being in mourning has spoiled their appetites," Ava said.

"No, it doesn't," Carmela agreed. "What's that the waiter's bringing to their table? You see that? In the covered dish?"

They watched as the waiter took the top off with a flourish and tipped it toward Vesper.

"I think that's Lobster Thermidor," Ava said.

"Hmm," Carmela said. "The specialty of the house."

"No holding back."

"Spare no expense," Carmela said. Then, "There's something not quite right about those two. They give off this . . . what would you call it? Vibe of suspicion. Their actions, their reactions, nothing seems normal."

"I hear you," Ava said. "And I personally believe the killer could be any one of three people: Edward, Vesper, or Naomi. Take your pick. Or maybe they're all in cahoots."

"Did you get a chance to really look at the Mourning Cloak show last night?" Carmela asked.

"Mmn . . . no, not exactly. I was pretty busy with other things."

"I think it's strange — and maybe telling — that some of the funeral clothing was actually on loan from Vesper's private collection."

"It's very hinky."

"It made me so suspicious and angry," Carmela said, "that I went back to Vesper's home this morning to confront her. I mean, she *knows* the killer used antique lace to strangle Isabelle. So why didn't she just come forward and tell the police about her collection? If she had nothing to hide, that is."

Ava narrowed her eyes. "Maybe she does have something to hide." She paused. "Have you mentioned any of this to Ellie yet?"

"No," Carmela said. "I didn't want to overwhelm her."

"Too much information, yet not enough of the right information."

"Something like that."

"You know what?" Ava fixed Carmela with an evil glint in her eyes. "I think we should pay a visit to Vesper's house and take a gander at that antique costume collection for ourselves."

"I already tried. Vesper barely let me past the front door."

"That's not quite what I meant."

"Wait a minute," Carmela said. "You mean *break into* her house? Into her mansion?"

Ava had a cool answer for everything. "It won't technically be breaking in, *cher,* since you were just there. It'll be more like . . . you overstayed your welcome."

CHAPTER 25

Vesper's home was dark as a tomb when Carmela and Ava pulled up in front.

"Are you sure you want to do this?" Carmela asked. She turned off the ignition and listened to the engine tick down.

"Absolutely," Ava said. "Why wouldn't we?"

"I can think of a half dozen good reasons why not. The least of which is we might get caught red-handed and hauled off to jail."

Ava pushed a hunk of hair off her face. "Babcock would never let that happen."

Carmela knew differently. "Oh yes, he would."

"Still," Ava said. "Don't you want to be privy to the mysteries inside Vesper Baudette's white elephant of a house? Don't you want to get a peek at her vintage clothing collection? Aren't you interested in seeing if she's got a spool of antique Belgian lace stuck in a cupboard somewhere?"

It was the notion of antique lace that finally got Carmela out of the car. If Vesper actually possessed some antique lace that matched the lace that had choked the life out of Isabelle . . . well, then, it would be case closed, wouldn't it? And that would be a very good thing for everyone concerned. Except, of course, for Vesper.

They stood for a moment, staring at the dark house. With just a sliver of moon casting light and dark shadows, the place looked foreboding. Dangerous. Then Ava grabbed Carmela's arm and said, "Let's sneak around back. See if we can pry open a door or force a window."

"Why does this seem like a horrible idea?" Carmela asked. She cast an eye at the mottled sky where low, gray clouds scudded by.

"Shh," Ava said as they headed down the driveway and disappeared into the darkness of the side portico. "Pipe down. We don't want to bring the neighborhood watch people down on our heads."

But breaking and entering proved to be much more difficult than Ava thought it would be. Five minutes later they were still stumbling through a tangle of shrubbery, searching for an open window where they might gain entry.

"This is awful," Carmela whispered. "My heels keep sinking into an inch of muck and I feel like I'm being shredded. There's, like, thorns on all these bushes."

"Suck it up, girlfriend," Ava said. "We can handle it."

"You really do have a criminal mind, you know that?"

"Huh?" Ava said as she stood on her tiptoes and batted at a screen. "Me a criminal? Naw, I'm a good girl."

"You're always trying to lead me astray."

"No way," Ava said. "You're the one who pulls *me* into these crazy murder mystery capers." She paused as her fingers scrabbled at the bottom of the screen. Jimmying it back and forth a couple of times until it hung loose, she said, "Hey, I think I just popped this one!" There was a loud ripping sound, and then Ava lifted off a window screen and lowered it toward Carmela. "Stow this sucker someplace, will you?"

Carmela grabbed the screen and leaned it up against what had to be a thornbush.

"Now get over here. Lace your fingers together and give me a boost. This inside window is *open.*"

"Ava . . ." Against her better judgment, Carmela came forward, her hands reluctantly clutched together.

"Hold me steady now."

Then it was just a matter of Ava alley-ooping up the side of the house, cranking her leg up and over the wooden sill, and then flopping inside.

"Ouch." Ava had made it inside, probably in a sunroom or back porch, but she'd clearly landed on something uncomfortable.

"You okay?" Carmela hissed.

"Yeah." Ava's voice sounded hollow and low. "I think maybe I grazed a Christmas cactus when I touched down. Ouch. There are stickles, anyway."

"Welcome to the club. We can rub hydrocortisone cream on each other's wounds when we're finished. If we ever finish."

Then Ava's head and shoulders appeared in the open window. "Come on, I'll pull you up."

Carmela grabbed Ava's outstretched hands and, as if she were making a technical alpine ascent, half walked up the side of the house while Ava strained and pulled.

"Jeez, you're heavy," Ava said. "What'd you eat tonight?"

"Shut up and pull harder."

Thirty seconds later they were both standing inside Vesper's house, their voices low and whispering, peering down a dark hallway.

Carmela lifted a hand and pointed. "I'm pretty sure this hallway splits the house in two. I think it leads directly through to the front entry."

"Good," Ava said. "That means it'll also lead us to a staircase. Did you happen to see a staircase when you were here before?"

Carmela had to think for a moment. "Yes. I saw one just before the maid showed me into the sitting room."

Ava froze. "There's a maid? A live-in maid?"

"I don't think she lives here, no. I don't think anybody could stand living with Vesper."

"Good point."

They tiptoed down the dark hallway until a staircase opened up just to their right.

"Here we go," Ava said. "Hang on to your undies."

The stairs were carpeted, but the aging wood beneath the carpet creaked and groaned like old bones as they slowly made their way up to the second floor.

"You know," Ava said, "I always wanted to live in one of these grand old homes, but now I'm not so sure. They're all so creaky. And they all have that old house smell."

"That's history for you," Carmela said.

"Or Vesper's lousy cooking."

They were at the second-floor landing and not sure what their next move should be.

"What do you think?" Ava asked. "Just open a couple of doors and peek inside?"

"We came this far."

Ava moved down the hallway toward the back half of the second floor. "Let's try this room. I think I see a dim light on inside." She pushed open a set of double doors, paused, and let loose a low whistle. "Take a look at this happy crappy. I think we just found Vesper's boudoir."

"Let me see," Carmela said, eager to have a look for herself. Would it be all prim and proper? Or just straight-ahead basic furnishings?

"It's decorated, like, in bordello style," Ava giggled.

Carmela gazed around. Ava was quite correct; Vesper's bedroom did carry a hint of bordello. There were tiered velvet curtains with tiebacks, an elaborate four-poster bed covered with puffy heart pillows, an honest-to-goodness fainting couch, and a vanity table with a huge circular mirror. Only instead of being done in crimson red, like a movie-style bordello would be, it was all blue. And not even Williamsburg blue or

Persian blue. The place was the blue of an ugly, fading bruise.

"Get a load of that painting." Ava was practically convulsing with laughter now, pointing at a painting of Vesper Baudette that hung over the white brick fireplace. It depicted her as a much younger, slimmer woman, wearing a long V-neck gown and doing a sort of peekaboo pose from behind an elaborate fan.

Carmela shook her head. "The things rich people do."

"She must fancy herself some type of movie star."

"No," Carmela said. "It's pure costume. This is a woman who gets off on costumes."

Ava looked around. "So where are they? The costumes, I mean."

"Time to check out the other rooms."

The bedroom next to Vesper's must have, at one time, belonged to Edward Baudette. It was decorated in a masculine blue-and-green-check wallpaper with matching bedspread. There was a heavy mahogany dresser and four-poster bed.

"Everything in this house is so blue," Ava complained. "Don't these people like bright colors? Maybe Hello Kitty pink? Or vivacious animal prints?"

"Not everyone has your keen sense of

style," Carmela said.

It was in a room at the very front of the house that Carmela and Ava discovered Vesper's costume collection.

"Whoa," Ava said as she swung the door open slowly. "This is spook city." She stepped into the room. "It's like being in an episode of *The Twilight Zone.*"

Carmela was right behind her, taking it all in. The room that housed Vesper's costume collection was huge, with three arched windows that let in a spill of yellow light from a streetlamp. It was populated by about twenty mannequins, all of them carefully arranged and wearing antique costumes.

"Doesn't it feel like Miss Havisham is going to come greet us at any moment?" Ava asked.

"*Great Expectations.* Except there's no rotting cake."

Ava was still put off by the bizarre spectacle. "Pretty weird, huh?"

"It's beyond that. None of the mannequins have heads."

Ava inhaled sharply and put a hand to her mouth. "Holy guacamole, you're right. No wonder everything seems so strange. They're all headless." She stretched an arm out and touched one of the dresses, a long velvet number that looked like it might even be from the Victorian age. "I wonder why no heads?"

"Why do I have a feeling that if we opened a closet door there'd be a pile of heads?" Carmela said.

"That is a seriously distressing thought."

Then Carmela's mind jumped back to the mission at hand. "Lace. We've got to look around and see if we can find some antique lace."

"Maybe over here," Ava said. She headed for a large glass display cabinet set against the wall.

Carmela was just steps behind her. "I wish we could see better." She could make out a few pairs of gloves, a hat, and what else was in that case? She didn't dare turn on an overhead light.

Ava reached a hand around the cabinet, fumbled, and flicked on a switch. Immediately, the interior of the cabinet was bathed in soft pink light.

"Better," Carmela said. Her eyes searched the display cabinet, looking for a spool of lace. There were lace hankies, gloves, shawls, and even a lace parasol. But no spools or strands of lace.

"You see anything?" Ava was searching, too.

Carmela shook her head. "No, nothing. Rats."

"Listen," Ava said, "if Vesper really used her lace as a murder weapon, she wouldn't have left it out here on display. It'd be secreted away in a closet or something."

But ten minutes later, after searching through all the closets and chests of drawers, no lace had materialized.

"We got nada," Carmela said.

"Disappointing," Ava said.

Carmela checked her watch. "And we've been in here way too long. Somebody's bound to come home soon."

"Okay, let's blow this pop stand."

"Same way we came in?" Carmela asked.

"It worked the first time."

They trooped back downstairs, but Carmela hesitated at the bottom of the staircase. "I wonder . . ."

"What? You want to search the downstairs rooms, too?"

"Only if we can do it in under two minutes. My warning radar is starting to bleep like crazy."

"Okay," Ava said. "I'll check out the rooms on the right; you do the rooms on the left."

Carmela ducked into Vesper's library, rifled through the desk drawers, and pulled open two floor-level cupboards. Still zilch. She dodged back out into the center hallway and dipped into the next room. That turned out to be a kind of media room with even less possibilities for hiding something.

She met up with Ava in the front entry.

"Did you find anything?"

Ava shook her head no.

"Time to go, then," Carmela said.

"Maybe we should just waltz out the front door," Ava suggested. She put a hand on the doorknob. "There doesn't seem to be any kind of security —"

Bleep, bleep, bleep! An alarm began bleating like crazy.

"— system," Ava finished. "Crap. Now what do we do?"

"I don't know!" Carmela cried. In her mind's eye she could see the two of them tumbling out the back window right into the waiting arms of the police. Arrests, booking, and disgrace would follow.

"We either have to run," Ava said, "or hide."

"Hiding's not a viable option. Vesper might come strolling in at any minute."

"Or she might get an alert on her cell phone!"

Carmela parted a curtain and glanced out at the street. "Uh-oh, too late."

"What?"

"See for yourself."

A dark-colored blue car with a gold shield painted on the front door suddenly glided up to the curb.

"We're starting to find ourselves in fairly deep doo-doo," Carmela said as she flattened herself against a wall.

But Ava was both bold and practical. She peered out the window, trying to see what was actually going on.

"What's happening?" Carmela asked. Her heart was hammering inside her chest.

"Not to worry," Ava whispered. "It's just some stupid rent-a-cop."

"Private security?" *That wouldn't be so bad. At least those guys weren't armed. Were they?*

"Yeah." Ava sounded hugely relieved. "I don't think he's gonna do much of anything. Oh, see, he's just shining his spotlight at the front of the house."

"Is he getting out of the car?"

"No, he's just sitting there like a blob."

Carmela breathed a sigh of relief. "Good. Let's just wait until he leaves and then we'll —"

"Oops."

"Now what?"

"Crap on a cracker, Carmela. You better take a gander at this."

Carmela flew over to the window and peered out. A New Orleans Police Department cruiser had just rolled up behind the private security officer.

"Now it's seriously serious!" Carmela cried.

"Time to exit stage left," Ava agreed.

"And pray that cop doesn't come stumbling around back."

They pounded down the hall — they were way past tiptoeing at this point — and tumbled out the back window. Ava managed a passable somersault while Carmela made a daring leap of death and landed (where else?) in a thornbush.

Clutching each other, panting wildly, they pushed their way out to the back cobblestone alley and clopped away, trying to put as much distance as possible between them and Vesper's house.

"Here. In here," Ava hissed. She grabbed Carmela's arm and yanked her into someone's backyard garden.

"Now what?"

Ava did a quick reconnoiter and pulled Carmela into a black wrought-iron gazebo that was covered with curling vines.

"Holy smokes," Carmela said. "That was close."

"Too close for comfort," Ava said. She

plucked a thorn from Carmela's hair, then surveyed her own sorry state. "Aw, my sweater's all ripped. Do you know how many acrylics had to give their lives for this?"

"Darn," Carmela said.

"You think you can darn it?"

"No, I . . . never mind."

"Listen," Ava said. "Now that we found a good hiding spot, I think we should just sit here and chill out."

Carmela wasn't so sure. "But what if those cops come looking for us?"

"They won't," Ava said. "Because they don't know it's us."

"That's completely terrifying."

"What is? The jumping and stumbling and hiding part?"

"No," Carmela said. "That you're starting to make sense."

CHAPTER 26

Memory Mine was busy for a Saturday morning. Customers swarmed in, regulars as well as an influx of tourists who had happily stumbled upon the charming little French Quarter shop by chance.

"What are those little boxes that you've got in your window display?" one woman asked. "Are they memory boxes? Are they decoupaged? Are they for sale?"

"I'm afraid not," Carmela told her. "But we carry all the materials, and I can show you how to make one for yourself."

Another woman wanted scrapbook paper with a newborn baby theme, so Carmela led her back to the paper racks.

And on it went. A woman who wanted handmade paper, another who asked about polymer clay. And through it all, Carmela worried about her little creepy-crawl last night.

Had she or Ava left any clues or telltale

signs at Vesper's house? Would the police find some evidence and, at Vesper's urging, come swooping down on them? Worse yet, would Babcock find out?

When there was a slight break, Gabby brought Carmela a cup of chamomile tea. "Here," she said, setting the cup down on the table. "I thought you could use this. You seem like you're a little on edge."

"Thanks." Carmela wrapped her hands around the cup and took a sip of tea. "Mmn, good. Yes, I am."

"What's that on your neck?"

"What?"

"Where you were just scratching," Gabby said. "Do you have a rash?"

"No, I just, um . . . had a close encounter with a thornbush."

"What? Maybe you better tell me what happened."

"Oh, Ava and I had ourselves a little adventure last night. One I might live to regret."

"Whatever it is, you know I'll stand by you," Gabby said. "Unless you're about to get hauled off to jail." She paused when she saw the expression on Carmela's face. "Wait a minute, it *was* something serious, wasn't it?"

"Ava and I went on a little creepy-crawl."

"You didn't. Not back to Lafayette Cemetery, I hope."

"Close," Carmela said. "But no cigar. Actually, we snuck into Vesper Baudette's house to get a look at her collection of antique clothing."

"And she let you in?"

"The operative words were *snuck in*," Carmela said.

"Ohhh. You mean you broke in?"

"Like common thieves under cover of darkness, yes. Only we didn't steal anything. But while we were taking a look around, we accidentally set off the alarm . . ."

Gabby looked stunned.

"And then the police showed up."

"Carmela!"

"And then we had to jump out the back window and run away."

"But first you landed in thorns," Gabby said. She frowned. "You two are courting disaster, you know that?"

"That's what everyone keeps telling me," Carmela said. "If I'm not careful I'll start to believe it."

Once there was a break, Carmela pulled out the gray silk shantung Tea Party in a Box scrapbook that she'd promised Jade Germaine. She knew she should be further along on it. Then again, she'd spent valuable time investigating Isabelle's murder. And that was important, too.

Jade had given her dozens of photos, so Carmela sorted through them, arranging them in individual piles. Photos of tea sandwiches on three-tiered trays, scones on a platter, a silver tea service, and one that she thought of as food porn, since the close-ups really did reveal the juiciness and freshness of the food.

Carmela settled on a photo of an antique sterling silver tea set for the album's cover. The silver popped on the pale gray fabric, looking elegant and tasteful. She knew Jade was pleased with the mauve and pink silk flowers she'd originally selected, so she affixed them permanently to the cover.

Working happily for a good half hour, Carmela ignored the ringing telephone and new influx of customers, letting Gabby handle any and all pesky details and inquiries. And just as she was feeling relaxed, just as she'd settled into a nice working rhythm, the jambalaya hit the fan. Babcock called.

"A very strange notice came across my desk this morning," Babcock growled in Carmela's ear. "It seems there may have been a prowler at Vesper Baudette's house last night."

"Wow, that's pretty scary. Is she okay?"

Babcock wasn't buying her act of supreme innocence. "She wasn't home." Pause. "You wouldn't happen to know anything about that, would you?"

"Me? No. I was at Baby Fontaine's party last night. Ask anyone. I gave a stellar performance in a one-act play called *Death on the Patio*. I . . . well, we . . . even got a standing ovation." She knew she was rambling and stopped abruptly. Swallowed hard.

"Are you sure you weren't doing a little freelance investigating?" Babcock asked. "I know it's difficult for you to keep your nose out of police business."

"That's so unfair," Carmela said, "when all I've tried to do is help poor Ellie."

"I'm quite familiar with your version of helpfulness. One minute you're holding Ellie's hand and the next you're out hunting for her sister's killer. After your ridiculous trip back to the cemetery the other night I've decided that you really don't know your limits. So I'm going to remind you — I am the detective, you are my girlfriend. And if you want it to stay that way, you better stop all this mischief."

"Goodness," Carmela said. "You sure

374

know how to turn a girl's head."

"I'm serious, Carmela. You need to be very careful. There's so much more going on right now that you don't know about. That I don't know about."

"Come on, what's up?"

"Carmela." Babcock's voice carried a warning note.

"No, seriously. Tell me what's going on that could possibly overshadow solving Isabelle's murder."

"I can only tell you that I've been hearing strange rumblings around city hall. About some impropriety that's been going on."

Carmela perked up. This was exactly what Prejean had told her.

"You mean like payoffs and bribery?" Carmela asked. "That's what Bobby Prejean has been saying all along. That Julian Drake and his Elysian Fields Casino buddies have been offering bribes to city officials in order to expedite their casino plans."

"All I know," Babcock said, "is that there's been a meeting called for late afternoon. The mayor just got back in town and he's asking the city council and top law enforcement officials to sit in."

"And you would be one of those top officials?"

"Don't play cute, Carmela. This is serious business."

"Okay, okay. Apologies."

"Just be careful, Carmela. And don't take any unnecessary risks."

"I will," she said. "I won't. Hey, let me know what happens with your meeting, okay?"

But Babcock had already hung up.

"Huh," Carmela said. She stood up, stretched, and rolled her head from one side to the other, trying to stretch out the kinks. Then she walked out into the retail area, in search of a teapot rubber stamp, her hand unconsciously brushing the itch on her neck where the thorn had stuck her.

Gabby glanced up from the front desk. "Everything okay? I couldn't help but overhear some of your conversation. It sounded like you were verbally jousting with Babcock."

"Oh, Babcock's got his undies in a . . ." That was all she was able to get out before the front door burst open and Naomi Rattler stormed in.

"How dare you!" Naomi screamed. She didn't even bother with a howdy-do. "How *dare* you!"

Carmela and Gabby exchanged glances and then looked back at Naomi. Her face was bright red, she was clenching her fists, and her nostrils were actually flaring out with every angry exhalation.

"How dare you try to put my life under a microscope!" Naomi shrilled. "Unlike you two, I have a reputation to uphold." Now she started shaking her finger. "And I warn you — you will *not* succeed in besmirching my good name."

Carmela blinked. This was a side of Naomi she'd never seen before. She'd seen her weird, snippy side, yes. But this was something else. This was pure, unadulterated, so-angry-you're-shaking rage. She wondered if Naomi could have directed some of that barely contained rage at Isabelle.

"What are you talking about?" Carmela asked, though she knew darn well what Naomi was screaming about. She'd found out that Gabby called about the poster. "There's no besmirching going on here, if that's even a word, so there's no reason to . . ."

"No reason?" Naomi's voice rose to an almost painful high C as she shouted at Carmela. "Your meek little assistant over there had the audacity to *call* the people at the Old Town Repertory Theatre. How dare you put her up to that! Those are my clients.

In fact, they've been important clients for years."

"Do you want to take it down a notch?" Carmela said. "Try to be reasonable?"

"I don't want to be reasonable," Naomi screamed. "I'm mad. In fact, I'm thinking of taking legal action against the both of you."

"Good luck with that," Gabby muttered.

Naomi turned on her. "You little weasel!"

That was enough for Carmela. She advanced on Naomi like Attila the Hun about to conquer the Eastern Roman Empire. "How dare you waltz in here and insult me, my friend here, and my shop. Gabby can call anyone she chooses for any reason she wants. And you, Naomi Rattler, can just stuff it. It's just too freaking bad if your feathers are ruffled."

Naomi fairly seethed with outrage. "Vesper Baudette warned me about you." Her voice was a dramatic hiss. "She said you were meddlesome and a troublemaker. I can see she was right."

Carmela finally found a hatchet she could throw back. "And the last time your name came up, Vesper referred to you as a simpleton."

"Liar," Naomi cried. "You're a liar."

"Your moment is over," Carmela said. She

threw an arm out and pointed toward the door. "Get out. And don't ever come back."

Naomi's mouth pulled into an ugly, grim line and her eyes blazed with fury. "Don't worry," she cried. "I will never set foot in your crappy little shop again!" And, with that, she jerked open the door and flounced out.

Carmela and Gabby looked at each other in the wake of Hurricane Naomi. Carmela was ready to burst into laughter, but she could see that Gabby was close to tears.

"I'm sorry," Gabby said. She shook her head regretfully. "I should have never called my friend at the theatre. I overstepped my boundary."

"You didn't," Carmela said, rushing to her side. "You were simply investigating."

"But still . . ." Gabby brushed away a tear. "I'm sorry I poked my nose in."

"Don't be," Carmela said. "You did good."

Gabby threw her an incredulous look. "I did? Really?"

Carmela nodded. "You were trying to help out and you did."

"And that's a good thing?"

"Yes," Carmela said. "In fact, you're getting to be as daring and suspicious and devious as I am."

"Thank you," Gabby said. "I think."

"And Naomi is a foolish child."

"I think so, too."

"Knock, knock," came a woman's voice.

They both looked toward the door, fearing that Naomi had made a return trip.

"Are you open for business?" a woman asked in a semiwhisper.

"We sure are," Carmela said.

The woman smiled. "Because I wasn't sure. You two looked so serious."

"We're always serious about scrapbooking," Gabby said, a big smile suddenly brightening her face. "Now how can I help?"

"Botanical paper?" the woman said. "The kind with fibers in it?"

Gabby perked up. "Mulberry, mango, or banana leaves?"

CHAPTER 27

Gabby took a quick peek at her watch, a stunning gold Chopard that Stuart had bought her just after he'd closed the deal on his sixth Toyota dealership.

"Time to lock up?" she asked. It was almost one o'clock Saturday afternoon and they'd agreed to close the shop early. Gabby was attending the Sweet City Charity Ball tonight and Carmela had the Elysian Fields Casino party. They'd both readily agreed that it took a girl a good four or five hours to bathe, steam, primp, curl her hair, apply a few layers of makeup, pick an outfit, and then accessorize it properly. Allowing, of course, for numerous revisions along the way. Gorgeous never came easy. In fact, it was a lifelong struggle.

"Okay," Carmela said as she shrugged her hobo bag onto her shoulder and scurried toward the front door. "I'm heading out right now." She hesitated. "Are you okay?"

Gabby waved a hand. "If you're asking about the Naomi incident, I'm totally over it. I'm not going to let her occupy any real estate in my mind."

"Good girl."

"So have a great time at the casino party tonight," Gabby said. "Just please don't go all in and lose your pocket money playing blackjack. And for gosh sakes be careful."

"Don't worry. Besides, I think they're handing out free chips. And I will be careful."

"Watch out for any weird guys."

"Hah," Carmela said. "All guys are weird. You should know that by now." She hesitated again at the door. "Are you coming? Or do you want me to wait for you?"

"I've got five more invoices to check against these orders and then I'll be out of here in twenty minutes — so no need for you to wait."

"You sure?"

"Go."

Carmela did. In fact, she was a woman on a mission. She planned to swing by Juju Voodoo, have a quick confab with Ava about what to wear tonight, and then go home. She figured she might even have time to take Boo and Poobah for a quick afternoon stroll before she had to throw herself full tilt into getting ready.

But first, Carmela was headed for Café du Monde to pick up her drug of choice — fluffy, soft, sugary, sinful beignets. If you lived in New Orleans, or if you were visiting New Orleans, you'd eventually wind up here — under the ubiquitous green-and-white-striped awnings. You'd listen to street musicians while you waited in line to grab a couple cups of chicory coffee and a cardboard tray (or two) of fresh beignets.

And then you'd dive in and launch yourself straight to heaven.

"Did you really?" Ava trilled as Carmela stepped into her voodoo shop. Her nose twitched like a bunny rabbit as the smell of powdered sugar–coated beignets wafted toward her. "Because I haven't had a bite of lunch yet and I'm starving." She grabbed a beignet from the tray, closed her luscious lips around it, and chewed. A beatific smile spread across her lovely face. "Mmn, na tha ith pr hvn." She was chewing while she rhapsodized, but Carmela picked up the basic gist of her words.

"Nothing like a good sugar high to propel you through the afternoon," Carmela said. "And probably into the evening." She'd already eaten one of the beignets on the way over. Who could resist! Now she reached for a pair of earrings that were sitting on the counter. "These are cute." They were gold hoops with dangles of pink crystals.

Ava waved a hand. "Take 'em. Wear 'em to the party tonight if you want."

Carmela held them up to the side of her face and glanced in the small oval mirror on the counter. "You sure?"

"I bought tons. For the holidays."

"Speaking of which," Carmela said, "I see you've strung twinkle lights among all your skeletons." Ava had an entire skeleton family, really an extended family, hanging from her rafters.

"Don't knock it. Voodoo stuff is very big during the holidays. Which is why I always lay in a huge supply of saint candles, too. Even if you don't believe in their magical powers, they always look pretty sitting on a fireplace mantel or decorating an outdoor patio." Ava pointed at the beignets. There were four left. "Are you gonna eat those?"

"They're all for you."

Ava's hand snapped out and grabbed a second one. "Thank goodness." She took a bite, said, "Hashtag yum." And then, "Hey, I've got something I want you to see." She set her beignet on the counter and dusted her hands together. "A dress I might wear tonight."

"Bring it out," Carmela said.

Ava ducked into her office and emerged with a crinkly bag. "It's something I borrowed. From my friend Bambi."

"The one who does the manicures, Botox injections, and weaves."

Ava snapped her fingers. "That's my lady."

"So I'm sure she has exquisite taste."

Ava pulled out a bright red ruffled dress that was a cross between a box of valentine candy and a naughty maid's outfit, if the maid worked at Hotel Hell. The neckline plunged to a deep V, the waist was cinched tight, and the skirt appeared to be multiple layers of stiff red netting.

"Holy smokes," Carmela said.

Ava grinned. "You like it. I knew you would. It's got that hint of saloon gal."

"Just like Miss Kitty." Carmela tried hard to stay upbeat. "Well, I guess it's, um, got a certain short and sassy factor going for it."

"Doesn't it?" Ava held it up. "Perfect for dancing."

Carmela eyed the length of the hem. "Only if your partner doesn't twirl you too fast or dip you back too far. Then all bets are off."

Ava's eyes twinkled. "That's the whole idea, love." She stuffed the dress back inside the bag and said, "That was a pretty close call last night at Vesper's house."

"Yes, it was."

"I can hardly believe we got away with it."

"We didn't," Carmela said.

"Whah?" Ava had taken another bite of her beignet.

"Babcock knows."

Ava made a face. "Ohmigosh, he knows we broke in?"

"He was gentleman enough not to push it too hard. But I know he suspects. Thank goodness he didn't make a big deal of it."

"Thank goodness is right." Ava reached for another beignet. Her third? "You know, that mess of costumes we saw at Vesper's last night got me thinking."

"About . . . ?"

"Narrowing down the killer. I still think the killer's gotta be either Vesper or Edward. They're the ones with the most compelling motives. They're the ones who could've gotten closest to Isabelle without her suspecting anything."

"They're also the ones walking around with guilty looks on their faces," Carmela said. "Still, it's hard to pry any information out of them. Short of using thumbscrews, we can't seem to pin anything down."

"What if we played one against the other?"

"How so?" Carmela asked.

"Well, if Vesper did it, Edward would have to be totally freaked. Right? I mean, knowing — or suspecting — that his own mother was a killer?"

"I see what you're saying," Carmela said. "And if Vesper thinks Edward did it, well, then she has to be scared out of her mind, too. That she raised her precious son to be a killer."

Ava's phone started ringing.

She wiped her hands on her jeans again and said, "But how do we approach them? How do we turn one against the other?" Then she snatched up the phone and said, "Juju Voodoo. Come on over and sit a spell. Or cast a spell." She listened for a few moments and then said, "Yup, she's here all right." She held out the phone. "It's for you."

"Me?" Carmela grabbed the phone. "Hello?"

"Carmela," said a cultured voice. "It's Mignon. You remember me? From Folly Française?"

"Oh yes, of course."

"I called your scrapbook shop," Mignon said. "And your assistant told me you'd already left for the day, but that you could probably be reached at this number." She hesitated. "I hope this doesn't cause a problem for you?"

"Not at all," Carmela said. "What can I do for you?"

"Well," Mignon said, "you were in here the other day asking about lace. Asking if anyone had purchased a piece of antique lace. And I was just going over my monthly sales receipts and saw something that might possibly interest you."

Carmela was suddenly very interested. "What's that?"

"There was a woman in here, oh, maybe three weeks ago," Mignon said. "Anyway, she was a Realtor, and she ended up buying a fairly large amount of lace. Something like fifteen yards."

"Was this antique lace?"

"No, I would never have had that much in stock. And this customer, this lady Realtor, said that the lace didn't have to be old at all. She just wanted it to *look* old. To match some other lace that was going to be used at an open house. I got the impression she wanted to decorate some invitations or something. Or maybe tie the lace around some fancy handouts — you know how Realtors are always trying to come up with some unique takeaway so you'll remember their property?"

"Yes," Carmela said. She'd once helped her own Realtor create some fun brochures and takeaways. "Do you remember the name of this Realtor?"

"No, I'm afraid not. Because she paid cash for the lace."

"Okay, do you by any chance know when the open house was going to be?"

"Sorry. I don't know that, either. I guess I'm not much help."

"No, that's okay," Carmela said. "It's good information. I appreciate your calling about this. Giving me a heads-up."

"It's just that you were so insistent about the lace," Mignon said. "It seemed so important to you at the time. I thought you might want to know about this. I wish I could have remembered more."

"Thank you," Carmela said. "Thank you very much." She was about to hang up, when something occurred to her. "Mignon, are you familiar with a local blogger by the name of Naomi Rattler? She writes a blog called . . . um . . ."

"Haute to Trot," Ava whispered.

"Haute to Trot," Carmela said.

"Yes, I have met Naomi," Mignon said. "In fact, when I first opened Folly Française, she came over and interviewed me. Did a lovely little piece about my shop.

About how vintage has become such a huge trend."

"But Naomi didn't buy anything from you? Like a piece of lace or anything?"

"No," Mignon said. "We just did the interview."

"Okay, thanks." Carmela hung up and gazed at Ava.

"What?" Ava asked. "What's going on?"

Carmela held up a finger, and then dialed the number of Miranda Jackson, her friend and Realtor. Miranda had recently helped her sell the Garden District home she'd finally pried away from Shamus in their rather acrimonious divorce settlement.

Miranda answered her cell phone on the fifth ring. "Hello?" She sounded harried.

"Hi, Miranda. It's Carmela. I have kind of a strange request."

"All the requests I get these days are strange," Miranda said. "What do you need?"

"Is there any way you can get me a list of all the open houses that are happening this coming Sunday? I know most of them are listed in the newspaper, but there are sometimes other ones, too, right?"

"Mmn." Miranda sounded like she was thinking. Or taking notes and thinking. "I can do that," she said slowly. "But at this very moment I'm right in the middle of a showing." She lowered her voice. "It's one of those dreary little cottages over on Piety Street. But I'm working with some all-cash buyers, investors, who are extremely motivated. I think I can lock this down today." Her voice rose again. "So the problem is, I couldn't get to your little errand until tonight."

"That's okay," Carmela said. "But when you get the information, call me, okay? Let me know."

"Sure. No problem."

Carmela dropped the phone into the cradle. Lace? And real estate? How on earth did those two things tie together? And did they have anything to do with Isabelle's death? Anything at all? All she could think of were the somewhat puzzling words that Babcock had spoken to her. *Stay tuned.*

CHAPTER 28

Carmela sat at her dining room table, watching her nail polish dry. Mostly, though, she was admiring the rich claret color that perfectly matched the glass of Pinot Noir she was drinking. As she was painting her toenails to match, two thuds sounded at her front door. Ah, Ava and her stash of dresses had arrived. Which, of course, jacked Boo and Poobah into high alert.

"Okay, okay," Carmela told her pups. "Chill, babies." She got up and waved her hands around in small figure eights. Maybe the extra air circulation would help the enamel dry faster?

Carmela gingerly opened the door using just the pads of her fingertips. Ava immediately tried to thrust an armful of garment bags at her.

"No, no, I just did my nails," Carmela screeched, jumping back. Which caused Boo and Poobah to lunge forward.

"Down, dogs," Ava cried. "Auntie Ava is *dying* out here." Like a pack animal trudging through the Gobi Desert, she dragged three garment bags into Carmela's apartment and piled them on the chaise lounge. "Dresses," she huffed, trying to catch her breath.

"Great," Carmela said. She was looking forward to trying on some party dresses.

"Take a gander and let me know which ones you want dibs on. Then I'll do a little picking and choosing for myself."

"What happened to the red dress? From this afternoon?"

"Ah, I decided it was plenty sexy, but maybe not quite classy enough for our big casino shindig."

"Ava, we're talking gambling and men who probably wear pinkie rings," Carmela laughed. She knew what kind of men hung around casinos. She'd been to Moonglow Casino over in Biloxi.

"Still, I want to look upscale," Ava said. "Like one of those rich society babes you see on the cover of *Town & Country.*"

"That might be a stretch."

"Hmm?"

"Never mind," Carmela said. "Let's take a look. Go ahead and do the big reveal."

"You got it." Ava hastily unzipped one of

the bags. Red, pink, purple, and black dresses spilled out, all in vivid Technicolor, like hybrid roses from some exquisite garden.

Carmela was impressed. "Where'd you get all these gowns? These are pretty high caliber." Ava's closet was jam-packed with sexy dresses, but these were a big step up in taste and design.

"I made a detour to the Latest Wrinkle."

"Ah," Carmela said. "Our favorite resale shop."

"Don't tell anybody, but I got all these dresses on approval."

"Meaning . . . ?"

"We don't have to pay for them."

"But aren't they expecting us to buy a couple?"

Ava put a finger to her mouth. "Shh. That's our little secret."

"Okay, let's see what we've got."

Ava pulled out a long black lace dress that was slit all the way up the front. "Lots of leg action going on here."

"Maybe a little too much."

"Okay, be a Puritan. I'll try it on." Ava pulled off her sweater and slipped out of her jeans. Within seconds she'd slithered into the dress. "Hah. It fits. And I didn't even have to use Crisco or fishing line." She did a pirouette and struck a runway-type pose, her legs looking long and shapely in the reveal from the dress.

"It's certainly more your style than mine," Carmela said. She picked up a bright blue dress with a flowing skirt and held it at arm's length, examining it critically. "This might work." She took off her blouse and jeans and slipped the dress over her head.

"Pretty color," Ava said. "Brings out the blue in your eyes."

Carmela smoothed the skirt down over her hips. "Not bad." Then she did a half turn and glanced in the mirror over the fireplace. "Oh no." Panic rose inside her. "There's no back."

"So what?"

"I mean nothing at all. I'm hanging out like a very naked lady."

"Shoulder blades and a hint of spine can be very sexy," Ava said. "Men enjoy a sneak preview."

"This isn't just a preview, it's a coming attraction."

Ava picked up a red dress that was spattered with sequins. "Maybe you should try this one, *cher*. Red is another color that looks *très jolie* on you."

"Sequins." Carmela made a lemon face. "You know I pretty much exist in a sparkle-free zone."

"Which makes it very difficult to find something that screams par-tay," Ava grumped. She slithered out of her long black dress and pulled on a skintight black leather dress. "Zip me up, will you?"

"Leather?"

"Leather says party," Ava said.

"Yeah, but what kind? S&M? B&D?" Carmela jerked and tugged at the zipper, but wasn't able to budge it. "You're gonna have to really suck in, kiddo."

"I'm trying," Ava said. "Wait." She held up a hand and inhaled deeply. Still holding her breath, she gestured for Carmela to go for it. The zipper started to move and finally slid all the way up to the top. "What do you think?" Ava gasped. "How do I look?"

"Honey, that black leather dress gives off such a dominatrix vibe that you're gonna need a safe word."

"I love it," Ava choked out.

"But can you breathe?"

Ava nodded. "Some."

"Okay." Carmela had just noticed a chiffon dress way at the very bottom of the garment bag. It was a long dress that was almost the same deep red color of her nails. She pulled it out and smiled. It had a sweetheart neckline and a nice flowy skirt.

She decided it was modest but not veering into Amish territory. It could probably work.

The dress slid over her body like hot butter on a biscuit. "What do you think?" Carmela asked.

"Good," Ava gasped. "Pretty. Even matches your nails."

"You want me to unzip you?"

Ava nodded. "I need a breather while we do our makeup. Then it's back to the old bondage and discipline." She picked up an oversized tote bag and dumped the contents onto the coffee table. Compacts shot out like hand grenades, and lipsticks glanced off the table like bullets. "I brought everything we need to get glam."

"The glam squad," Carmela said. She was usually okay with just lipstick and mascara, but this was a special occasion.

Ava held up a silver compact and twirled a fluffy pink brush. "How about we add a touch of shimmer to your décolletage?"

"You think I need it?"

Ava cocked her head. "Please."

Carmela threw back her shoulders. "Okay, let's go for it."

They patted on makeup base, lined their eyes, arched their brows, and spackled on highlighter.

"This is fun," Ava said. "Like playing

dress-up." She swirled a flat brush in a palette of blusher and aimed it at Carmela. "You need powder on your cheekbones, too."

"Just a dab," Carmela said, as Ava dabbed away.

Ava pursed her lips and studied them in the mirror. "My lipstick. Should I go with lilac or lavender?"

"Which color's more of a cool blue?" Carmela asked.

"Um, probably the lavender."

"Then that's the one." Carmela finished with a hit of Dior's lip gloss in Vertigo. Then she fluffed her hair, which was always easy, and said, "What do you think?" She was waiting for a critique from Ava. Instead she got praise.

"You look fantastic," Ava declared. "If Babcock saw you now he'd never let you leave the house without himself as your escort."

Carmela laughed as she threw her lipstick into her black satin clutch and then set it next to Ava's larger beaded bag. "Now if we can just . . ."

The telephone rang, interrupting her train of thought.

Carmela snatched it up. "Hello?"

It was Babcock. Which instantly put her

on high alert. "How'd your meeting with the big muckety-mucks go?" she asked.

"It got delayed," Babcock said. "I'm just heading in there now."

"Okay."

"Listen, when I'm done here I'd like to drop by."

Carmela wavered. "Um. I'm not sure . . ."

"Wait a minute," Babcock said. "Are you on your way out? For the evening?"

"Something like that."

There was a slight edge to his voice. "Where are you off to?"

Carmela hesitated a fraction of a second longer than she should have, allowing Babcock to pretty much figure it out.

"Holy crap, Carmela, you and Ava are headed for that casino party, aren't you?"

"Uh . . . yes."

"Carmela, I don't think you should go to that party."

"Oh, come on. It's just a silly casino party. With a bunch of local politicos."

Babcock was firm. "I'd rather you not mingle with that particular crowd."

"Really," Carmela said. Now there was an edge to *her* voice. "I'll be fine."

"Then I'm going to send someone over there."

"To keep an eye on me? Are you serious?"

"Completely."

"Don't," she said. "Just . . . don't."

When Carmela hung up the phone, Ava said, "That didn't sound good."

Carmela flapped a hand. "That was just Babcock being overly protective."

"Nice of him," Ava said.

"Sometimes."

The phone rang again.

"There," Ava said. "I bet he's calling back to apologize."

"You think?" Carmela grabbed the phone for a second time.

But it wasn't Babcock at all. It was Boyd Bellamy, her landlord at Memory Mine.

"Carmela?" he said in his squawky old-man voice.

"Yes?"

"There's a problem."

With the rent? No, I just sent it in. "What's wrong?"

"Some jackhole smashed your front window," Bellamy said.

"At my shop? At Memory Mine?" Carmela was stunned.

"Better get down here," Bellamy said. "And deal with the problem."

"Is . . . is everything ruined?"

"Ruined?" Bellamy said. "The place is a shambles!"

Ten minutes later, Carmela and Ava stood on Governor Nicholls Street peering at what remained of Memory Mine's front window. Boyd Bellamy was pacing back and forth on the street, red-faced and angry, arguing with a rotund man who was apparently an insurance adjuster.

"You really got bashed," Ava said.

The gently curved bow window wasn't just cracked, it was completely smashed. Jagged shards of glass lay scattered on the sidewalk, creating kaleidoscope reflections of neon signs from across the street. Fragments of glass had fallen inside the bay window, too. A miniature theatre, a couple of albums, and three collaged memory boxes were completely destroyed.

"It's toast," Carmela moaned. "Our projects are toast."

"I'm so sorry," Ava said. "If there's anything I can do . . ."

"Maybe call that hardware store down the street from you? See if they can come over and nail some plywood across the windows?" She paused to correct herself. "Nail it across where the windows used to be."

"I'm on it," Ava said.

Bellamy seemed more upset than Carmela. "Look at this," he said, gesturing wildly. "Ruined. This fine bow window is completely ruined."

"Was that your insurance adjuster you were talking to?" Carmela asked.

Bellamy ignored her question. "You have business insurance, don't you?"

"Yes." A long time ago, Shamus had urged her to get it. Now she was glad she'd listened to him.

"Good," Bellamy said. "Of course, this is still gonna be a damn mess to straighten out." He looked around, as if he might catch a glimpse of the perpetrators. Then his eyes landed on Carmela. "Why are you so dressed up?"

It was Carmela's turn to ignore his question. Mostly because it was none of his business and partly because she wanted to know what *he* was going to do about the broken window. He was the landlord, after all. The legal property owner.

"You're going to restore the window, right?" Carmela asked.

"We'll see, we'll see." Bellamy rocked back on his heels and let loose a sigh. "You've turned into a not-so-desirable tenant, it seems."

Carmela was incredulous. "What? You're upset with *me*?"

Bellamy gave a guttural harrumph that Carmela took to be an affirmative answer.

"I didn't have anything to do with this," Carmela said, furious now. "A pack of crazy vandals did this. Probably a bunch of marauding drunks from one of the bars on Bourbon Street."

Bellamy wasn't convinced. "You never know. You could have brought this on yourself."

"What?" Carmela said again. "I offended somebody with my floral scrapbook designs and miniature theatres? Are you serious? Are you crazy?"

Ava tapped her on the shoulder. "The hardware store guy is here."

"Thank goodness," Carmela said. She watched as the True Value Hardware pickup truck pulled to the curb and a tall guy in white coveralls got out. He had a drooping mustache and an unlit Camel cigarette stuck in one corner of his mouth.

The hardware store guy surveyed the window, scratched his head, and said, "I hope I brought enough plywood."

Carmela and Ava watched as the man angled big hunks of plywood over the windows and began nailing them in place.

It was slow going, but the plywood was thick and all the pounding and banging made it seem fairly secure. Carmela figured the whole thing would hold for a few days, until they sorted out how to replace the window. And who would pay for it.

When the last nail had been driven, Ava looked at Carmela and said, "There's nothing more we can do here. Now what?"

Carmela shrugged. "Go to a party?"

CHAPTER 29

The first thing Carmela and Ava saw when they arrived at the casino party was an enormous white tent rising up in the middle of a field like a just-grounded UFO. Moonlight shone down like silver icing, while four giant searchlights scoured the night sky, casting long beams and adding to the carnival atmosphere.

"That tent looks like a giant Jiffy Pop," Ava said. "You know, when the popcorn is all popped and the tinfoil bubble top is ready to burst?"

Carmela figured that with Babcock being so tense, something else might be ready to burst. But after sniping with Babcock, and the shock of seeing her front window destroyed, she was ready to turn a blind eye to the problems of the universe. At least for tonight, anyway. Tonight she was going to relax and have a good time. And what better place than a gala to celebrate the groundbreaking of the new Elysian Fields Casino?

Thanks to valet parking, they were able to exit their car right at the entrance to the tent. And, wouldn't you know it, there was a plush red carpet for guests to walk down and a couple of hired photographers to add some glam and sizzle.

"This is fantastic," Ava squealed. "A genuine red carpet. With paparazzi and everything." She clutched Carmela's arm. "We so deserve this."

"You realize that all the guests get this same treatment," Carmela pointed out.

"Still, a girl can pretend she's a star, can't she?"

"Then enjoy it to your heart's content," Carmela said. She lifted her eyes and saw, in the background, the jagged, dark ruins of the old Enchantment Amusement Park. The half-demolished roller coaster poked up, looking ominous and spooky behind the white tent. The bones of other attractions were starkly visible, too. The humped roof of the fun house, the peaked roof of an old shooting gallery. *Sad,* she thought. All the families that had enjoyed riding the roller coaster, shooting the log flume, taking pictures there. Gone now. Just a faint memory.

Ava gripped her arm as they were carried

along with the crowd into the giant white tent. "This place is a madhouse," Ava cried.

And it really was. Off to their left, a group of tuxedo-clad men and evening-gowned women, all dignitaries, no doubt, posed with shiny silver shovels. They hunched together, giving a token dig into the wooden floor, grinning like mad for a gaggle of news photographers.

"Look," Ava said. "There's Zoe and Raleigh from KBEZ-TV."

"Here to cover the symbolic groundbreaking," Carmela said. "I guess a press turnout is de rigueur for any big new building project."

Ava pantomimed a yawn. "That part is kind of boring." Then her face lit up with sudden delight. "But look at all the good stuff that awaits us."

Spread out before them, like jewels in Ali Baba's cave, were gambling tables, a glittering bar, waiters passing out hors d'oeuvres, a full orchestra, and a genuine dance floor.

Caught up in the excitement, Ava did a little jig. "Good thing I wore my dancing shoes."

"But first a drink," Carmela said. "I need to calm my nerves."

"I hear ya," Ava said.

They sauntered over to the bar where five

white-coated bartenders were working frantically.

"You want a Cosmopolitan?" Carmela asked.

"Absolutely," Ava said.

"Two Cosmopolitans," Carmela told the bartender. She slid him a five-dollar bill and, a few minutes later, two Cosmopolitans slid across the bar to them.

"Thank you, ma'am," the bartender said. "But you know it's an open bar."

"Goody," Ava said.

Carmela smiled at him and he gave a little salute as he tucked the tip in his shirt pocket.

"Come back anytime. I'm Tony."

"Tony's cute," Ava said.

"Tony's working," Carmela said.

"Hey, so am I."

"You made it!" a jubilant voice called out. They both whirled around to find Julian Drake bounding toward them, arms spread apart in a heroic welcome, a big smile on his face.

"Of course we did," Ava said. She stuck out a hip. "You made the evening sound so appealing."

"Isn't this something?" Drake asked, gesturing at the elaborate setup. "We've got gaming tables for roulette, blackjack, and even baccarat. Just like we'll have at the new Elysian Fields Casino. Only that one will be very real and exceedingly plush."

"I can't wait until it's built," Ava said.

Carmela thought she might have to wait awhile. If Julian Drake and his cronies were proven guilty, that is.

"Let's get you ladies set up with some chips," Drake said.

They followed him across an elegant Aubusson carpet into the roped-off gaming area. He ducked behind a roulette table, whispered something to the pit boss, and returned with two enormous stacks of blue chips.

"These ought to get you started," Drake said.

"Jeepers," Ava said, thoroughly impressed.

"Thank you," Carmela said. "But you've given us . . . what? Two hundred dollars' worth of chips?"

"No problem," Drake told them as he backed away. "Enjoy and good luck. Don't spend it all in one place." And he was off to glad-hand some other guests.

Ava was stunned by their windfall. "We're rich," she said. "Let's go cash these in and paint the town red."

"I think Drake really meant for us to gamble," Carmela said.

"Oh. Okay." Ava looked around. "I'm not exactly an experienced casino-type gal. What do you think we should try first?"

Carmela looked at the blackjack table. No empty seats. So not there. She glanced at the baccarat table and was stunned to see Vesper and Edward Baudette sitting there, liberally pushing out stacks of red and blue chips as they studied their cards.

Well, why wouldn't they be here? Carmela thought. Julian Drake was supposed to be the best man in Edward's wedding. So it was only logical that they'd be invited to this big wingding. She and Ava would just have to stay away from the Baudettes. Ignore them as best they could.

"Over there." Carmela gestured to Ava. "We'll play a little roulette."

They slid onto stools and stacked their chips in front of them.

"Now what?" Ava asked.

"Chips placed on red or black pay two to one," Carmela told her. "Or you can play the numbers."

"I wanna play the numbers."

"Then you can put chips directly on the numbers, or you can corner the numbers or halve them."

"Which pays more?"

"Directly on the numbers," Carmela said.

"Straight up pays thirty-five to one."

"Then that's what I'm going to do." Ava put six chips on six different numbers, while Carmela placed ten chips on the red field.

The wheel was spun, and the white ball zipped around, endlessly circling the roulette wheel. Finally it slowed down, clattering and bouncing from number to number.

"Exciting," Ava said.

"Twenty-four red," said the croupier as the ball landed. He swept all the chips toward him, but put a matching stack in front of Carmela.

"You won," Ava said. "I lost."

"Try again."

"Maybe I should just play red or black."

"It's a strategy."

This time Ava put five chips on black. And it came up black.

"Okay," she said. "Now I'm getting the hang of this game."

They played for another ten minutes, winning some, losing a little, until Ava said, "We should try another game."

"Sure," Carmela said.

They gathered up their chips and wandered through the casino area. Carmela was happy to see that Vesper and Edward were gone, but she was nonplussed when

411

she turned and found herself staring into Shamus's smiling face.

"You're here," Shamus said.

"And you're like a bad penny," Carmela said. "Always turning up where I least expect you."

"Did you bring a date tonight?" Ava asked him.

"Naw," Shamus said. "I'm . . ."

Carmela arched an eyebrow. "Playing the field?"

"C'mon, Carmela," Shamus said. "Don't be that way. Where's that sweet girl I know and love?"

"I don't know," Carmela said.

"Hey, we had some good times together, right?"

"Sure," she said. "A few."

"Are you still happy hanging out with that cop?"

"Detective first grade," Carmela said. "Just to clarify."

But Shamus had been drinking and was starting to get nostalgic. "You were good for me. I miss you."

"Water over the dam," Carmela said.

"No chance at all?" Shamus asked. "You know, a lot of couples get divorced and end up getting back together. Reconnecting."

"Fat chance of that."

"Really?" He tried to look hopeful.

"Really," Carmela said. She glanced at Ava, who was busy counting her chips and stuffing them into her purse. "Ava, I think it's time to check out the hors d'oeuvres."

Ava clicked her purse closed. "Sounds good to me." When they were out of earshot, she said, "Was that silly boy mooning over you again?"

"Shamus pours two drinks down his gullet and starts remembering all the good times," Carmela said.

"But not the bad times."

"You got that right."

"Not to change the subject," Ava said, "but I see that handsome D.A. over there. I'd sure like to club him and drag him back to my lair."

"Bobby Prejean," Carmela said, as they suddenly came face-to-face with him. "What are you doing here?"

Prejean chuckled. "You keep asking me that."

"I'm sorry," Carmela said. "I do, don't I? When you have a perfect right to a social life." She grinned at him. "To be a gadabout if you feel like it."

Prejean leaned in and said in a low voice, "You might say I'm here to keep an eye on Julian Drake and the rest of these casino people."

Carmela thought about the meeting that Babcock was in right now. "I take it your office finally found some hard evidence?"

Prejean nodded. "We're getting very close to nailing the whole organization."

"So all of this — this casino thing — won't ever happen?" she asked.

"Oh, it'll happen all right. On this very spot." Prejean winked at her. "Just not with this particular company."

For the first time in a week, Carmela felt herself beginning to relax. The knot she'd been carrying in her stomach eased. If Julian Drake really was guilty of financial impropriety, it felt like Prejean would finally nail him. And if Drake had been the one who murdered Isabelle, because she'd been watching him closely . . . well, then that would get sorted out, too. Justice would eventually be served.

Prejean smiled at both of them. "But just because I'm here in an official capacity doesn't mean I can't have a good time."

"That's some pretty toe-tapping music they're playing right now," Ava said.

"Then would you like to dance?"

"Would I ever."

Ava shoved her clutch purse into Carmela's hands as Prejean grabbed her and spun her out onto the dance floor.

Well, okay, Carmela thought. So . . . maybe it was time to enjoy another refreshing beverage? Yes, she definitely thought it was.

But just as she was about to give the high sign to Tony the bartender, Naomi Rattler loomed in front of her.

"I'm still ticked off at you, you know," Naomi said.

Carmela shrugged. "Whatever." She thought of Naomi as small potatoes.

"You think you're so smart," Naomi hissed. "Running all over town, playing amateur detective."

"Naomi, shut up," Carmela said. "If I was a good detective I would have figured Isabelle's murder out by now."

Naomi eyed her carefully. "Do you think you're close?"

"Oh . . . I don't know." Carmela gave her a cool glance. "Could be."

"I know you've been suspicious of Edward all along. But he's really a very sweet, gentle guy. A pussycat. He would never . . ."

"Sure. Okay," Carmela said. "That's why you're always cozying up to him? Because he's so dang sweet?"

"Because he's needful," Naomi said, her voice rising an octave. "I'm trying to help him recover from his tragedy. Get over his grief."

"I saw him playing baccarat before. He didn't seem particularly grief stricken."

"But he is. Just in his own way."

Carmela regarded Naomi. Just when she'd started to discount Edward as a viable suspect, Naomi had come charging in to stir up her suspicions again. Could the murderer be Naomi or Edward? Or had she overlooked the fact that the two of them might have been in collusion?

Carmela muttered an, "Excuse me," and brushed past Naomi on her way to the bar. She found Tony, grabbed a second Cosmopolitan, and surveyed the crowd.

Ava was still out on the dance floor dancing with Bobby Prejean. Maybe, she thought, Ava had finally connected with a good, solid guy. Although hanging out with a party girl like Ava might not be the best thing for Prejean's reputation.

When her cell phone rang, Carmela had to juggle her drink and the two clutch bags to answer it. When she finally answered, her Realtor, Miranda Jackson, was on the line.

"I did that checking like you asked," Miranda said. "There aren't a lot of open houses on the books. In fact, there are just sixteen scheduled for tomorrow."

"Can you read me the names of the sellers?" Carmela asked.

"You want the names?" She paused. "Well, okay."

But when Miranda read her the names, Carmela didn't recognize a single one.

"Did that help?" Miranda asked. "For whatever you're up to?"

"It kind of did. On the other hand, I may be way off base."

"I'm sorry to hear that."

"Okay, thanks," Carmela said. She was about to hang up, when another thought popped into her head. "No, Miranda, wait. I know this is a long shot, but what about the open houses that were held last Sunday?"

"Mmn, you'll have to give me a minute if you want that information."

Carmela waited patiently, watching the gamblers crowd around the roulette wheel, catching sight again of Ava and Bobby Prejean over on the other side of the dance floor. A slow dance was playing now — "The Lady in Red" — and they were snuggled together, cheeks touching, looking very cozy.

Miranda was suddenly back, talking in Carmela's ear. "I'm afraid I came up with an even smaller number. There were eight open houses last Sunday."

"And the sellers were?"

"You want those names, too?"

"If you could," Carmela said.

Miranda started mumbling the names. Edward Ames, Charles Ross, and so on.

But it was the fifth name that rang Carmela's bell.

In fact, Carmela was so shocked she asked Miranda to repeat it.

"Oh sure," Miranda said. "It's Bobby Prejean."

CHAPTER 30

Carmela's heart lurched. If Bobby Prejean was selling a house, had his Realtor been the one who'd bought all that lace? Then she realized it was new lace, not old lace. So what exactly did that mean?

"Miranda, what's the address of the Prejean house? Do you have that in front of you, too?"

"It's on Chestnut Street in the Uptown area. Here it is. One twenty-two Chestnut. As I recall, it's one of those cute little West Indies–type cottages."

Carmela was still too dazed to respond to Miranda's chitchat.

"Wait a minute, let me scroll through my e-mails," Miranda said. "I think they had a broker's open house and I still might have the invitation." After a few moments she mumbled, mostly to herself, "I never seem to get around to clearing out all my old e-mails."

Carmela was holding her breath, almost afraid of what she might learn.

"Yes, here it is," Miranda said. "The invitation's in the form of a JPEG. In fact, it's very creative. It looks like something *you* might have designed. A little image of lace and parchment with all the details printed on it. Really cute."

"Who's the Realtor?" Carmela asked, her heart in her throat. She knew she was getting close to unearthing information that would point in a direction she'd never considered before.

"Let's see. The invitation came from Connor-Fleming Realty. Let me find . . . Here it is, the listing Realtor is Abby Grover."

"Would you happen to have her number?" Carmela was getting more and more wound up. Her words tumbled out like marbles rolling downhill.

"Well . . . sure." Miranda was quiet for a few seconds. "But if you want to take a look at the property, or possibly make an offer, don't you want me to feel them out first?"

"Miranda, it's not about the house right now. Please, I just need the number for this Abby Grover. I'll . . . well, I'll explain it to you later."

"If you say so. Okay, got a pen?"

"Go."

Miranda rattled off a phone number and then hung up.

Carmela prayed that she'd heard the number correctly. She dialed hastily and when a woman answered, "Abby Grover," she let loose a sigh of relief.

"Ms. Grover, my name is Carmela Bertrand. I understand you're the listing Realtor for the Prejean house over on Chestnut Street?"

"Yes?" Grover said.

"I need to talk to you about the invitation for that listing. And it's really important. Like life-and-death important."

Clearly taken aback, Abby Grover hesitated before she answered. "I'm at a wedding reception right now and my husband is . . . just a minute, just a minute. Jack, I asked you to *wait.*" Then she was back with Carmela. "Um, I think it would be better if we talked tomorrow. Or perhaps on Monday when I'm back in my office."

"Please," Carmela said. "This won't take long. And it's really important."

"Excuse me, you said it was life-and-death important?"

"Yes, it really is."

That seemed to intrigue the Realtor. "In

that case, what exactly did you want to know?"

"You created some sort of invitation or announcement for one of your listings? The property on Chestnut Street?"

"Yes, that's right. I'm a big believer in creative marketing. If you want to sell property in a tough market like this, you have to reach out and grab your audience. Whether you're appealing to fellow Realtors or prospective buyers."

"And this invitation you created was printed on parchment paper?"

"Yes. But . . ."

"And it was wrapped in lace?"

Grover was suddenly cautious. "Excuse me, I thought you were interested in the property itself. But you make it sound like the *invitation* is what's important."

"It is," Carmela said. "I really want to know everything about it."

"Really?"

"Please?" Carmela implored.

"Well, I found this hunk of old lace at the Chestnut Street property. It was stuffed into a drawer with a musty old fan and some other trinkets. Anyway, I decided it might be fun to run with that theme, since the house has a turn-of-the-century Caribbean cottage feel to it. Anyway, we added lace to the invitations and tied it around our handouts. And decorated the place with palmetto fans, palm trees, that kind of thing. We staged the patio with wicker furniture and served iced tea. With a bit of effort, we made the place look like a cottage that a British viceroy would have lived in in Antigua or something."

"Abby . . . Miss Grover. Thank you very much."

"Are you okay? You sound kind of stunned by all of this. But I assure you, fancying up a house for sale is what any smart Realtor does. No mystery there."

"I understand," Carmela said. "And thank you." She stood stock-still and tried to catch her breath. All around her the crowd was upbeat and excited. Croupiers paid off winners, party goers joked with one another, waiters dashed about with gleaming trays filled with crawfish pâté, tiny cornbread muffins, and blackened catfish kabobs.

And yet . . . Bobby Prejean. Was it possible that the lace that strangled Isabelle had come from his house? Could he have murdered Isabelle?

No, Carmela told herself. It just wasn't possible. He'd been a huge fan of Isabelle's, had praised her work sky-high.

And yet . . .

Carmela moved slowly through the crowd, the fun and revelry suddenly lost on her. Her mind was going in a million different directions. Trying to follow a thread . . . trying to make sense of . . .

She spotted Julian Drake just ahead of her. He was talking with two silver-haired men dressed in well-cut tuxedos. Carmela gave him a wan smile, caught his eye, and eased her way into his group. "Can I talk to you?" she asked.

Drake gave a roguish grin. "When a pretty girl wants to talk to you, you never say no," he told the two men.

Carmela grabbed his arm and pulled him aside. "We have a problem."

Drake looked suddenly perplexed. "What?"

She decided to fire her question at him point-blank. "Are you under investigation by the city or state?"

Drake reared back as if she'd smacked him in the face with a cream pie. "Me? What . . . are you crazy? No way."

"What about your company, Consolidated Gaming?"

"Hey, what is this? Where are these questions coming from?" Drake furrowed his brow and puffed out his chest. "Because I don't appreciate them one bit."

"Bobby Prejean isn't trying to shut you down?"

This time Drake gave a derisive snort. "Are you serious? The D.A.? I sincerely hope not, since the governor is slated to be here tonight. And, hopefully, the mayor will show up fairly soon." He frowned again and glanced around. "Something must have kept him."

Suddenly, Carmela's cell phone rang. She jerked it out of her purse and put it to her ear as Drake said, "You have to tell me where all these rumors are coming from."

"Carmela?" It was Babcock calling.

"What?" she said as she turned away from Drake, the better to hear.

"Listen to me, Carmela. You and Ava need to leave that party immediately." When she didn't respond — she was almost too shocked to respond — he said, "Promise me you'll get out right now. In fact, I'll send a patrol car to pick you up. Get into it and don't ask any questions."

Everything came together for Carmela like a tsunami wave gathering its strength from the ocean's floor and then curling up toward the sky. Babcock would only order her to leave if she was in grave danger. Which meant he must have just learned something in his meeting with the mayor and the chief of police.

"Is this about Bobby Prejean?" she asked.

"Good Lord, Carmela, how did you know? Are you psychic? Never mind, don't answer that. If you see Prejean, just stay as far away from him as possible. In about five seconds he's going to be under federal indictment for racketeering, bribery, and extortion."

"What?" Carmela was stunned.

"Your friend Isabelle? Turns out she'd been secretly compiling evidence against Prejean."

"Oh no," Carmela groaned. "Prejean must have found out about it. That's why he killed her!" Now she knew why Prejean had been pointing his finger at Julian Drake. To throw everyone off the track. She gulped and said to Babcock, "And I just found out about the lace!"

"Lace?" Babcock said. "The *lace*? Carmela, I want you to listen carefully . . ."

But Carmela didn't need to hear any more. She dropped her phone into her bag and dashed through the crowd, frantic with fear. She was on the lookout for Bobby Prejean now. And Ava. Because, dear Lord, the last time she'd seen him, Ava had been with him.

Carmela bumped and dodged her way through the crowd. Drinks spilled, waiters glared, people muttered after her, but still she doggedly went on. Angling toward the dance floor where the orchestra was playing Lionel Richie's "All Night Long."

Stopping abruptly, Carmela caught her breath and looked around. Couples floated by as if in a dream. But for Carmela it was the worst kind of torment.

Then, she spotted Prejean across the room, holding on to Ava. His head was bent toward her and he was smiling, as if he was hanging on her every word. His arm circled her waist possessively.

Carmela ground her teeth together and sliced through the melee of dancers like a great white shark on the hunt. Twenty-five feet, twenty feet, she was closing in.

When Carmela figured she could be heard above the music, she shouted, "Ava, get away from him! Run!"

Ava heard Carmela's shout and cocked her head to one side, as if to ask, "What's wrong?"

And then Prejean saw Carmela steam-rolling toward him, eyes blazing, her entire body quivering with rage.

Prejean and Carmela locked eyes for an instant, and Prejean's expression clouded. He suddenly knew he was in trouble. Realized that he'd somehow been found out.

"Ava," Carmela cried again. "Get away from him."

Flustered now, Ava took a step back from Prejean. But it wasn't far enough. Like the snap of an alligator's jaws, he reached out and pinched Ava's arm. Then he grabbed her and spun her around so hard that one of her gold earrings flew off and hit the floor.

Dragging a protesting Ava, Prejean propelled her toward the narrow back entrance of the tent. Ten seconds later they disappeared through the slit and were swallowed up by the night.

Poof, they were gone!

CHAPTER 31

Pushing aside the canvas, Carmela left the glittering party lights behind and slipped into the night shadows. She was mere seconds behind them. And yet, Ava and Prejean seemed to have completely disappeared.

Where are they? Where could they have gone?

Carmela peered into the inky darkness, trying to get her bearings. But all she could see were the ruins of the abandoned theme park. The ravaged roller coaster had a gaping hole where support beams had once stood. A Tilt-A-Whirl had tilted off its axis.

Listening carefully, trying to alert herself to any telltale sound, Carmela thought she heard a little squeak.

Was that Ava being dragged through the ruins by Prejean?

"Ava, is that you?" Carmela called out.

But there was no response save the wind

whipping the tattered canvas of a carnival booth and the ripple of faint laughter from the party behind her.

Carmela made a split-second decision and dashed across the gravel into the abandoned theme park.

She knew they had to be in there. It was the only possible place Prejean could have taken Ava. Not only was it dark and spooky, but it offered a million twisty little hideouts.

Carmela shuddered as she walked past a dilapidated kettle corn stand. This run-down amusement part was anything but amusing. Once the grounds had been jam-packed with folks out for a good time, enjoying a heart-stopping ride on the giant Ferris wheel. Now it was a pile of trash with a murderer hiding in its midst.

And the murderer has Ava.

Carmela ducked around a web of thick black cables that dangled precariously from a metal stanchion. More cables were lying in fetid rain puddles. Carmela gave them a wide berth — who knew if any of the wires were still live.

Pieces of track from broken rides littered the ground. Bumper cars were scattered about the landscape as if Godzilla had grabbed them and tossed them like Tinker-toys.

Carmela stumbled on, past another ride and what was left of a carnival ringtoss game, half of the wooden pop bottles rotted away. Just past that concession her right foot sank into a sticky pit of mud and trash.

She fought to pull herself free and ended up slipping and sliding. Then she lost her balance and, arms flailing, went crashing down. She landed with one knee half in a puddle, the other on the cracked blacktop.

Shaken by her fall, scuffed and hurting now, her anger flared even hotter. Hobbling along on mud-slicked shoes, Carmela yelled out to Prejean, "Let her go, Bobby. It's all over. You're under federal indictment." She hesitated. "And we know you killed Isabelle."

Her voice echoed hollowly in the vast, deserted amusement park. There was no answer.

"Prejean," Carmela called again. "The police are on their way."

Prejean's voice finally floated out to her. "Go away."

"I will go away. I just need to take Ava with me."

"That's not going to happen. She's my ticket out of here."

"A hostage situation isn't going to help you," Carmela called back. Maybe if she tried reasoning with him?

But Ava was completely hysterical. "Help," she screamed. "Carmela, get me out of here!"

But where are you?

Carmela could hear Ava struggling. It sounded like she was slapping at Prejean, struggling mightily to escape from his grasp.

They must be about fifty feet away, Carmela figured. On the other side of a forlorn merry-go-round, its brass poles stolen and most of its wooden animals destroyed.

"Ava," Carmela called out.

"Carmela!" came Ava's scream.

Prejean snarled at Ava. "Shut up. Or I'll snap your arm like a twig."

Carmela crept forward slowly. At the same time, luck was with her and a puff of clouds parted. A brief sliver of moonlight shone down, illuminating their faces. There was a sound of scuffed gravel.

Prejean was dragging Ava into the abandoned fun house!

Carmela glanced up and saw two ugly orange clowns grinning down at her. And suddenly remembered the Ouija board spelling out C-L-O-W.

Was that word supposed to have been clown? Had some prognosticating spirit actually been tossing her a clue?

Carmela shivered and glanced around. There was no help in sight. Nothing. Just an abandoned shooting gallery.

Shooting gallery.

That gave Carmela a lightning bolt of an idea. She quickly dug in Ava's clutch purse, hoping it was still there. It was! She almost grinned to herself as she pulled out Ava's paintball gun. It was time to level the playing field.

Gripping the gun, Carmela dashed into the fun house. There was an enormous cutout of a clown directly in front of her. To enter, she had to dive through the clown's gaping mouth, braving a dirty, shredded curtain.

Carmela took a deep breath and jumped through, batting away the stinking curtain and thick strands of spiderwebs. She was in a long, dark hallway now, creeping along. She could hear faint sounds of Ava and Prejean somewhere ahead of her. Ava whimpering, Prejean barking at her.

Sneaking along, Carmela hugged the rough wall until her right hip bumped hard against the edge of a frame.

A mirror? It was a mirror, one that was stained and discolored and cracked. She eased her way past it, the fun house mirror making her appear three feet tall and five feet wide. The next mirror made her look nine feet tall and one foot wide.

Carmela was beginning to feel like Alice in Wonderland — that she'd tumbled down the rabbit hole. This place was awful and strangely disconcerting. Tiptoeing along, she went from the mirror room into a room where the floor canted at a steep angle. Hanging on to tables and chairs that were bolted to the sloping floor, Carmela picked her way through, her head spinning from this strange encounter.

Emerging into a narrow hallway, Carmela crawled into the lower half of an enormous wooden barrel-of-fun. The barrel no longer rotated, thank goodness, and the roof above it had caved in. The hole allowed just enough moonlight to seep in for Carmela to catch sight of Prejean dragging Ava into the next room.

"Stop right there, Bobby Prejean!" Carmela screamed in her most command-ing voice. "Don't take another step!"

Prejean's disdainful laugh came back to her. "Or what?"

Carmela gripped her gun harder and stepped out of the barrel where she could be seen. "Or I'll shoot." She raised the gun to shoulder level and aimed it directly at him.

"You don't have the guts to . . ."

Carmela pulled the trigger. The gun kicked like a mule in her hand and then, a millisecond later, she heard the sound of a loud splat.

"Oh my God, I've been hit!" Prejean screamed. "I'm really hit!" As Prejean stumbled backward, Ava wrenched herself out of his grasp and scurried toward Carmela.

Prejean, stunned beyond belief that he'd been shot, touched the center of his chest where the paintball had whacked him hard and exploded. His eyes goggled as his hands came away smeared with red and his jaw worked furiously.

"Help me," Prejean cried out in a piteous voice. "Don't let me bleed to death." He sank to his knees and croaked out, "I am bleeding to death."

Ignoring Prejean completely, Carmela grabbed Ava and pulled her along. "Come on," she urged. "We've got to get out of here."

Prejean stretched an arm out, begging for help, but they never looked back. They scampered back through the barrel, back through the tilted room, past the mirrors, and finally came shooting out the clown's mouth.

As they greedily gulped fresh air, the night exploded with red and blue flashing lights.

"What?" Ava cried.

A siren rose and fell like one of Prejean's screams.

"I think Babcock just arrived," Carmela said. She was flooded with relief. "And it looks as though he brought the cavalry."

Two uniformed officers jumped from the nearest squad car, guns drawn.

"Where is he?" one officer demanded.

"Fun house," Carmela said. "Inside. Just follow the wailing."

"Are you ladies okay?" the second officer asked.

Before Carmela could answer, she heard a familiar, calming voice.

"Don't worry, I've got this."

And then Babcock was pulling Carmela close to him, letting her bury her head in his chest while he reached out to put an arm around Ava's shoulder.

"You two okay?" Babcock asked. "You're not injured? You don't need an ambulance? Carmela? Ava?"

"We're okay," Carmela said. But her knees wobbled and she felt like she was on the verge of collapse.

"Is your arm okay, Ava?" Babcock asked. She'd been rubbing it where Prejean had pinched her.

"I'm okay," Ava said. "But Prejean . . . I think he's in a bad way."

Carmela glanced back at the fun house where more cops were pouring in. "Good," she said.

CHAPTER 32

Police officers swarmed the old amusement park like mosquitoes hovering over the bayou after a heavy rain. Some wore SWAT uniforms complete with helmets, but most were in crisp blue uniforms. A welcome sight, indeed.

Carmela watched two burly officers drag Bobby Prejean, hands cuffed behind his back, out of the fun house. He was fake-bloody and filthy and struggled like crazy as he let fly an angry barrage of curses and insults.

"You're making a grievous mistake," Prejean screamed to anyone who would listen. "I'm warning you. My office will have your badges for this." His voice rose into a shrill screech. "Do you know who I am?"

"You're a nasty jerk," Ava scoffed.

"No, he's a killer," Carmela said quietly.

When Prejean caught sight of Carmela and Ava, he doubled up on the drama.

"You two," Prejean screamed. "I'm coming after the two of you first."

Carmela hefted the paintball gun up in front of her so he could see it. Offered him a thin, chilly smile.

Babcock stepped in front of the two women. "Enough," he shouted at Prejean. "You're going straight to jail."

"Do you have enough to hold him?" Ava asked.

"Can you pin Isabelle's murder on him?" Carmela wanted to know.

"Here's how it shakes out," Babcock said. "And you're hearing this for the first time, just like I did a half hour ago."

"Okay," Carmela said.

"Apparently, for the last six months or so there'd been an undercurrent of rumors about Bobby Prejean," Babcock said. "That he was operating fat and sassy in his own private fiefdom. Spreading a few bucks around, lining his pockets, profiteering wherever he could. But he was slick and nothing ever stuck. The man was like Teflon."

"Wow," Ava said, engrossed in the tale.

"Anyway," Babcock said, "this was all very hush-hush. Only a handful of people in the mayor's office had their suspicions about him. But two months ago they caught a break. A brave, young assistant D.A. stepped forward."

"Isabelle," Carmela said.

Babcock bobbed his head. "Isabelle volunteered to be the whistle-blower, the insider who would try to provide the mayor with the ammunition he needed to come after Prejean. If she could uncover solid links between Bobby Prejean and several high-level drug dealers, and could expose a couple million worth of bribes to city officials, then they would have him."

"But Prejean found out about Isabelle's clandestine snooping," Ava said.

"It was *suspected* that Prejean found out," Babcock said. "But there was no *proof.* So the mayor still couldn't go after him."

"But how did you guys find the proof that *was* needed to expose Prejean?" Carmela asked.

"Isabelle's cell phone," Babcock said. "One of the techs called just as our meeting was breaking up. She'd stashed a bunch of her notes on her cell phone. Enough to incriminate Prejean and probably even send him to prison for good." He smiled at Carmela. "And, strangely, at almost the exact same time, Carmela got the poop on Prejean the old-fashioned way. By snooping."

"When I found out about the lace," Carmela said, "and the parchment invitation . . . I knew we had him."

"Parchment and old lace," Babcock said. "Amazing."

Of course, KBEZ-TV rushed out to catch the excitement. Zoe with her microphone and battery pack, Raleigh with his camera. Lights flared brightly and Babcock gave a quick statement, made all the more dramatic by his standing in front of the crumbling fun house. Then Raleigh managed to press his camera lens up against the back window of the squad car where Prejean was being held.

Thanks to a quiet word from Babcock, the two officers in the car took their own sweet time in pulling away.

"Think he'll get a fair trial?" Ava asked as they watched the taillights slowly disappear.

"Who cares," Carmela said. "Prejean robbed the city, murdered Isabelle, and faked his own car accident. It's over."

"Not quite," Babcock said to Carmela.

"What?" she asked.

He reached for the paintball gun she held in her hand. "Time to give it up, 007."

Carmela grinned as she relinquished the gun. "So I don't have a license to kill?"

Babcock bent down and kissed her. "Just a license to thrill."

Ava cleared her throat. "Excuse me, but we do have one more thing to take care of."

Ellie opened the door to her apartment slowly and gazed at them wide-eyed, a great big question on her face. "What happened?"

"It's over," Ava said. "Carmela apprehended Isabelle's killer."

"The *police* apprehended the killer," Babcock corrected.

"But . . . who?" Ellie asked. "Who was it?" She tried to smile bravely, but started crying at the same time.

"It was Bobby Prejean," Babcock said.

"Isabelle's *boss*?" Ellie was stunned.

"That's right," Carmela said. "Edward and Vesper may be crackpots, but they're not killers."

"And Naomi is a terrible blogger," Ava said. "And event planner . . ."

Carmela smiled gently. "But she's not a killer, either. And neither is Julian Drake."

"Then how . . . Why?" Ellie asked.

"Isabelle was a whistle-blower," Babcock said. "She was investigating Prejean from the inside out. Seems he was negotiating with drug dealers and bribing certain city officials. Even a judge."

442

"So she died doing what she'd vowed to do," Ellie said slowly.

"I suppose you could look at it that way," Carmela said.

"But how . . . how did . . . Wait, you said *Carmela* apprehended him?" Ellie looked confused. "How on earth did that happen?"

"Carmela figured the whole thing out," Ava said. "She kept asking questions and found out all about the lace and parchment invitation to an open house at one of Prejean's properties."

Ellie looked stunned. "Goodness."

"And then she came after Bobby Prejean at the casino party," Ava said. "But he kidnapped me and dragged me into the old fun house. I thought I was a goner, but Carmela came running in and saved the day by shooting him."

"You killed him?" Ellie asked. She touched a shaking hand to her heart. "Shot him dead?"

"Not exactly," Carmela said. "I shot him with a paintball gun."

"But it probably hurt like crazy," Ava said. "Maybe even broke a rib or two?" She looked eagerly at Babcock.

"Maybe," he said. "If you want to put that kind of positive spin on it."

"That's . . . that's just amazing." Ellie took

a step back. "You'd all better come in. I think I need to hear the whole story on this. Would you . . . can I fix you a cup of coffee or . . . ?"

"You got any Chardonnay?" Ava asked. "Or Merlot would be okay, too."

Ellie smiled. "Why . . . I suppose."

While Ellie went off to get the wine, Babcock put his arms around Carmela and pulled her close to him.

"There's something I need to ask you," he said.

Uh-oh. A warning bell sounded in Carmela's head as she gazed up at Babcock and sighed. She loved this man. Yes, she did. She loved him with all her heart. *But please, please, please,* she thought to herself, *don't ask me that one particular question.* Because, truth be told, she just wasn't ready for a full-time commitment. Edging toward it, surely. But just not there yet.

"What did you want to ask me?" Carmela stammered. Her heart was in her throat.

Babcock suddenly looked as serious as he'd ever looked in his life. He licked his lips and then said, "What I want to know is . . . are you *ever* going to listen to me?"

Carmela's blue eyes gleamed and a smile flashed across her face as Ava looked on with approval.

"Yes!" Carmela cried. "Of course! Just give me a little more time."

Babcock furrowed his brow, puzzled by her response. "Wait a minute, did I . . . ? Did you . . . ? Are we talking about the same thing here?"

"You two," Ava grinned, "are *totally* on the same page."

SCRAPBOOK, STAMPING, AND CRAFT TIPS FROM LAURA CHILDS

Prestige Soap

Small soaps that you purchase at outlet stores or craft fairs look like a million bucks when you wrap them up in fancy paper. Just find some paisley or patterned paper at a craft store and wrap them up like tasty little gifts. Be sure to add a gold medallion sticker or tie them with elegant gold cord or ribbon. Your soaps will look lovely in any bathroom or serve as a nice hostess gift.

Bottle Cap Charms

If you have a taste for funky jewelry, bottle cap charms are perfect. Start by placing your bottle caps, ridge side down, on a sturdy surface. Flatten each one using a wooden or rubber mallet until the ridges are completely flat and form a kind of frame. Punch a hole through the flattened rim of each bottle cap. Now cut out your images (or photos) in about a 1" circle to fit inside the frames. Glue the images in and seal with your favorite sealant or glaze. Use jump rings to attach each bottle cap charm to a chain necklace. (Hint: think thematically. Comic book charms, vacation charms, floral charms, grandkids, etc.)

Wine Gift Bags

Instead of paying for wine gift bags at the stationery store, why not make your own? Find plain white or brown kraft paper bags at a craft store and decorate them yourself. You can enhance them with decoupage, rubber stamping, freehand painting, or gluing on photos or other images.

Get a New Slant on Your Page

Why not try a scrapbook page that has your entire composition set at a slant? Start with your photos set at about a 40 degree angle, then build around them. Use postcards, stickers, paper mementos, and all the elements you usually use on one of your scrapbook pages. When your composition is arranged, just glue it carefully. The neat thing is, when you tilt your composition, you achieve a sense of movement that makes your page feel fresh and fun.

Spatter Backgrounds

Have a little fun à la the artist Jackson Pollock. Start with a plain sheet of paper (color is great, too) and spatter on paint. And I mean *really* spatter it on. Or if you'd rather drizzle your paint, then have at it. Just go wild with the pattern and your design. Once it dries, you've got a nifty one-of-a-kind background page to highlight all your "action" photos. For example: kids splashing in water, dirt bikes, race cars, soccer games, puppies in the mud, etc.

Anniversary Keepsakes

To make an anniversary memento to celebrate a milestone anniversary, start with an elegant piece of paper that has an antique gold or silver pattern. Lay down your photo of the anniversary couple and frame it with lace or gossamer ribbon. In the lower left-hand corner, add an elegant silk bow, some golden leaves, some tiny mementos (keys, charms, etc.), and perhaps the word *Celebrate* or *Anniversary*. Now frame your entire composition, but leave off the glass (you want your 3-D effect to shine through).

Matchless Matchboxes

Small or even large matchboxes go from ugly to glam when you cover them with pretty paper. Then add embellishments such as lace, beads, wax seals, or ribbon. You can do Christmas-themed matchboxes as stocking stuffers, or even Valentine-themed matchboxes with a "Light My Fire" theme.

FAVORITE NEW ORLEANS RECIPES

PECAN PIE MINI MUFFINS
1 cup brown sugar, packed
1/2 cup flour
1 cup chopped pecans
2/3 cup butter, softened
2 eggs, beaten

Preheat oven to 350 degrees. Grease and flour a mini muffin tin (18). In medium bowl stir together brown sugar, flour, and pecans. In separate bowl, beat butter and eggs together until smooth. Add wet mixture to dry mixture and stir until just combined. Spoon batter into muffin tin, making sure cups are approximately 2/3 full. Bake at 350 degrees for 20 to 25 minutes. Yields 18 mini muffins.

PASTA PRIMAVERA
1/2 cup olive oil
1/2 cup carrots, chopped

1/2 cup celery, chopped
8 oz. chopped spinach
1/4 tsp. basil
1/8 tsp. garlic powder
1 lb. fettucini noodles
1/2 cup Parmesan cheese, grated

Cook pasta according to directions. Heat olive oil in frying pan, then add carrots and celery and cook until tender. Add chopped spinach and cook until just tender. Add basil and garlic powder. Toss cooked fettucini into frying pan with vegetable mixture and stir, heating all the way through. (You may add a little extra olive oil if needed.) Serve immediately in bowls and garnish with Parmesan cheese. Yields 4 servings.

CARAMEL SHORTBREAD BARS
1 cup butter, softened and divided
1/4 cup sugar
1 1/4 cups flour
1/2 cup brown sugar, packed
2 Tbsp. light corn syrup
1/2 cup sweetened condensed milk
1 1/4 cups chocolate chips

Preheat oven to 350 degrees. In a medium bowl mix together 1/2 cup butter, sugar, and flour until crumbly. Press into a 9-inch square pan and bake for 20 minutes. In a

2-quart saucepan, combine 1/2 cup butter, brown sugar, corn syrup, and condensed milk. Bring to boil and boil for 5 minutes. Remove from heat and beat vigorously with a spoon for 3 to 4 minutes. Pour mixture over baked crust (crust can be warm or cool), and let cool. Place chocolate chips in microwave-safe bowl and heat for 1 minute. Stir and continue to heat and stir every 20 seconds until chocolate is melted and smooth. Pour chocolate over firm caramel layer and spread evenly. Chill for 30 minutes and enjoy. Yields 20 small bars.

BIG EASY BUTTER CHICKEN

2 eggs, beaten
1 cup crushed butter-flavored crackers
4 small chicken breasts
1/2 cup butter, cut into pieces
salt and pepper to taste

Preheat oven to 375 degrees. Place eggs and cracker crumbs in 2 separate bowls. Dip chicken in beaten eggs and then dredge in cracker crumbs. Arrange coated chicken in a baking dish. Place pieces of butter on top of and around the chicken. Salt and pepper to taste. Bake for 40 minutes. Serves 4. (Tip: serve with rice or pasta.)

SWEET POTATO CASSEROLE

3 cups sweet potatoes, cooked and mashed (canned okay)
1 cup white sugar
2 eggs
1/2 cup butter, melted
1 tsp. vanilla extract
1/2 stick butter
1 cup brown sugar
1/2 cup self-rising flour
1 cup chopped pecans

Preheat oven to 350 degrees. Mix together sweet potatoes, white sugar, eggs, melted butter, and vanilla. Pour into a buttered baking dish. For topping, melt 1/2 stick butter and stir in brown sugar. Add the self-rising flour and pecans and mix together until crumbly. Spread this topping on the sweet potato mixture. Bake for 30 minutes. Yields 4 to 6 servings.

EASY APPLE FRITTERS

2 cups Bisquick
2/3 cup milk
1 egg
2 cups apples, chopped well
oil for frying
powdered sugar to sprinkle on top

Mix Bisquick, milk, and egg together. Add

in apples and stir. Drop teaspoonfuls of dough into hot oil. Turn and fry until golden brown on each side. Drain on paper towels. Sprinkle with powdered sugar and serve hot. Makes 24 fritters.

CREAMY RICE PUDDING

1 cup uncooked rice
2 cups milk, divided
1/2 cup sugar
1/4 tsp. salt
1 large egg, beaten
2/3 cup golden raisins
2 Tbsp. butter
1/2 tsp. vanilla extract

Bring 1 1/2 cups of water to a boil in a saucepan. Add rice and reduce heat to low. Cover and let simmer for 20 minutes. In a separate saucepan, combine 1 1/2 cups cooked rice, 1 1/2 cups milk, sugar, and salt. Cook over medium heat until thick and creamy, about 15 minutes. Stir in remaining 1/2 cup milk, beaten egg, and raisins. Cook for 2 minutes, stirring constantly. Remove from heat and stir in butter and vanilla. Yields 4 servings.

BOURBON STREET COCKTAIL SAUSAGES

1 pkg (16-oz.) miniature smoked sausages
1/2 cup brown sugar, packed
1/2 cup ketchup
1/2 cup bourbon

In a large skillet, add sausages, brown sugar, ketchup, and bourbon. Heat mixture and simmer until sauce is bubbly and sausages are heated all the way through.

OLD ENGLISH CRUMB CAKE

2 cups brown sugar, packed
1 1/2 cups flour
1/2 cup butter (softened)
1 tsp. baking powder
1 tsp. baking soda
1 cup buttermilk
2 eggs
1 tsp. vanilla extract

Preheat oven to 350 degrees. In medium-sized bowl, mix together brown sugar, flour, butter, baking powder, and baking soda. Reserve 1 cup of this mixture to use for topping. Now add buttermilk, eggs, and vanilla extract to the dry mixture in the bowl. Stir well, then pour into greased cake pan (about 9-by-11-inch). Sprinkle crumbs over top of cake batter. Bake for 35 to 40 minutes, or until a toothpick comes out clean. (Hint: delicious with a fruit topping or fruit on the side.)

SASSY JALAPENO POPPER SPREAD

2 (8-oz.) packages of cream cheese, softened
1 cup mayonnaise
1 (4-oz.) can chopped green chilies, drained
2-oz. can jalapeno peppers, drained and diced
1 cup Parmesan cheese, grated

Stir cream cheese and mayonnaise together in a bowl until smooth. Stir in green chilies and jalapeno peppers. Pour mixture into a microwave-safe serving dish and sprinkle with Parmesan cheese. Microwave on High until hot and bubbly, about 3 minutes. Serve with crackers and chips. Yields about 2 1/2 cups.

ABOUT THE AUTHOR

Laura Childs is the *New York Times* bestselling author of the Tea Shop Mysteries, Scrapbooking Mysteries, and Cackleberry Club Mysteries. In her previous life she was CEO of her own marketing firm, authored several screenplays, and produced a reality TV show. She is married to Dr. Bob, a professor of Chinese art history, enjoys travel, and has two Shar-Peis.

The employees of Thorndike Press hope you have enjoyed this Large Print book. All our Thorndike, Wheeler, and Kennebec Large Print titles are designed for easy reading, and all our books are made to last. Other Thorndike Press Large Print books are available at your library, through selected bookstores, or directly from us.

For information about titles, please call:
(800) 223-1244

or visit our Web site at:
http://gale.cengage.com/thorndike

To share your comments, please write:
Publisher
Thorndike Press
10 Water St., Suite 310
Waterville, ME 04901